Where Past Meets Present

Capulin Cabin. Photograph by J. D. Marston.

Edited by James B. Hemesath

Where Past Meets Present
MODERN COLORADO SHORT STORIES

UNIVERSITY PRESS OF COLORADO

Copyright ©1994 by the University Press of Colorado

Published by the University Press of Colorado
P.O. Box 849
Niwot, Colorado 80544

The University Press of Colorado is a cooperative publishing enterprise supported, in part, by Adams State College, Colorado State University, Fort Lewis College, Mesa State College, Metropolitan State College of Denver, University of Colorado, University of Northern Colorado, University of Southern Colorado, and Western State College of Colorado.

The support of Adams State College is much appeciated for the timely completion of this project.

Special thanks to my family, my wife Jayne and our children, Andrew and Charlotte.

Cover photograph and frontispiece: *Capulin Cabin* by J. D. Marston. Copyright ©1993 by J. D. Marston. Used by permission of the photographer.

Library of Congress Cataloging-in-Publication Data

Where past meets present: modern Colorado short stories /
edited by James B. Hemesath
   p. cm.
   ISBN: 0-87081-330-7 (cloth) — ISBN: 0-87081-331-5 (paper)
   1. Short stories, American — Colorado 2. American fiction — 20th century.
   3. Colorado — Fiction. I. Hemesath, James B., 1944–
   PS571.C6W48   1994
   813'.01089788 — dc20

                                    94-8411
                                        CIP

10 9 8 7 6 5 4 3 2 1

The stories and poems reprinted here remain the property of the individual copyright holders or their designees.

"Sand Creek" by Simon J. Ortiz. From the book *From Sand Creek* by Simon J. Ortiz. Copyright ©1981 by Simon J. Ortiz. Used by permission of the publisher, Thunder's Mouth Press.

"The Chinook" by Richard Broderick. First published in *Night Sale,* New Rivers Press. Copyright ©1982 by Richard Broderick. Reprinted by permission of the author.

"The Lucero *Requiem*" by Joanne Greenberg. First published in *Rites of Passage,* Rinehart and Winston. Copyright ©1972 by Joanne Greenberg. Reprinted by permission of the William Morris Agency, Inc.

"The Can Men" by Robert O. Greer, Jr. First published in *Writers' Forum.* Copyright ©1990 by Robert O. Greer, Jr. Reprinted by permission of the author.

"Private Debts / Public Holdings" by Kent Haruf. First published in *Grand Street.* Copyright ©1986 by Kent Haruf. Reprinted by permission of Sterling Lord Literistic, Inc.

"Clare" by James B. Hemesath. First published in *South Dakota Review.* Copyright ©1989 by James B. Hemesath. Reprinted by permission of the author.

Contents

Where Past Meets Present

Editor's Introduction

Where Past Meets Present: Modern Colorado Short Stories is, for Colorado, the first such publication of its kind — a gathering together of contemporary, post–World War II stories, all set in the Centennial State. The anthology's fifteen stories are about the land, the mountains and plains, and the small towns and cities of Colorado in the second half of the twentieth century. They take place in southern Colorado, Front Range cities, on the Eastern Plains, and the Western Slope.

Most of the works first appeared in literary or small press magazines from around the country: John R. Milton's fine *South Dakota Review* published three of the stories; *Prairie Schooner, Grand Street,* and *Southwest Review* each published one; and Alexander Blackburn's *Writers' Forum,* from the University of Colorado–Colorado Springs, published two.

In each of the stories, the opening and closing poems that frame the anthology as a whole, and the stark black-and-white beauty of J. D. Marston's cover photograph, *Capulin Cabin,* I saw something truly Colorado.

The opening frame, the narrative poem "Sand Creek" by Simon J. Ortiz, speaks of daily life at Fort Lyon Veterans Administration Hospital in the mid-1970s. The Sand Creek Massacre of 1864 proves not that distant from modern Fort Lyon, either in time or miles.

"The Chinook" by Richard Broderick is a sixties tale that many in their early to late forties will surely identify with. It involves a young couple; she's pregnant, they're probably not married, and they have a scheme to "get back to nature." That's the gist of this not-so-long-ago tale.

Joanne Greenberg of Golden (also author of the famous novel *I Never Promised You a Rose Garden*) contributes "The Lucero Requiem," an intensely imagined exploration of the meanings of creativity, genius, and compassion. The particulars concern the works of Greenberg's fictional creation Naçencio Lucero, a southern Colorado composer and army infantryman killed in Italy in World War II. The time now is twenty or twenty-five years after his death, and Lucero's work is about to be premiered on the Front Range.

Robert O. Greer, Jr.'s, warmhearted "The Can Men" details a wintry Denver afternoon in the faded lives of two rodeo cowboys far past their prime. For Dittier and Morgan the thrills and glory of the National Western Stock Show, the Cheyenne Frontier Days, and the Calgary Stampede are long gone.

Kent Haruf's "Private Debts / Public Holdings" is a deadly tale of transgression, retribution, and forgiveness, a biblical tale, an Old Testament tale set in a small farming town on the open vastness of the Eastern Plains. "Private Debts / Public Holdings" proves reminiscent of Shirley Jackson's classic "The Lottery"; it depicts the unthinkable, and yet it is something more.

My piece, "Clare," depicts one family's life in the San Luis Valley, life at 7,500 feet. As in much fiction of the American West, the geographic setting of the story, "the Valley" in this particular instance, might arguably be viewed as the tale's central character or protagonist.

The early 1980s — the first years of the Reagan presidency with its promise of riches for the bold, and the beginning of the "me" decade — provides the backdrop for Baine Kerr's "Jumping-Off Place." This is a story that one might find funny, with its outdated clothes and dreams, if it weren't so true for its time.

Russell Martin's 1988 novel, *Beautiful Islands,* opens with NASA astronaut Jack Healy from Durango *up there* in a tin can, far above the Santa Fe Trail, Interstate 25, and the mountains, taking a look at Colorado from space. Martin's story, "Matter and Energy," adapted from the novel, takes Jack on another journey, to a bustling, crowded Denver on an early summer day and an encounter with his past.

Against the towering immensity and cold beauty of the southwest's San Juan Mountains, the college and tourist town of Durango provides the setting for Antonya Nelson's "Mud Season." A young woman dies in a highway accident, and her parents, months later, come to see where it happened.

Colorado Springs native Kent Nelson's "Winter Ascent" has its literary antecedents in the Hemingway–Jack London mystique: a young man confronts unrequited love, a mountain, and his mortality. This is a story in which anyone who hikes or climbs in the mountains can readily imagine himself or herself a character, pitted against terrain and weather.

In "His Mother's Image" Manuel Ramos interweaves the nightmare of the Vietnam War with the Hispanic folkloric tradition of *la llorona* or "the crying woman." The Arkansas River just outside Florence provides the dreamlike backdrop and a strong sense of place for the tale's unfolding.

People come to Colorado for all sorts of reasons — a broken heart, a new beginning, and the good fishing, to name just three. Dan Schoenholz's deceptively simple story, "The Black Canyon," incorporates those three and more.

Gladys Swan's "Backtracking," set in Salida, concerns itself with manhood myths of the West that were derived from dime novels of the late 1800s, and that live on today in the mass-market Western novel: *a man's a man, a man's gotta do the right thing.* A teenage boy's life, and that of his mother and his sister, his luckless father, plus that of the would-be deliverer of the mother, the daughter, and the boy, are all destroyed by tale's end.

The annual two-week family vacation, a much treasured excursion for many of us, has been the source of considerable dollars for Colorado's tourist industry. Robert Love Taylor's "Sentimental Journey," set in the mid-1950s, depicts such an excursion from flat Oklahoma to magical Colorado. This gentle, bittersweet story, with its intimations of the coming social unrest of the sixties, includes a family "educational" stop at an Alferd Packer roadside marker between Slumgullion Pass and Lake City.

Steve Rasnic Tem's "Dinosaur," set in Rangely and Meeker, is the one story that I knew I had to have for this anthology. Originally published in *Isaac Asimov's Science Fiction Magazine,* "Dinosaur" combines sense of place, character development, and plot into a sad yet wondrous tale of northwestern Colorado.

Forgotten old mining towns in the Colorado Rockies — ghost towns (or nearly so) transformed into world-class ski resorts — during the expansionist years after World War II: that's the gut of the fifteenth and final story, Thomas Zigal's "Leave-Taking," a memory tale set in the late 1940s. The narrator, an old man, was a young man "back then," a young man who failed to see the future.

The closing frame, the jazz poem, "ears popping over la veta pass" by Tony Moffeit, speaks of the open road, the geological past, and hope for the future.

All eighteen contributors — the fifteen story writers, the two poets, and the photographer — have written autobiographical afterwords especially for the occasion. Regarding *Capulin Cabin,* the jacket photograph, I quote from J. D. Marston's afterword. About the quality of afternoon light on the lonely cabin he photographed in the San Luis Valley, Marston writes: "The clouds kept shifting and growing higher in the sky until they created a form that pointed right into the roof of the cabin and at the same time seemed to emanate the history within the cabin." *Seemed to emanate the history within the cabin* . . . Those words strike me as key not only to the photograph, but to the larger meaning of the anthology itself.

Every story in *Where Past Meets Present: Modern Colorado Short Stories* has a strong tie to the past, to history. This tie, in many cases, is to frontier Colorado; in others it is to a more personal past. Colorado has a certain lure. People want and expect something from Colorado; they want new beginnings. In 1893, speaking amidst the glories of the World's Columbian Exposition in Chicago, historian Frederick Jackson Turner lamented the closing of the U.S. frontier. But now, over a century later, the lure of the frontier is still around. More and more people are coming to Colorado, it seems, looking for the frontier itself or their derivation of it, and probably will be long after this book has turned to dust.

I greatly enjoyed editing *Where Past Meets Present: Modern Colorado Short Stories*. I hope these stories add to your reading pleasure and enrich your vision of the West as much as they have done for me.

These are our stories.

James B. Hemesath

Sand Creek
Simon J. Ortiz

La Junta: in this town, we are not dangerous anymore, and the towns-people know it; they volunteer nothing, no compassion, no love.

Passing through, one gets caught into things; this time it was the Veterans Administration Hospital, Ft. Lyon.

Like many other Americans, I love movies, and there were movies at the Veterans Hospital. Watching, men and boys throbbed and ached, passionately, hopelessly.

In the VAH, you can't be anything but alien to the combat soldiers if you don't know the glaze and sour sweat; all Billy would talk about was going to Kansas City and freedom.

We all called him Apache. They said all he did was carry out orders in Korea. The only thing he ever talked about was dawn at Dulce and freedom, just like Billy.

The Polka Dot Kid said, "I was born dirt poor and religious in Raton, New Mexico and forty-two years later I found myself in a skidrow hotel in Amarillo; I thought I was in Denver."

Autumn is beautiful in Colorado, like a golden dusk, rich with smell, the earth settling into a harvest, and one could feel like a deep story.

Buffalo were dark rich clouds moving upon the rolling hills and plains of America. And then the flashing steel came upon bone and flesh.

There was a recurrent dream for a while of driving east, passing near Sand Creek; tension was a tight string straight as the Kansas border.

The blood poured unto the plains, steaming like breath on winter mornings; the breath rose into the clouds and became the rain and replenishment.

THE CHINOOK

Richard Broderick

It began as a kind of impatience. She would wake up at three or four in the morning, impatient for the day to begin. She didn't know why. Morning would bring no change, just the same routine, the same loneliness. She knew that, but was still impatient. Gary had always been a sound sleeper, a much better sleeper than she. It was a kind of gift, the way he could drop off like that. But now, as she lay beside him, the slow draw of his breathing pulled back and forth across her nerves and the moon staring in the window, she felt resentful.

Hello moon. One night, she dropped the silent mental conversation between her and Gary and addressed the baby. Hello moon. Hello baby. At other times, horrible dreams plagued her, bloody and turbulent. What sort of mind could dream up such dreams? She knew. It wasn't her mind at all, but her body, flooded by strange hormones. Whatever the source, the dreams frightened her, waking her with a start. Sometimes, she'd rise in the brooding darkness of the old house and tiptoe down to the kitchen. It was the only room that felt like home, that felt domesticated. She'd sit in the dark, the mice scratching behind the baseboard, propane billowing out of the wall heater. In Denver, this house would have been condemned. Up here it was a "vacation retreat." At first light, she'd sit and watch the world materialize. There was the bird-feeder out behind the kitchen, its plexiglassed interior taken over by squirrels. Then, the toolshed, the water pump, the irregular pattern of pines. And, somewhere in the distance, the upper slopes of Longs Peak. It was all there, every morning. The solidity and shape of things calmed her.

• • •

They heard about the Chinook on the radio.

They were driving down to Denver for her weekly visit to the obstetrician. Her obstetrician was a Dr. Nhys, a man in his forties with a salt-and-pepper beard and a fatherly manner. It was her only chance to talk to someone besides Gary, or old Mr. Nestor on those rare occasions when he'd come up to the house.

They hit the plains at dawn. To the east, the sky was a rim of pink pressed against a rim of gold, as if the sun were just now beginning to show through the raised lid of a trunk. Before them lay a broken countryside of open fields, mesas and ravines.

Gary was racing the dial through different bands, trying to locate a high-voltage rock station beamed out of Denver. It was a way to avoid conversation this early in the morning. By chance, he hit a station on which she heard the word "Chinook" pronounced very distinctly. Gary pushed the dial into a cloud of static.

"Hold it," she said. "Back up a little. I want to hear."

A reporter gave the story in a measured cadence. A 200 mph Chinook slammed into pre-dawn Boulder, devastating many businesses and a mobile home park west of town. Twenty people believed dead. Many more missing. Damages estimated in the millions.

Another voice came on, this one hoarse and self-conscious. It was a scientist from the National Center for Atmospheric Research, located just outside Boulder. The scientist gave a garbled explanation of what he termed "the Chinook and Chinook-like phenomenas." He talked about warm air currents rising against the rim of the western slope. He described the way the cold air in the upper atmosphere pressed the warm air down until it welled up, spilling over the Continental Divide, rushing down faster and faster, channeled into the narrow canyons threading their way toward the prairie floor. He mentioned other "Chinook-like phenomena" in other mountainous regions around the world, the Santa Anas in California, the foehns in Switzerland. It was Boulder's misfortune, he said, to be situated so close to the Divide. Little screened the city from the full brunt of the winds.

The report moved into a commercial for breakfast sausage. Gary put his hand on the dial.

"Heard enough?" She nodded and snuggled into the corner where the car seat met the door, wrapping her arms around herself for warmth. The sky was turning blue — a cold, total blue.

The heat in the VW was finally working. She started drowsing off. They came to a stretch of concrete highway, passing a tree-covered slope on the right, its lower reaches coming down to the ditch that stretched alongside the road. A bank of brown grass flashed by the window. The tires clicked against the pavement, rhythmically, monotonously. "Chin-OOK," they chanted over and over. "Chin-OOK. Chin-OOK. Chin-OOK."

. . .

It hadn't been her idea to come to the mountains. Gary had proposed it. The notion had never really appealed to her, but since she had had nothing to offer in its place, she said nothing.

"Here's the plan," Gary had told her. "We'll find some old place along the front range. This time of year, lots of places will be empty. We'll rent it for a couple of months, then come down a week or two before the baby's due."

She nodded, biting her lower lip. Her signal of hesitance, of reservations. Gary was oblivious. He was very good at being oblivious to things like that.

They found a place through the classifieds. "Country hm. near Estes Pk. Beaut. vw., avail. Feb. 1." Gary gave up his job search — "Only temporarily," he assured her. "I'll find something when we get back." She called Martin Marietta and told her boss she'd be out of town for awhile. Early in the pregnancy, she'd been sick frequently, nothing serious, just dizzy spells and constant nausea, but enough to interfere with her work, and so she had taken an extended leave. Everyone had been very kind, assuring her that she'd have her job back in such a way that they raised serious doubts in her mind. Right now, she didn't care. They could live on her savings, at least for a few months.

The house belonged to a Mr. Nestor who stayed there during the summer and spent winters at his son's dude ranch near Longmont. Can't take the cold anymore, he explained cheerfully when she called. Getting too old.

He was waiting for them when they arrived at the dude ranch. He led them into an office whose walls were decorated with antlers and stuffed fish and glossy wooden plaques bearing inspirational or humorous messages. "To make a friend you have to be a friend," one advised her. "Caution, Jackalope crossing," joked another. Beside it was a photo of Mr. Nestor next to a smiling John Love, longtime popular Colorado governor. On the pine counter was a nameplate that said "Wild" Bill Nestor. She couldn't resist smiling at it, or at Mr. Nestor's bola tie and flannel shirt. He reminded her of her father. The same pared down look, the same deep voice made rheumy by cigarettes. As soon as he saw she was pregnant he adopted a Westerner's air of easy courtliness. Just like her father.

"When are you expecting?" he asked with a shy smile. She told him and he beamed, his face breaking into a complex pattern of seams and creases. "Oh, that's just wonderful," he exclaimed.

"Just wonderful."

. . .

She was dreaming.

She was dreaming about the Chinook. A sea of warm air billowed up to the rim of the Divide, pressing against the rock. She could feel the pressure, like something inside her. The rock gave way, bellied out, like flesh. There were things swimming in the warm air, vague shapes just beneath the surface. The mountains parted, letting the warm air spill forth with a tremendous roar. The shapes in the warm sea became people, houses, trees, tumbling, tumbling down the mountainside.

"Holy Christ!" Gary exclaimed. She woke with a start. "Will you take a look at that?"

Sweat settled in the hollows above her collarbone. Her hand came up to her chest, fingers touching the button on her coat. She made a noise in the back of her throat, half a reply, half an attempt to clear her head of the dream. She ran a tongue across her teeth. Her mouth was dry and sour.

"God, what a mess."

It took a moment for her to figure out where they were. The car was just outside Boulder now, on the south side of town. Here the road climbed an overpass and curved in a long sweep to the east before mounting the tableland that separated the city from Denver.

"I must have dozed off," she apologized.

"I guess. Look down there."

The mobile home park lay below them. It had the look of a shattered egg. Scraps of furniture, drapery, clothing had been blown — exploded — across an area a quarter of a mile wide. Shards of aluminum siding, sheared off into threatening shapes, were strewn everywhere, incongruously gay in their white and pink and bright yellows. Near the far edge of the park, a giant billboard sagged, ripped in half as if by a giant pair of hands, the torn part lying atop a roofless home with the word "Welcome" facing the sky. A fire truck and two ambulances stood near the center of the scene — she could not see how they got there — red lights stuttering slowly as several men in orange boots picked their way through the rubble with the casual attitude of shoppers at a flea market.

"Incredible, huh?" Gary intoned.

"Yeah." She watched as the park disappeared from view, cut off by a blue car hovering next to her door.

"I wouldn't be surprised if they don't find some more people under all that junk."

"Neither would I." Closing her eyes, she touched her head against the cool glass of the window and thought about the baby.

"You all right?" Gary touched her arm.

She looked at him and managed a smile. "Yeah, just fine." Up ahead, the sky had turned to a milky blue. Wispy clouds flattened toward the horizon. The mildness of the sky, as they began the long slow climb up onto the tableland, seemed like a lie. How precarious life is, she thought, and placed a hand across her stomach.

• • •

After Gary had signed the rent agreement they went directly to the house. It was a three-story, New England style structure halfway down a snowy road. A cul-de-sac at the far end of the road overlooked a wooded ravine. The plastic sheets covering the porch window billowed and collapsed, making the house look as if it were breathing. Pine trees filled the whole lot. In clearing the road, snowplows had constructed a high barrier of gravel and ice in front of the place. No one had shoveled the walkway leading to the porch.

"First thing we do is clear off a path here," Gary told her.

He got out and clambered ahead, in his excitement forgetting to help her. Climbing the ice drift proved difficult for her. Belly interfered with knees and arms were constricted by her parka. On the far side, having conquered the drift, she paused and tried to catch her breath.

"How — high — are — we?" she gasped.

Gary looked at the sky as though it might have the answer printed across it.

"I don't know," he mused, frowning speculatively. "Probably around 8500 feet. Maybe higher."

After some fumbling with the lock, they entered the porch. The plastic covers kept it very still and even colder than outside. Their intrusion disturbed a pair of jays on the roof. The birds protested noisily.

"Cozy," Gary announced behind plumes of steam.

The paneling in the living room had been turned black with soot and there was a smell of rotten eggs from the propane heaters. The built-in bookcases along the three walls were empty save for a mouldering collection of Carlyle's *History of the French Revolution*. Something had nested in the fireplace. A fine layer of dust lay over everything. Gary scooped up what looked to be burnt matchheads off the end table.

"Mouse turds," he said upon closer examination. He looked around, his hands on his hips. "Been awhile since anybody's cleaned the place."

"You realize," she told him, "that we didn't even bring a broom." Sensing the implied reproach, he stomped off into the kitchen. She had wanted to bring a broom and mop, but in his haste he'd thrown things into the car in a heap and there hadn't been any room.

"Great."

While she stored the groceries and started lunch, Gary drove down to Longmont for cleaning supplies. After eating, they cleaned the rest of the day, then fell into bed exhausted. The next morning, they started in on the second floor. Late in the morning, Gary announced that he was going for a walk. He'd brought some snowshoes and was eager to try them out.

"Where are you going?" she asked.

"I don't know. Around."

He was gone until dusk. She worried for awhile, then figured that there was not much that could happen to him. He'd dressed warmly and taken some food. She knew that in concentrated doses she made him nervous. Sweeping out the fireplace, she built a fire out of some kindling she found in a box. She took down a volume of Carlyle and read about the French Revolution until Gary came home.

• • •

Her labor commenced in the oddest way, almost like a practical joke.

On the way back from Dr. Nhys' office, they'd stopped at Boulder for some lunch. The mobile home park had been cleaned up and there was no other sign of the Chinook's passage except for some boarded up windows at the shopping center where they ate at a fast-food place. She wasn't very hungry, but Gary urged her to eat, to put something in her stomach. Over his objections, she ordered an Orange Julius — it was one of the house specialties — arguing that, if nothing else, the eggs and cream and orange juice would do her and the baby good. Gary sulked through his hamburger. He didn't like having his advice disregarded.

Now they were in the car again and had just left the prairie as they climbed a stretch of winding road. On either side, dwarf pines clung to sheer rock faces and the granite promontories were twisted into grotesque shapes. A stream, flush with the first spring runoffs, hurtled down the side of the road. Just ahead, the blacktop narrowed into two shoulderless lanes with no place to turn.

It began as a case of uncontrollable hiccups, followed by what she hoped were gas pains. For a brief period of mounting anxiety, she tried to convince herself that the pains were merely the result of the Orange Julius. But they were too regular for that. They came in waves now, a sensation something like conventional cramps but gripping a much more generalized area of her abdomen. At the crest of each wave, she felt as if the contents of her stomach were being sucked toward the floor.

Then her water broke.

It was not a particularly dramatic moment. Just a feeling of giving way, of a released pressure and then a warm flow progressing, spreading rapidly down the inside of her thigh. She leaned forward, feeling like a schoolgirl who's just wet her panties.

"Turn around," she said, trying to keep her tone flat and unpanicky.

"What?" There was a trace of petulance in Gary's voice. He was still annoyed with her for drinking the Orange Julius.

"I said *turn around.*"

"Why? You forget something?" He glanced at her now, flashes of his aggrieved expression alternating with quick checks of the road.

Breathe deeply. Evenly. Through your mouth. Normal rate. "I'm having the baby."

"What?" Gary hooted. "You aren't due for a month."

Another wave of contractions, this one the strongest yet. If you don't shut up and turn the car around, she thought, I'm going to —

"I think," she said with a gasp as another wave of pain rolled over her, "I'm in the best position to judge the matter."

He looked at her, the last vestiges of skepticism erased by the sight of her flushed face and the way she braced herself, one arm on the dash, the other against her stomach. "You sure?" She nodded, biting her lip. "Well, I'll be damned," he muttered, decelerating rapidly and swinging the car over the crown of the road. They were headed in the opposite direction, back toward the prairie. She gritted her teeth, hoping she could hold on until they reached Boulder.

• • •

They just made it to the community hospital not that far from the University of Colorado campus. The trees were all bare save for a cluster of pines outside the emergency entrance. Gary had driven around campus, lost, until she made him ask for directions. Students in down parkas with day-packs on their shoulders hurried to class or toward the shabby housing up on the Hill.

In the emergency room, she lost sight of Gary. Her last glimpse of him was standing in the entranceway to a long, tiled passage, wearing his parka and looking, she thought, very much like a student himself except for the anxious expression on his face. Absurdly, he waved to her as she disappeared down the hall.

She called out to assure him she'd be back.

In the fish-eye mirror hanging above and slightly astern the obstetrics table in the delivery room, she looked a mess, her legs parted, her hair soaked as if by a sudden downpour — a disaster victim awaiting relief. Figures in green scrub robes and sterile masks bobbed and probed between her knees, anonymous as firemen about to enter a burning building.

Afterward, they placed the baby on her chest and then took it off to the nursery. A pair of orderlies rolled her up to a semi-private room on a gurney with a bad wheel. She slept. When she woke Gary was standing by the bed with his hands folded in front of him. He looked self-conscious.

"How are you feeling?" He seemed diffident all of a sudden, almost as if he wanted to be forgiven for something. But for what?

"A little washed out. Sleepy." She felt a conciliatory urge. She wanted to forgive him for whatever he'd done or not done. He leaned over and kissed her cheek. "I must look awful," she fretted, touching her hair.

Gary shook his head and his smile relaxed. "No, you look wonderful. Beautiful."

"Have you seen the baby?"

"Yes," he grinned. "She's beautiful too."

She thought of the purplish, wrinkled child they'd placed on her chest. "She's kind of wrinkled, don't you think?"

"I like wrinkles. Didn't you know that?"

"That's good," she said, raising her head a few inches off the pillow. The effort exhausted her. "Did you call my dad?"

"Uh-huh. He's catching a flight tomorrow."

"That's good." She closed her eyes and stretched gingerly. "Everything's good."

• • •

Gary went off to find a motel. A half-hour later, a nurse brought the baby in for another feeding. Doctor Nhys looked in to see how she was feeling. She was touched that he'd come all the way from Denver to see her. Another nurse came and gave her a sponge bath. An orderly adjusted the sheets on her bed. When they'd all gone, she lay back, her hands folded beneath her breasts, washed in the sweet warmth of fatigue. So far she was the only occupant in the room, which sat at the end of the corridor. It was very quiet. She was exhausted but also — what? Happy? No, drained of discontent. She felt free of all distractions, free to lie there and be herself.

She thought of a day the summer before when she and Gary had taken an outing to a prairie park east of Denver. The day had been clear and still. Climbing to the top of a low mesa, they paused in a little swale where the grass was stained deep green, a vibrant, moving color with a trace of fire in it. To the west, a bank of dust signaled the beginning of the mountains. Neither of them spoke and the silence seemed to gather around them in dense clouds of golden particles. A meadowlark's call, clean and astringent, pierced the silence. She remembered how inseparable she felt from her surroundings, how she and Gary and the lark's song and the mesa all had seemed part of a continuum. For some strange reason, she felt the same way now. She looked around the room. She would be happy to stay there, just the way she was, forever.

She turned toward the window which overlooked part of the campus and a section of Boulder that rose along the base of the Flatiron Range. The sky looked as if it had been scrubbed clean — stripped bare like the beds of an abandoned house. As she watched, a small cloud, small and soft and ragged, drifted in from the East, filling the room with a kind of nimbus of anxiety. She closed her eyes. Gripping the chrome rails of the bed, she willed away thoughts of Gary, her job, what would happen when she was released, thoughts which now crowded around her like unwelcome guests.

THE LUCERO *REQUIEM*
Joanne Greenberg

T he weary chorus was going over it again, and the four soloists waited in vain for their entrances. The music lacked form and rhythm, and the chorus' notes seemed to have been chosen at random. During a break, Harold Bropes, the tenor, leaned over to Max and whispered, "Where did they dig this thing up?"

"I don't know." Max shrugged. "I never heard of it."

"Somebody said the composer was a local bird, Spanish, Southern Colorado somewhere. Sponsor the minorities, but this is ridiculous!" Harold guffawed softly and flipped back the pages of his score. The thought crossed Max's mind that Harold hadn't exchanged so many words with him since rehearsals had begun and that dislike of the music was probably the only thing the four soloists would agree on.

The chorus stumbled again. Had work ever gone this badly? Max remembered times when he hadn't liked the music or the conductor or another singer, but usually an excitement came with the thought of performance, and there was a general camaraderie, even of despair, that overrode whatever else there was to complain about. He couldn't remember any other time when people just nodded good evening to one another and went home after a rehearsal. Joan Gideon, the soprano, was new and very young, worried, no doubt about her first big role, but Max had worked with Harold before and been friendly enough. Down the row was Abby Denicek, the contralto, with whom he'd worked more times than he could remember; yet from the beginning of these rehearsals there had been none of the usual joking between the soloists or among the chorus, and no horseplay. Perhaps it had something to do with the music itself. Maybe its formlessness and lack of continuity was being translated into a feeling of separateness and distance between the singers. He wondered if his own slight depression was a function of the music, like another set of overtones.

Max found himself sitting up after the rehearsal that night, studying the score. No wonder Halvard, the conductor, was getting disgusted. They were still unable to work out the transitions between chorus and solos. He flipped through his part impatiently. It wasn't the first night he had taken the score to bed with him and tried to see intelligibly somewhere. Who in hell was Naçencio Lucero? He wasn't one of the new young Denver composers, or one of the old ones, and he wasn't connected with the University. What had gotten the Music Department interested? It was probably, as Harold had said, someone pushing the idea for the novelty of a premier performance.

At the next rehearsal Max went out to the campus early and stopped in at the library to look in Rollinder's *Musicians' Supplement.* There it was:

Lucero, Naçencio: 1923–1943
Born Blanca, Colo. Choral setting of Pueblo rain prayer, 1940. Strong Spanish-Indian influence. Served U.S. Infantry WW II. Three choral works: *Missa Azteca, Missa Kiva, Native Requiem* for Voices and Chorus. Mss. bequeathed to Music Department Univ. Colo. Died Italy, Aug. 16, 1943. 7 compositions extant. *Missa Azteca* performed Vienna Academichor 1952, Harvard-Radcliffe Chorale 1960.

Not much help there. Max went on to rehearsal dutifully and did his best, but he was still irritated with the music and the people who were working with him. The only joy was in listening to Joan sing.

She was young, arrogant, and too impatient to spend much time with phrasing or interpretation, but it didn't seem to matter. She covered octaves as easily as single steps — never straining for a note or ending short of breath. Her ease was thrilling; her voice had abundance, certainty, and strength and no tedious compromises. Max was a good musician and he knew it. The pleasure he got from listening to her made him a little confused; the vocal shading was poor, the phrasing rudimentary, yet . . .

Rehearsal was over; he sighed and closed his score. Whatever musicianship Joan learned, it wouldn't be from this.

• • •

The next rehearsal was no better, although Max had practiced his part with bitter determination. When the session was over, he nodded absentmindedly to Halvard and the others and began his elaborate preparations for going out into the icy night. He had minded all this a great deal when he was younger — the muffler, hat, and the scarf to protect his chest, throat, and ears. It had made him feel pampered and sissified, such elaborate care of his body, such concern over the right foods, the breathing, the exercises. He had tried to equate this with the fuss orchestral musicians made over their instruments, protecting them from shock and temperature changes. Now this care had become habit and he dressed slowly.

When he was ready, he saw with no particular surprise that everyone else had gone. Pushing out into the foyer of the auditorium, he met Abby adjusting the funny fur cap she often wore.

"Cold night," he said and smiled. He liked Abby. Her contralto voice wasn't powerful, but it was rich and well placed and she used it intelligently. Over the years he had come to value her knowledge, her musicianship, and her opinion on points of style. It occurred to him that after the first few rehearsals she had stopped waiting for him so they could walk to the parking lot together, picking over the work or talking shop. It bothered him that he hadn't noticed this before, and he suddenly found himself shy with her. "Uh — you going to the car?"

"Yes," she said smiling. "I think so."

They laughed, and he relaxed. "What's wrong, Abby? What's wrong with the four of us?"

They had come out into the night and the cold air shocked them. Max was so bundled up that he had to turn his whole body in order to look at her. She was facing straight ahead, impassively, as though she hadn't heard him.

"You must have felt this too," he said, "unless it's all in my mind, but I can't figure out why I feel so — so damn lonely. I don't like the music, but it's not the first time. I've sung with Halvard before; he's no George Szell, but he's competent. Harold is okay; you're fine; Joan is weak on experience, but she sings like an angel. Why is there this — this deadness among the four of us? We're jarring; the voices don't blend; and when we sing those damn trios and quartets, it's as though we're singing against one another. After rehearsal everybody scowls good night and goes home."

"Can't you figure it out?" she asked. He thought he heard bitterness in her voice.

"No. The only singing around here is Joan's."

"Joan is a bitch," Abby said quietly, "a petty, opportunistic, self-centered bitch."

Max was shocked and then embarrassed at the rawness of her hatred. "Let's see . . . you're trying to tell me something. . . ."

But she didn't laugh and Max dropped his bantering tone. "Abby, I've never seen you so violent about anyone. I don't know what's going on between you two, but it may be part of what's ruining everything for all of us. I mean, besides the music."

"We sing as if each of us were singing alone, but we sing duets too, Max. What about the duets — yours and mine?" Her voice sounded tight, but whether from the cold or not, he didn't know.

"Well?"

"Well nothing. We're gracious with each other. . . . Don't laugh — it's the word I mean. We play to the lead phrases in each other's part. In the *Sanctus,* you throw me that D flat and then you sing quietly so that I can echo it two bars later. And sometimes I pull up quickly so you can get a good running start when you need the power."

"That kind of thing takes years of experience, working together, knowing the music. This is Joan's first big role. She has four solos, as many duets and trios; it's the equal of a starring role in an opera. She's brand-new. Give her a chance."

"*I can't,*" Abby insisted. She was sounding a bit shrill, not bothering to protect her voice. "She won't let me. Max, have you ever been cut off a half-second before your note ended? It's like coming down flat-footed. It makes you sound bad and the one who pulls the stunt gets off scot-free. She and I have a dozen spots that are natural for echo and re-echo, but when her voice is supposed to fade a little, playing to my part, she rides over me like the Roman army. I've tried again and again and it's always the same." They had reached the parking lot and for a minute she hesitated. He knew she was embarrassed. She had sounded malicious and bitter, but she was also dead serious. "I know, Max, she's very affecting and very young, and I'm jealous of her voice." She smiled at him. "Why should that surprise you? I may be middle-aged, but I'm not deaf."

"I'm sorry," he said. "I guess I didn't think you knew it. I've been jealous often enough, but I never had the guts to say so."

"She's a shark," Abby said quietly. She had gotten into her car. She closed the door and they waved good night through the window. As Max pulled away in his own car, he saw Abby still fumbling in her purse for her keys.

Leaving the lot, he turned left, off campus, and half-unconsciously a melody started to grow in his mind and free itself. He turned the car out onto the highway, a long, straight stretch, deserted at this time of the night. He was doing seventy and the motor was giving him a C-sharp. He was suddenly aware that the music in his mind was one of his solos, one he hadn't practiced for weeks. As he followed it, it began to rise in him until it burst from his throat, full voice. He drove through the darkness singing, the melody wheeling and turning at the top of his range like a huge, primeval bird that circles and, in syncopated beats, follows over a hundred hills and valleys the invisible contours of the air.

• • •

Max waited excitedly for the next rehearsal. The single bit of music had rooted itself in him and now it wouldn't let him go. At work, he found himself humming it, dipping and sliding joyfully over his notes; feeling a rhythm, a pattern he had never heard before. Maybe there were more secrets hidden in the music, waiting for him. When he sat down in his chair at rehearsal and opened the score, it was with an excitement he hadn't felt since the work began.

Halvard started with the chorus. Max listened intently, trying to hear what he had heard in his solo. It wasn't there. The voices still sounded hollow and disconnected. The choral part led into Joan's solo and, with Abby's words in his mind, he found himself listening under the brilliance and being bothered by something more than faulty phrasing and flashiness. Studying the score, he followed as Joan began a duet with Harold. At each entrance and release, she was hanging on her best notes a fraction of a second overtime, putting Harold off his entrances and taking his releases before he finished them. When she trilled over his voice, she drew too much attention to the ease of her performance, singing about the fires of hell in a bright, almost operetta style. And she was magnificent. Her youth and talent somehow made the excesses work. There she hung happily, like a kid balanced on a fence, showing off, delighting in the danger. When Harold took up what should have been the major voice, she didn't relinquish the lead, and all Max could think was: God, is he outclassed!

Luckily for Harold, he didn't realize how consistently he was being overreached. When the duet ended, he turned and grinned at Joan. She hesitated for a moment and then gave him a dazzling smile. Max could have sworn there was nothing arch or cynical about the smile; it was a look of pure happiness, and the whole bass section of the chorus which had seen it break over Harold in his fool's paradise, was warmed. Most people hearing the subtle contest lost and lost again by the tenor would simply conclude that he had a second-rate voice. Even then, Max couldn't agree with Abby all the way. Joan was young and inexperienced and full of the newness and wonder of her gift. Who could blame her for wanting so much?

The chorus hit flat behind him, and Halvard stopped them and turned to the soloists. "I'll have to work this part out from the beginning," he said. "You might as well take the rest of the evening." They gathered their things and began to leave the stage.

The thing to do, Max knew, was to take everyone out for a beer. A few laughs would reduce the tension. They had to sing together; they might as well start trying to get through to performance in a decent way. He wanted to say the words easily and casually, but suddenly he found he couldn't. He didn't really want to go out for beer; he wanted to go to the back of the auditorium and listen to the chorus. Standing away from it, he might be able to hear in the blend of voices some pattern that was eluding him. It was a rare chance; he might not have another.

"Joan" — he caught up to her, still undecided what to say, and then he blurted — "let's go back and listen."

She smiled at him, flattered a little by the attention. "You're a glutton for punishment." They were offstage and at the word "punishment," Abby and Harold turned, caught by the word. Joan gave a little shrug of disinterest. "There's nothing until the *Lacrymosa*."

Abby smiled coldly, a smile that showed how intense her hatred was. "Music is made," she said, "even when you are not singing."

"Really?" Joan laughed as though she had said something witty. Then she turned and pretended to be listening to the chorus. "They're flat again. Ugh!"

Harold had suddenly put his knuckles to his mouth. "I just realized — we have to sing this in two weeks!"

For a moment they all stood shocked, counting off days. The chorus went flat again and they looked at one another grimly. The hundred and fifty voices could not be dismissed as mere background anymore. Like a precocious and unpredictable child due to appear in company, its moods were suddenly a source of dread. They listened in silence and then, one by one, slipped away and went home. No one said good night.

· · ·

Now everyone realized how close the time was. Rehearsal nights were doubled. Halvard began to pick and quibble and make the chorus repeat phrase after faulty phrase. After rehearsals they looked keelhauled, the soloists grim and strained. Harold began to wear loud ties; he got jauntier in an irritating way. Joan seemed more brittle; Abby more rigid and pedantic; and Max found it harder and harder to concentrate. He couldn't figure out whether the heaviness he felt was fear of a bad performance or disgust at the childish conflict among the four of them. They tested one another, giving and taking little vindictive remarks with strangely avid pleasure, and the more Max tried to help, the more he blundered. Once, after Abby made a crack about the arrogance of young singers, he had tried to lighten it, saying that Joan was naturally proud of being young. He had spoken carelessly, quickly, to ease the moment, but it was a tacit acknowledgment that Abby's remark was correct, and it had earned him a place in the war from which he couldn't step without creating rancor on both sides. Harold had also been drawn in, on Joan's side, and they all faced the last rehearsals and the concert itself in a grim tension, hiding behind the pages of their scores and riding out angrily on the staff lines that carried their music.

Max was more and more taken with that music. It began to echo in him against the rhythm of his steps — a beat, beat, then a dropped-beat-upbeat, one-two, da-da-*dum*. He had had to make peace with the dissonances and hollow intervals in his part, and now he was becoming used to them and to a new kind of order in what he sang.

But the choral parts wouldn't come. On Wednesday night Max asked Halvard if he could take a break and go back in the auditorium. "Who will sing your part?" Halvard asked.

"I could sing it from there."

Halvard looked disgusted. "Do you want to hear the balance or just get away from whatever is going on among the four of you?"

Max was surprised. He hadn't realized that the coldness of their performance had been so noticeable. How foolish to imagine that it hadn't! He was about to say something, but Halvard was gesturing him to go back.

The chorus began, as Max walked down the aisle singing at half-voice the random, staccato notes that were written for him. He didn't like this section and even now had to fight a tendency to burlesque his part. As he went, he softened his voice and softened again in order to listen. The sounds had begun to blend and merge. They were doing the *Dies Irae,* chorus and solo voices singing of the souls of the dead rising for judgment, and from the bare, cavernous intervals, Max heard, like a vast echo, what seemed to be numberless, pinpoint-separate voices rising to whimper, gibber, plead, and harangue at the Gates of Heaven. As the other solo voices came and went in the clamor, he could hear that Joan and Harold were putting their sounds by rote, without phrasing.

"Sing scared," he muttered, "it's Judgment Day."

When the section was over, Halvard turned to Max, who walked back to the group. They were waiting for his word; only he had heard what an audience would hear. He shrugged and then looked up at the stage. "It's beautiful!"

The chorus, tense with exhaustion and ready for betrayal, broke into relieved laughter, and Max laughed too. "It does fit — really. The voices come out in those little staccato passages like little cries. . . ." The three other soloists were looking at Max with tolerant amusement. "You — you'll just have to hear it yourselves."

So they went back, one by one, dutifully, to "hear" and when they returned, nodded dutifully at Halvard. Abby gave Max a quick smile as she stepped past him and back into her place, but it was for encouragement, not agreement. She had liked his joy, not the music.

• • •

That night as Max lay somnolent in his bath, he listened to the music again. His mind began a daydream of the words of it. There were the Souls of the Dead; as far as the eye could see, old people, babies, parents, children, warriors, lovers, rising naked for the Last Judgment. None had yet been through the purifying fire; all were wearing their arguments and reasons and sins and glories tangled around them. Victims were crying for justice, villains for justification; the humble were begging, the arrogant demanding. Lovers were. . . . He sprang out of the tub and ran to the phone, leaving a trail of water and dripping large drops on the phone book as he looked up Abby's number. Her husband, Frank, answered, and by the time she came to the phone, Max was feeling sheepish and irritated with himself.

"Hello?" It was obvious that his call had wakened her.

"Hello, Abby. This is Max. Uh — do you know the bit we do right in the middle of the *Dies Irae?*"

"What is it?" she said sleepily.

"I just figured it out, the staccato notes there . . ."

"That's good, Max," she said vaguely, and yawned. "Well, good night, then." And she hung up.

• • •

They tried it at the next rehearsal, as Max had heard it in his mind. Abby had listened to his idea, shrugged, and said, "Why not?" So when his voice rose against hers, he bit off the ends of the notes and she answered as he had suggested, stridently, in a hard, almost toneless series of ascending cries. Up and up they went, louder and shriller. They began to sound like squabbling lovers, each blaming the other and shouting his innocence before the Judge of the Last Day. Behind them the chorus began to get the idea; it wailed and stung and here and there the single voices of gifted ones broke as if by force from the mass of sound to cry and be swallowed up again. The pitch rose. They could see Halvard looking at them, smiling. They went louder and more strident until they couldn't contain their joy and both Abby and Max burst out laughing, the chorus petering out behind them.

"Good God!" Halvard said into their dying sound. "Of course! Of course!"

Then, everyone laughed, the first spontaneous and healing sound Max had heard since rehearsals had started; but as he looked around, he noticed that Joan seemed puzzled, and later, when he asked her how she liked their interpretation, she said, "I can't understand how Abby could fall for such a trick — making her voice sound ugly on purpose. You sounded good, though." There was no use trying to explain.

There were only two more rehearsals before the concert. Max could feel fear in the chorus and an awful tension in Halvard. He knew he had to talk to Abby, to work for some kind of unity in the week left. So he called her. "Let me take you to dinner. We could 'dine out' at that three-two beer place off campus and then go to rehearsal."

"Sounds great," she said. "I'll wear my beanie."

• • •

It wasn't great. The jukebox was so loud they couldn't talk without shouting, and they were afraid of the strain on their voices. In the end they talked in the pauses between paroxysms of amplified Rock.

"You know, we should *all* be here," Abby said, "drinking, talking, and dropping names."

Max glared at the jukebox. "We should all be somewhere where we could work it out. . . . Are you scared?"

"Yes." She nodded. "Every year a dozen singing groups spin Bach and Haydn in their graves, but that music is familiar; people know how it's supposed to sound. The mind corrects a sour note or a wooden baritone. I don't like this music as much as you do; but if we kill it now, we may be killing it outright and forever, and that isn't fair. If only that bitch——"

"Cut it out," he said. The jukebox stopped her. Afterward: "Look, I don't want to talk about you and Joan, but about the music. Last month I didn't like it either and now I wonder how I could have been so deaf to it. I think you could learn to like it too, but there just isn't time."

"Well, what *is* there time for? If you talk about the work, you'll have to talk about Joan. She's out to kill me. I tried to help and then I tried to leave her alone. What else is there?"

Jukebox again. They waited.

"One more thing." Max softened his tone so that the words might shock her less. "There is one more thing to try and that is to give in, to let her have it all her way."

"Do you know what she wants?" Abby said with quiet fury. "She wants all her singing to be solo; duets and trios just provide her with a muted undertone, a harmony."

The jukebox again. Again they waited.

"All right. Why don't we give in? You and I still have our parts. Last night I counted seven — no nine — sections where she doesn't sing at all. We can do whatever we want in those, and when Joan sings, we'll pull back and let her have it all to herself. How about it?"

"You say you like the music, yet you want it unbalanced that way?"

"If it has to be," he said grimly. "I have a feeling Lucero didn't write it for people like us to sing, but for people like her. The temperament wouldn't matter to him because she's brilliant enough."

"Then music is for showmen, not musicians."

The jukebox again. . . . The food came. They ate angrily and then left, finding it easier to talk as they strolled toward the campus.

Max realized that he would have to put the situation personally, as it had come to him. He said, "You know, when I was Harold's age, I was sure I could be great if only the conductor was right and the roles were right. If I didn't get famous, or wasn't given top roles, it was because my voice wasn't being brought out correctly. It hurt for a while. I saw plots, intrigues; but somewhere along the line I found I had begun to listen to the music for its own sake. I was like a man marrying for money and then falling in love with his wife. I began to yearn to belong to a career I already had. I started working very hard because I wanted knowledge to bring me greatness. It didn't. It brought me competence. I'm grateful for that, but suddenly, greatness — a greater talent than mine — comes along, and I find I have to shut up and get out of the way."

"Max, your voice is better than mine, and God knows, hers is. Lots of people's voices are. But I always thought that at least my musicianship made up for a lot I didn't have. Now you're saying it doesn't — that it has no value."

"Who said it has no value? How many great ones are there? If the Bach and the Lucero are going to get sung, our kind are going to have to do nine tenths of the singing because there aren't enough top musicians with great voices to go around."

"Is that *all*?"

"Well," he said, and found himself grinning, "maybe it's not *all*. We get to listen to them, to learn."

"And do what, when they make our duets solos, when they ride us down?"

"Wear the wheel marks and try to smile."

"Oh, *thanks*."

The campus was full of young people out in the unseasonably mild night.

"I feel like Methusaleh's mother," Abby said disgustedly. "Methusaleh's mother with wheel marks."

Max laughed.

"Max, I just remembered the first time I ever saw you. Good Lord, fifteen years ago. . . ."

"You thought: There goes one hell of a handsome fellow!"

"Not exactly. It was an audition for the Verdi *Requiem*. Frank and I had just moved here and I didn't know anybody. They were holding the audition at some church, I remember. I went early; you were standing in a corner singing the *Confutatis Maledictis* — up to your neck in contrition, remorse, stench of sin — and grinning from ear to ear."

"I like to sing," he said sheepishly.

She smiled in the dying light. "You do, don't you?"

He nodded.

"Okay," she said. "You win."

• • •

The singing had a quality of panic to it. They had all suddenly become aware of how close the performance was. Halvard, usually placid, raged and barked, and the chorus shifted nervously while he scolded them, sighing over repeated stops for correction.

During the second hour they took the whole work straight through for the first time. With the experience of perfected parts, the members of the chorus found that they were beginning, slowly, to understand the whole. They were on key, moving toward a vague but present form in the work, and they were rewarded with a humble amazement at their own power to move.

In the *Domine Jesu,* the bass section felt for the thunder it was meant to produce — and found it. The tenors took their cue, Halvard crying, "Fine!" Altos and sopranos followed. The upper voices blew into a gale, "Deliver us." The basses rumbled, "from the Lion's mouth. . . ." Then unison built — forte, fortissimo — and suddenly all the voices exploded in desperate joy — the *Sanctus.*

At the end of the choral part some of the singers were in tears; and the conductor, sweating and exultant. "Now!" he cried, over the sound he dared not break, "tempo will increase, sound diminish. Until the soloists come in. Keep it taut . . . taut." And he cued the soloists, who began fortissimo, as Max had once said scornfully, like four five-hundred-pound angels shot out of a cannon.

The chorus gradually stilled; the quartet faded as if those angels were beating in unison, slowing as they rose higher and still higher.

Max heard Joan beside him, too loud. She wasn't following the mood. Halvard waved her down slightly, but didn't want to stop. The sound seemed off, somehow, but the four went higher and softer still, until they had merged into a single beam of sound that slowly faded and was gone.

There was dead silence; a spontaneous, breath-caught gasp of awe. And in the silence, Abby's voice, a stage whisper. It had been pitched loud enough to be heard above talk and rustling scores; in the silence, it filled the room. Abby was leaning over to Joan helpfully, and whispering, "You were singing B-flat there. It should have been A-flat."

The room burst into uncontrollable laughter. Joan surely knew it was release from the tremendous power of the music that made them laugh so wildly, but her face went stiff with rage. Abby tried an apology, but there was really nothing to say.

The rehearsal continued and when it was over, Joan left immediately. The rest of the singers stayed on, not wanting to leave a place where they had been surprised in the act of creation. When they did go, they were quiet. No one wanted to disturb the sounds that hung shimmering in his mind.

Max saw Abby to her car. Looking out at him she said, "I wasn't trying to . . . I didn't mean . . . I was trying to *help*."

"I know," he said. "Don't worry about it."

• • •

By dress rehearsal, Max hoped that the moment would be lost in everyone's excitement at the music. He knew Joan wouldn't forget, but a good rehearsal could put the embarrassment in perspective.

Joan came late and sang her part looking straight ahead. Whenever the others worked with her, they gave ground; Abby so much that Halvard had to keep motioning her up, and afterward, spoke to her about it. "I don't want to keep pulling the sound from you."

Abby apologized and said she would work harder. Joan watched them from her place and then left quickly.

• • •

On Sunday afternoon Max dressed carefully in formal clothes. He wore a thick undershirt beneath the starched dickey because he sweated heavily when he did a concert. Before he left for the auditorium, he swallowed the tablespoonful of honey dictated by custom (energy, memory, richness in the tone). With all his years of performing, he was still nervous before he sang and wanted no one around him but other singers. When he got to the auditorium, he went backstage and sat down among the knots of nervous chorus members who were trying to chatter away their fear. Someone mentioned Abby's immortal comment to Joan at rehearsal, and the group laughed. Max looked around quickly to see if either of the women was there to hear it. They weren't, and he was relieved.

By the time all the soloists had arrived, it was only fifteen minutes to performance; time to go downstairs and warm up. They went quickly and no one spoke. Max remembered having done the Beethoven *Solemnis* more than once in a cascade of practical jokes, the Verdi *Requiem* with a roaring joy that took the soloists a mile past the beer joint one night, arm in arm, singing the *Hostias* at the tops of their lungs. Even when conductors were tough and temperamental, which this one wasn't. . . . He shrugged and began to get ready. He took several deep breaths and let them out slowly and then began a series of vocal eases, starting softly and never opening to full voice. He sang slowly, listening with care, testing the balance and richness of his tone.

He was in good voice today; the fact was clinically objective but reviving, and it caused him to smile so that he went a little sharp.

When it was time, he picked up his score and started back upstairs. The chorus was already arranged onstage. He saw Joan waiting in the wings, worrying her hair over her finger. He went to her smiling. "Ready?"

She turned toward him, coolly professional: "Of course."

He didn't know what to say. He had always left the wings for battle, giving and taking a quip or an insult to break the tension, but even in her first solo performance, Joan wanted nothing from him. They stood together in silence until Halvard walked onstage from the other side. Abby and Harold came up, and the four of them went, one after the other, into the glare and the sound of applause.

Halvard called the chorus' attention with his eyes; he smiled at the four soloists, and then, putting his hands wide for the choral entrance, mouthed to them all, "Sing like hell." His hands cut down; the music began.

It went quickly. The entrance was hesitant, but soon the chorus forgot itself in the music. By *Te Decet Hymnus,* the singers had hit their stride, a wild, happy, syncopated roar of sound in which the soloists found themselves carried to their quartet by sheer momentum. There they took breath to dig in and work. Max and Abby haggled and nagged in their duet and fed each solo as lovingly as they could to bring out the subtle currents of the music. Solos and combined voices wove into choral parts — they were going to make it. Abby was letting Joan have her way, all of it; Joan was singing wide open, overriding everyone's part and punishing Abby until it seemed she had been reduced to an echo. Max knew the audience wasn't familiar with the music and probably wouldn't know the difference. They were going to make it solidly. The difficult parts were almost all behind them. The chorus was at *Libera Eas,* thundering and confident and exactly on pitch. From their tidal sea of sound the quartet rose again to its hushed single note, then the *Agnus Dei,* and *Lux Eterna.*

As Max sang, he heard his own voice filling the hall. There was a depth and timbre in it he had never known he could produce. Cadence by cadence he opened. All the power he needed was there at his will, his restraint of it, an almost palpable delight. He knew he had perfect command of breath, tone, range. For these few moments he felt himself working at height, and it was this music which had given him his glory. He was full of joy and gratitude. When it was finished, he turned, slightly in awe of what he had been allowed to do, to share it with the others.

He saw that Joan had stepped back and was bringing her score up to close away the audience. Then she turned toward Abby with a look of withering hatred. The chorus missed it; Halvard, busy with their entrance, missed it, and Max was left standing alone and helpless, his mind repeating stupidly: But we're almost through . . . we're almost through.

Halvard gave them a cue, Joan's score came down, the entrances were made and the beat moved them on. Abby began, Joan followed. The first four bars were past, the second. Then, minutely and relentlessly, Joan sharped her pitch and began to sing louder, making Abby's voice seem heavy and flat. For a moment Abby looked puzzled, standing in her place and producing sounds that were without depth or tone. Then her eyes went to Joan. She shook her head once, looking straight at the soprano and singing the flat-sounding sequence.

When Max's entrance came, he moved in loudly, hoping to pull them both back, but Joan had edged her voice like a razor. It was too late to restore tonality. No one would believe the pitch that Abby was singing as she resisted Joan's almost irresistible power. Max's cadence ended and the warring duet swept on relentlessly toward its end in the choral fugue. With one last agonizing syllable, Abby sounded her A-flat true, but beside Joan's sharped, brilliant voice it sounded like a mistake, tinny and off-tone. The full chorus overrode it and, pitching itself from the soprano note, turned into the final fugue a whole tone sharp. Halvard scowled, then winced, his left hand trying to fan them down.

As the fugue went on, the chorus realized that something was wrong — it was going too high. Some tried vainly to correct while others, pushed to the limits of their vocal ranges, shrieked falsetto notes to the marooned conductor. There was no reality, no up or down, only waves of sound on which they choked and groaned, breasting again to look for some marker in that ocean of mad tides. Abby, exhausted, hopeless and on pitch, gave a dozen dull-sounding cues, until Max himself began to wish she would give in.

After an endless passage without laws or boundaries, the fugue was over and the chorus stood shaken. There was no more for the vanquished contralto to do. She had ended her performance sounding old, and her look of cornered bitterness was a look of old age. Beside her, radiant and vivid, stood the soprano, her last notes triumphant. Max and Harold had a small linking part, unison, in support of the final choral *Requiem Aeternam.* It was a ringing statement, an affirmation of life in the presence of death. The four soloists stood still as it sounded past them, the power of it vibrating the floor beneath their feet. When the last note died, there was a silent moment of awe and then the audience broke with applause.

• • •

They were leaving. A ripped score, a dozen wads of Kleenex, and someone's forgotten raincoat were scattered in the dressing room. Most of the singers had gone home. Max was about to leave too when he saw Abby sitting very quietly just outside the dressing room in the little alcove where the stage lights were controlled. The chorus members must have trooped by her, still keyed up with the music and the excitement, leaving her in the little hollowness of their departure. He felt her exhaustion and had to warn himself against treating her like an invalid. Pity would give a reason to what Joan had done. "Hi," he said, "want a ride home?"

"My car's outside," she answered absently. "Frank worked today, thank God."

"Leave the car. My sister is making lasagne. Come on. We can get the car later." She looked so much a victim that he found himself getting annoyed. "Oh, Abby, come on. Not everybody fell for that trick — it isn't the first time a career got launched with a foot in someone else's face."

"So much," she said bitterly, "for competence."

Max began to feel tired; he always did after a concert. And he couldn't ask her if she had heard what he had done — the incredible thing he had done. "Come on," he said. "We'll eat and get plastered and plan revenge."

"I'd like to dedicate my first drink," she said quietly, "to Mr. Lucero. He writes a beautiful score. Why did I take so long to realize it? I knew I wasn't a great singer, but I thought I was a good musician. Imagine — to be in music for so many years and not be able to feel that strength or hear that beauty until you'd sung the thing fifty times. I'd like to write him a letter of apology, but I don't know where he lives. Who is he? Is he still writing?"

"He has three compositions for chorus and soloists. He died in World War II, in Italy."

"One of my generation after all," she said, and smiled. "Now I'll have to have that drink to the War Dead, although he isn't through being a casualty. Imagine having to depend on people like Joan, and people like me."

"To Immortals!" Max said, raising his arm, "who have to take their lumps forever."

"To a voice" — Abby smiled — "whose lousy, crummy, vindictive, sharped-up note can sound so true that a chorus of a hundred and fifty people follows its lead——"

"To Competence!" Max shouted and gave a Bronx cheer.

"To A-flat!" Abby howled.

"To Muzak!" Max cried.

"To Muzak!" she shouted after him, and, remembering the phrasing of something they had done together, she whispered the echo, "To Muzak!" Then a three-beat rest "*In excelsis!*"

THE CAN MEN

Robert O. Greer, Jr.

The alleys behind the high-rise office buidings downtown were prime locations for the can men to enjoy a good night's sleep, and not have to watch out for the police, or for thugs looking to rob them of their last quarter. If they arrived early enough, between 6 and 7 P.M., they could prop up their cardboard houses in the back doorway of one of the businesses; then stuff the corners with newspapers and rags to block out the wind, pull out their bedrolls, and settle in for the night. There were always easy pickings in the trash dumpsters, too. The business world didn't place the same value on aluminum cans as Morgan and Dittier.

"Come on Dittier, my cart's half full," said Morgan. "Quit your slow-assing. It's gonna snow."

All afternoon, dark clouds had been drifting over the front range of the Rockies into Denver. Morgan could feel the sharp bite of the first hard December freeze. Four bitter months were on the way. The temperature was still in the mid-thirties, not nearly as cold as it would get. In an hour or two, the can men knew the air would turn perfectly still. An eerie calm would settle. Then it would start to snow. It was always the same when a cold front came through. Now there was a stiff breeze from the northwest, and the air was filled with the nauseating smell from the Purina rendering plant. From late October until early April, that odor served as their first warning to seek shelter. It was a scent Morgan and Dittier had learned to fear.

"Come on, Champ," repeated Morgan, a muscular cigar stump of a black man with a shaved head and skin as smooth as a carnival nubian's. "If we hurry up we'll be early enough to stake out a spot behind First National. We get one of those and shit — in the morning we'll be dry as a bone. Quit your moping. I told you yesterday to let me pull that tooth. Now you're paying the price."

Dittier pulled his empty shopping cart up next to Morgan's.

"Better get to looking harder or the only thing you'll have to show for a day of scarfing is a cart full of snow," joked Morgan.

On their trip down the alley between Sixteenth and Seventeenth Avenues, they struck gold. Morgan spotted a man emptying trash. They stepped back into a doorway. Peeking around the corner, they watched the man finish. Then, very deliberately, the two of them approached the dumpster.

"Keep a lookout, we don't want to get run off," whispered Morgan. He shinned the side of the eight foot high dumpster and dropped down inside. It was empty except for a corner filled with greasy shopping bags, papers, and a treasure chest of aluminum cans. The wind was already howling through the dumpster, causing the trash inside to swirl around. A sudden gust filled Morgan's eyes with dust and grit. Winter gnats buzzed around his head. The bottom of the dumpster was wet and slick. Morgan had to step carefully or risk falling into the ooze that covered the floor. He started tossing cans over the top to Dittier. Some still contained soda or beer. Their contents spilled onto Morgan's hands. He swatted at a bug, missed, and wiped his sticky hands on the front of his coat. When he finished hurling out the last can, he knew they almost had their limit.

Morgan climbed from the dumpster, smiling. His cart was full. Dittier's was halfway there. Two full carts of cans, at two dollars a pound, would bring twelve dollars. Since the Safeway up on Thirteenth Avenue had installed a can crusher, Morgan no longer ran the risk of cutting up his hands or jamming a heel from smashing a day's collection of cans. Now, he simply dumped them in the crusher and waited for the machine to spit out their money.

The can men made two more sweeps down the alleys behind Fourteenth and Fifteenth. Morgan surged ahead, carefully surveying every possibility. Dittier dragged behind.

"Damn it, you still ain't but half full," said Morgan, dropping back and examining Dittier's cart once again. "One of these days, I'm gonna quit looking out for you. You got me pulling all the load."

Dittier grimaced in pain, then looked sheepishly over at Morgan. Dittier's face was a dry wash of wrinkles from too many years in the sun, his eyes were bloodshot from lack of sleep, and he had a four day patchy growth of beard.

"I didn't mean that, Dittier. I just want us to beat the weather. If we have to drag these cans over to the Safeway in the snow it'll be too late to get a good spot, and we'll spend the night freezing our asses. Understand?"

Dittier nodded yes.

"Come here, Champ, let me take a look at that jaw," said Morgan.

Dittier screwed up his face while Morgan patted his swollen jaw. "Shit, it's twice as big as yesterday and it's real warm too. Better let me take a look inside."

Dittier opened his mouth wide, like a child showing off a new tooth.

"No wonder it's killing you. There ain't no top part of that tooth left. The damn thing's broke off down to the gum. You better let me pull it. The pain ain't gonna stop till I give what's left of that sucker some fresh air and sunshine."

Dittier gave Morgan a long questioning look, then nodded OK.

Morgan walked around to his cart and opened up the smaller of two plastic bags he kept attached to the sides. Inside were a few tools, an oily parka, and a blistered leather shaving kit. He pulled out a pair of pliers. Then he walked over to the other bag and rummaged through old boots and shoes until he found some mildewed paper towels. Morgan's house, an old Amana freezer box, painted with Thompson's water seal, was neatly folded flat and tied to the bottom of the shopping cart. The clothesline holding it down was unraveling. Morgan teased out an extra flap of cardboard from inside the box and tore off a piece the size of a half-dollar. He wrapped two paper towels around the cardboard and handed it to Dittier.

"Hold on to this, Champ," said Morgan. He reached into his coat pocket, took out a half empty pint of Old Crow and soaked another towel for rubbing down the pliers.

"Now, hold out your towel," he said.

Dittier obliged. Morgan poured half of the remaining whiskey over it.

"You can kill what's left of it, Champ." He handed Dittier the bottle. Dittier swallowed the rest of the whiskey in one gulp, and gave the empty bottle back to Morgan. Morgan looked at it for a moment, shook his head, and tossed the bottle aside.

"The things I do for you," said Morgan, mussing Dittier's thinning blond hair. "When I'm done pulling what's left of that tooth, I want you to bite down on that paper towel, but not too hard, OK?"

Dittier nodded his head up and down rapidly.

"It'll be good for disinfecting the wound, and biting on it will help stop the bleedin'. Now open up."

Dittier opened his mouth with a grunt. Morgan struggled with the tooth for over fifteen minutes, while Dittier stoically endured the pain. Neither of them expected bleeding to become a complication. Morgan always claimed that getting a wound "dirty" was the risk. During their years on the streets every cut, scrape, and gash had always stopped bleeding. This time was different.

"Hell, I can't figure it. I got the rest of that tooth right here," said Morgan, rolling the bloody root between his thumb and forefinger. "Let me take another look. Maybe I can see where the bleedin' is coming from."

Morgan took a makeup compact from his shaving kit, opened it, and held the cracked mirror inside up next to Dittier's pale thin face.

"Maybe I can get a better look with this." He pushed the mirror as far back into Dittier's mouth as he could. "Try not to breathe, Champ, you keep fogging up the mirror."

Dittier took a gulp of air and held his breath.

Morgan angled the mirror around until it was covered with blood. "Beats me. I don't know where the bleedin' is coming from, Champ. It don't look real good." He wiped off the mirror with a towel and closed the compact with a snap.

Dittier let out a long warm stream of air and a trail of condensation rose in front of his face.

Still puzzled, Morgan took off his faded Navy watch cap and rubbed his forehead. "We better head for Denver General and have somebody there take a look before you bleed out on me like a stuck pig. At least it's on the way to the Safeway. We'll get you patched up and with a little luck still have time to dump our cans and scope out a good spot for the night."

He handed Dittier another paper towel. "Bite down on this. And button your coat up all the way. Ain't summer out here."

The can men stashed their carts under a wheelchair ramp at a side entrance to the hospital. Inside the building, they followed the blue line on the floor to EMERGENCY. A tiny woman in her early twenties was seated behind the counter in the waiting room, thumbing through medical charts. She hardly took notice when Morgan and Dittier walked in.

"The Champ here is bleedin' and it don't seem to want to stop. How about a little help?" asked Morgan, leaning on the counter.

"Where is he bleeding from?" She looked up briefly from a chart.

"His mouth, I had to pull a tooth for him," said Morgan.

"You what!" She stood up and walked around from behind the counter.

The blood soaked paper towel was poking from the corner of Dittier's mouth. He was chewing on it, slowly wavering back and forth. His eyes were glazed and his face was ashen grey.

"You better come with me," she said, taking Dittier by the arm.

"I'm coming too," said Morgan.

"Not so fast. See that desk over there in the far corner?"

"Sure," said Morgan.

"We'll need you to fill out some forms for your friend. He's in no shape to do it. Ask for Molly and hurry up. The doctor will need the information pretty quick." She steadied Dittier by his arm for a moment and then ushered him into the emergency room.

Morgan rolled his eyes in frustration. He didn't like being separated from Dittier. He distrusted doctors and hated hospitals. Chewing nervously on his lower lip, Morgan walked over to the desk to complete the paperwork. As soon as he finished he rushed back outside to check on their carts. Their cans were safe, but the temperature had dropped ten degrees, and the first wet flakes of snow had started to hit the pavement. The streetlights had just come on, and the tubes inside still flickered. Filtered through the light, the snow looked like tiny flecks of silver. The streets were still warm enough to melt the snow, but Morgan knew the temperature would keep dropping, and eventually the snow would begin to stick. Shit, he mumbled. He pulled up the collar on his coat, covered the carts with two ragged plastic bags he pulled from his pocket, and headed back inside.

Dittier was slouched on an examination table, still dizzy, with an I.V. in his arm when Morgan entered the emergency room. The instant he saw Morgan, Dittier sat up straight and grinned. Morgan smiled back and patted Dittier's knee.

The room was a brightly lit aseptic white box with five examination tables. Gurneys lined the walls. The floor was institutional grey tile, waxed and buffed to a glossy shine. Morgan noticed a strong alcohol smell. Dittier's table was the one closest to the back wall. A canvas drape hung from a track in the ceiling and surrounded the table on three sides. The drape shifted, floating in on them every time someone walked by.

Dittier's legs dangled from the edge of the table. He was swinging them freely, back and forth. They would rotate five or six times, then Dittier would let his heels bang against the side of the table. Intermittently Morgan would send Dittier a piercing glance, but his stares only brought an ear to ear grin from Dittier, who would stop momentarily, and then start his game all over.

The doctor attending Dittier was a serious faced first year Resident — starchy and formal. He pulled the drapes shut around them as he walked in and quickly scanned Dittier's medical chart.

Then, several times he tried to get Dittier to open his mouth, without success. He returned to the chart and puzzled over it for a moment before he was interrupted by another one of Dittier's loud bangs.

"I won't be able to determine what's wrong with your friend if he won't cooperate," said the doctor, looking over at Morgan.

Morgan shot Dittier a look and Dittier's leg stopped in mid-swing. "He won't open because every time he does it starts bleedin' all over again, Doc. Ain't like him to bleed. I seen him cut a hundred times worse bulldoggin' a steer. Never like this though. Ain't right."

Morgan's response unsettled the doctor, so he picked up the medical chart and read it again.

> Name: Dittier Atkins.
> Address: Garth Hotel, 1621 Blake Street, Denver, CO.
> Age: 52.
> Occupation: Professional Rodeo Cowboy.
> Insurance: None.
> Patient's Appraisal of Health: Excellent.
> Smoking History: Two packs a day (Lucky Strikes).

"Have you ever had bleeding problems before, Mr. Atkins? Just shake your head yes or no," said the doctor.

Morgan interrupted. "I told you before Doc, quit wasting our time, just patch him up. This ain't no social visit."

The doctor ignored Morgan and continued reading the chart.

> Bleeding Disorders: None.
> Weight: 190.
> Medications: Don't use drugs, only beer.
> Name & Address of Responsible Party:
> Morgan Williams, same.
> Method of Payment:

He asked Dittier a few more questions, but in response he got only a series of head nods and grunts. Finally, he persuaded Dittier to take the blood soaked paper towels out of his mouth. The extraction site was still oozing. The doctor removed a gelatinous clot and covered the wound with a 4x4 gauze. Dittier clamped down on the gauze with enough force to crack a jawbreaker and gritted his teeth.

"Not so hard," instructed the doctor. Still perplexed, he took a last look at Dittier's chart.

Operations: Gallbladder (and once on my back).
Fractures: Several.
Diabetes: No.
Recent gain or loss of weight: No.
History of Heart Attack or Stroke: No.
Ulcer: No.
Psychological or Emotional Disorders:
Personal Physician:

Fifteen infectious diseases were listed near the bottom of the history form. Morgan had circled Tuberculosis.

"Do you know when he had Tuberculosis?" asked the doctor, finally accepting the fact that Morgan would have to be his interpreter.

"When he was a kid, Doc, and he healed up just fine. You don't think a man could get to be a world-class bullrider with consumption, do you? It ain't possible. You wouldn't have the strength. Besides T.B. don't make you bleed, just cough."

The doctor turned away from Morgan for a moment and partially opened the drape. "I'm going to need some jaw films on this one, stat," he said, to a short squat radiology technician. He turned back to Dittier, perfunctorily changed the bloody dressing, and once again shook his head in puzzlement.

The technician returned, pulled back the drapes, and rolled in a portable X-ray unit. Morgan stepped aside as the technician pulled the machine to a standstill in front of Dittier. Dittier looked frightened and started to edge toward the end of the table.

"It's all right, Champ, they're just gonna take some pictures," said Morgan, his tone soft and reassuring.

Dittier looked directly into Morgan's eyes, and when Morgan nodded it was OK, Dittier inched back to the center of the table.

"I need one periapical and a lateral jaw," said the doctor to the technician. "James, here, is going to take some X-rays, Mr. Atkins. I need you to cooperate."

Dittier squeezed his eyes shut tightly and tensed up all the muscles in his face. The technician slipped the first film packet in Dittier's mouth smoothly. He quickly exposed it and moved rapidly to take the second. In less than three minutes he was finished. He opened the drapes to back the X-ray machine out as one of the nurses walked by. The doctor stepped out and stopped her.

"Sharon, I may need some platelets on this one," he added. "Would you bring me back a lab form?"

She nodded yes, and hurried away.

The doctor turned, closed the drape, and directed his attention back to Morgan. "Why on earth would he try to take out a tooth on his own, and exactly how long has he been bleeding?"

"He didn't do it. I did, and he's been bleeding steady — for a good thirty minutes," said Morgan.

"Playing dentist wasn't a wise idea, Mr. Williams."

"Hell, I seen it done before. I watched a dentist pull a tooth for Dittier up at Frontier Days, in Cheyenne, back in '74. But the bleedin' stopped right away. Everything was going right that year. Seventy-four — that's the year we won the bullriding title — earned over seventy grand. Dittier's wearing the championship buckle."

The doctor looked down at Dittier's belt. Just below his sunken stomach was a tarnished, pockmarked, silver buckle. In the center, set in high relief, was a cowboy riding a steer. Dittier grinned with pride as he put his two thumbs inside the belt on either side of the buckle and pushed it out for the doctor to get a better look. The doctor looked at it for a second or two, then turned his attention back to Morgan. He continued to listen carefully, hoping for some clue to Dittier's bleeding.

"He was the best, Doc, the best. And me, I was his clown, right there with him, living the high times, never expecting to touch down. We had a drop top Electra 225 and a top of the line Stiedham trailer — for hauling our horses. Lots of times, back then, the motels and hotels was free. We got breakfast, for nothing, and big dinners on occasion too. We had it good, Doc. We was rodeo superstars."

A stoop shouldered technician pulled the drape partially open and handed the doctor Dittier's first X-ray. The doctor placed it on the viewer. The bright white light from the view box showed a black empty socket where the tooth had been.

"Has your friend ever injured his jaw?" asked the doctor.

Morgan hesitated a full fifteen seconds before he answered. "Once. Broke it down in New Mexico, in Gallup, near the tail end of our career. We was still doing pretty good, wearing hundred dollar Stetsons, the custom kind, steamed and creased to our order. Dittier drew a bull — name of Piston. A real shit-ass of an animal. Piston threw him on his face and busted the Champ's jaw. That bull would've stomped his head too, if I hadn't suckered it from over in my barrel. Anyway, we collected $1500. It saw us through the winter — that and selling the Electra. We hung on to the horses until '79. After that ain't much to tell."

"That's strange. There's nothing on his X-ray that looks like a healed fracture."

"Must have healed real good, that's all," said Morgan.

"Maybe," said the doctor, examining the X-ray closely once again. "How long have you two been on the streets?"

"Since Dittier hurt his back in '80. But we do okay. Ain't that right Dittier?"

Dittier nodded yes.

"He can't work because of his back. But I get enough labor pool jobs to keep our bellies full, and if our food situation gets too bad — I tell them old ladies down at the Salvation Army we found Jesus. Now that you know our life's history, could you get back to fixing him up?"

"It's not quite that simple. I still don't know why he's bleeding. He may have to be admitted."

"Not on your life, Doc. We don't separate that easy. I ain't leaving him here for you to practice on. I'll take him with me and tend him myself. Let's go, Dittier."

Dittier hopped up from the table and pulled the I.V. from his arm.

"Don't!" shouted the doctor, grabbing Dittier's arm and blocking his exit. "At least wait for the other X-ray."

Dittier gave Morgan a confused look. Morgan, who had the drape already halfway open, closed it slowly. He rubbed his cheek several times and then let out a sigh.

"You ain't gonna do nothing to hurt him, are you?" asked Morgan.

"Certainly not."

"How about it Dittier, you want to stay?"

Dittier rapidly nodded his head up and down.

"OK. But I ain't budging from his side till he's fixed."

"Fair enough," said the doctor, adjusting Dittier's I.V. "Have a seat back here." He patted the table top a couple of times. Dittier sat back down. "And Mr. Williams, you can watch everything from right down there," he added, pointing to the foot end of the table.

One of the technicians stepped in and handed the doctor the second X-ray of Dittier's jaw. He slipped it on the view box and recognized the dark spiderweb pattern of a small ruptured artery.

"I've found the problem. It's a broken blood vessel. I can have you out of here in forty minutes," he added, a tone of satisfaction in his voice.

Dittier and Morgan looked at each other and grinned.

The doctor walked out, and in five minutes a technician rolled in a cart with an electrosurgery machine. It was about the size of a typewriter, and extending from one end there was a long black wire with a silver attachment that looked like the kind of pick used to remove the insides of a walnut. The doctor walked back in with a surgical assistant who tested the machine. When the doctor was sure everything was set up and working properly, he turned to Morgan.

"This will take about twenty minutes. I just have to cauterize the wound. You might be more comfortable outside in the waiting room."

"No way, Doc, I'll just stand right here." He looked over at Dittier. "You OK, Champ?"

Dittier nodded yes. Morgan gave him a thumbs-up sign.

The doctor injected the right side of Dittier's mouth with a local anesthetic, waited a couple of minutes, and began. Morgan moved down from his position at the foot of the table as soon as the doctor started. He squeezed between the doctor and the assistant who was running the suction. After three or four attempts to look Morgan off, they gave up. For the next fifteen minutes Morgan was breathing down their necks. When they finished, the assistant quickly removed the electrosurgery unit from the room.

"I'm through, Mr. Atkins. The bleeding has stopped, but I want you to keep biting on this gauze for another twenty minutes. Am I clear?"

"Don't worry, Doc, I'll make sure that he does," said Morgan, feigning a punch to Dittier's shoulder.

Dittier reared back and smiled. Morgan took a pack of Lucky Strikes from his coat and tapped out a half smoked cigarette.

"You can't do that in here. If you really must smoke, you can do it in the hall or in the back half of the waiting room," said the doctor.

"OK with you Dittier, I'll just be a minute," said Morgan.

Dittier nodded yes.

Morgan put the pack of cigarettes back in his coat pocket, stuck the half smoked Lucky behind his ear, and headed through the drape.

The doctor turned his attention back to Dittier. "I still can't put this whole thing together, Champ. Your X-rays and your medical history just don't match. There's no old fracture, and between you and me, I don't think you weigh anywhere near the 190 pounds it says here on your chart."

Dittier held his head down, staring at the floor.

"Are you certain about the broken jaw?"

Dittier raised his head and his eyes drifted slowly over to the X-ray view box. He inched his arms down across his stomach until his weathered hands covered his belt buckle. Finally, he glanced over at the doctor and started swinging his legs. On the fourth swing both of his heels hit the table with a loud bang.

The doctor looked at Dittier's hands and smiled. "You know, Champ, that buckle *is* pretty interesting. How about letting me have a second look?"

Dittier shook his head no several times.

"Just one look — how about it — for a rodeo fan?"

Dittier smiled and removed his right hand from over the buckle.

Five minutes later Morgan was back. The doctor met him as he parted the drape. He was holding Dittier's belt in his hand.

"I believe the buckle is yours, Mr. Williams."

"Ain't mine. It's Dittier's."

"But it has your name engraved on the back."

Morgan gave Dittier a disappointed look and shook his head. Dittier began nervously biting his lower lip.

"Why the charade?" asked the doctor.

Morgan hesitated a moment before answering. "I just figured you might do more for Dittier if he was a champion instead of a clown. Same way it works out on the streets."

"This isn't the streets," said the doctor.

Morgan gave the doctor a sympathetic smile. "Doc, I'm sorry but people got to stick with what they know."

Morgan helped Dittier on with his coat and pulled the skinny rodeo clown's collar up tightly around his neck.

"It'll be freezing outside by now, Champ, bundle up," said Morgan. He looked back over at the doctor. "Better let him have his belt back," he added.

Dittier rubbed the belt buckle across Morgan's dirty coat sleeve several times. Then he reached under his own baggy coat and put the belt back on. Morgan offered up a punch to Dittier's midsection, pulling it at the last second. Dittier feigned collapse, then sprung erect and burst into a series of wheezy snickers that quickly escalated to a booming unrestrained laugh.

PRIVATE DEBTS / PUBLIC HOLDINGS

Kent Haruf

When Jessie Burdette became public property in Holt that spring, it was a matter of community honor. Her husband, Jack Burdette, had disappeared in January with a suitcase full of new clothes that he hadn't paid for. It wasn't this particular fact that bothered us, however. On the contrary, most of us were rather amused by it.

Jack had been the manager of the Farmers Co-op Elevator for about seven years. He had grown up here, we all liked him and were willing to accept a local boy's temporary indiscretion. But after he had been gone for about a month, we discovered that, besides shirts and pants and three packages of blue underwear, he had stolen $150,000 too. This money belonged to the Co-op Elevator, and since the elevator was owned in shares by half the county, we were naturally mad as hell about it. But none of us knew where he was anymore; the police couldn't find him; all of the all-points bulletins failed to turn him up; we grew increasingly outraged and hostile. In his absence, then, we sought our revenge on someone whose whereabouts we did know. We turned on his accomplice: old Charlie Soames.

Charlie Soames was a local accountant, a seventy-year-old man with wire glasses and a paunch, and we all knew him, just as we had thought we had known Jack Burdette. But at about the same time we discovered the facts about Jack's embezzlement of co-op funds, we also learned that it was Charlie Soames who had helped him: Charlie had juggled the books. He had been doing this for about three years. And now Charlie had pretty good reason to be mad himself — Jack hadn't told Charlie he was leaving either, so Charlie was still in town. Consequently, he was apprehended almost immediately and put in jail. And that contented us for a while. We looked forward to gaining something satisfying out of him at least.

But then in March when Charlie was temporarily released on his own recognizance to await the trial, the first thing that old man did was, he climbed up into the attic of his house on Birch Street and shot himself in the head with a .22 single-shot rifle. And it didn't kill him. It merely scrambled his brains in such a way that any thought of further prosecution or eventual imprisonment was out of the question. So we felt doubly cheated then. It was as if we'd been deceived by two of the people in town we had always believed we could trust.

As a result of these events and these feelings, we declared a kind of open season on Jack Burdette's wife. She was the only person left to us who might offer a sense of local redress. She seemed to understand that too. At times she even seemed to welcome it. Anyway, she stayed in Holt.

· · ·

It began in April. At the beginning of April that year she appeared one afternoon at the elevator beside the railroad tracks. She walked up the steps into the outer office and scale room and told Bob Thomas she wanted to see Doyle Francis. This surprised Bob Thomas. It was just after lunch and no doubt Bob had eaten too much as usual and was half asleep. He was slouched at the desk behind the counter, shuffling through some shipping receipts. When he looked up there she was. "What?" he said. "What'd you say?"

"I'd like to see Doyle Francis, please. I believe he's still working here."

"I'll go get him. No, I'll go tell him. Hell. You wait here."

She had her information right: Doyle Francis was in fact still working at the elevator. In the months after her husband had left town the board of directors had begun to advertise for a new manager, but they hadn't hired a permanent replacement yet because in the intervening months they had become suspicious of their fellow man. Deeply, excessively suspicious. They had begun to insist on researching each applicant's past — and not just his work experience, as is customary when hiring somebody new, but his ethical and moral and religious history as well. It was as if they had begun to suspect everybody, to believe every man in the world who applied for the manager's job at the elevator wanted only to take their money, to skip town with it. In the end, however, what they really only wanted to ask these men was: "Goddamn it, if we hire you now, how long are you going to be here working for us before you think you have to add to what we pay you, before you turn out to be another son of a bitch like Jack Burdette did? You ought to at least be able to tell us that much."

We didn't blame them for this attitude, this new profound mistrust of others; we felt similarly ourselves. But, because of their suspicions, Doyle Francis, who had been the manager before Jack, was still there in April, still waiting for the board to hire someone else so he could relax into retirement again. That afternoon he was still in his old office when Bob Thomas burst in.

"She's here," Bob said. "She wants to see you."

"Who does?"

"Her. That son of a bitch's wife. She's out there in the scale room."

"What does she want?"

"How the hell do I know? She just said she wanted to see you. That's all she said."

"Well," Doyle said. "Show her in, Bob. Or are you scared, if you get too close to her, she might steal your pocketbook or something?"

"By God," Bob said. "I don't trust none of them no more. That's a fact."

"Never mind," Doyle said. "Ask her to come back here. Go on now, try to act like a gentleman for once in your life."

"I don't need to act like no gentleman. Not with her, I don't."

He turned and went back out to get Jessie. She was still standing at the counter.

"He said he'd see you. Come on, I'll show you where he's at."

"Thank you," Jessie said, "but I know where the manager's office is."

"Well, don't take too long. Some of us got to work for a living."

Jessie walked around the counter and down the narrow hallway past the toilet and the storage room. She was wearing slacks and a loose green blouse. When she entered, Doyle Francis stood up. He was one of the few men in town then, at least of those connected to the elevator, who still treated her with respect and minimal courtesy. He offered her a wood chair with armrests.

She sat down, heavily, a little carefully — she was still pregnant then, still carrying that little girl of hers that Jack had left her with; she was in her seventh month. She set her purse on her shortened lap, in front of her stomach.

"Now then," Doyle said. "What can I do for you, Jessie?"

"I don't want anything. If that's what you think."

"No," he said. "I don't think that. They don't pay me enough to worry about what other people think."

"Well, I don't," Jessie said. "I didn't come here to ask for anything. I came here to give you something."

"Oh?" he said. "What is it you want to give me?"

"Not you. The board of directors. The elevator. All these people."

"What is it?"

"Here." She opened her purse and withdrew a legal document. She pushed it across the desk toward him. Doyle picked it up, looked at it.

"Wait a minute," he said. "Hold on now. This is some kind of a deed, isn't it?"

"They said it was legal."

"Who said it was legal? What are you talking about?"

"The people down at the bank. They said I could sign it over to whoever I wanted to, even if Jack wasn't here to co-sign it. They said considering the circumstances it would be all right."

"Did they now?" Doyle said. "I'll bet they did too."

He looked at the document again, read it this time. It was a quitclaim deed transferring the title of a house and property over to the board of directors of the Holt County Farmers Co-op Elevator. Her signature was at the bottom in fresh ink.

"All right then," he said, "I suppose it is legal. I wouldn't know; I'm not a lawyer. But then I don't suppose anybody around here would protest it very much, would they? Even if it wasn't legal?"

"No, they wouldn't protest it."

Doyle laid the deed down on the desk. He folded his hands over it. He said: "How old are you, Jessie?"

"I'm twenty-six."

"And you have two boys?"

"Yes."

"How old are they?"

"They've just turned four and three. But why are you asking me these —"

"And you're going to have another one pretty soon, aren't you?"

"In June," she said. "But —"

"Do you believe in hell?" he said. "Is that it?"

She stared back at him.

"Is that why you're doing this? Because, let me tell you, I don't think there is any hell. No, I don't. And I don't think there's any heaven either. We just die, that's all. We just stop breathing after a while and then everybody starts to forget about us and pretty soon they can't even remember what it is we think we did to them."

"I don't know what I believe," she said.

"Then why are you doing this? Will you tell me that?"

"Because," she said.

"Because? That's all. Just because."

She continued to stare back at him, to watch him, her eyes steady and deep brown. Finally Doyle said:

"All right, you're not going to tell me. You don't have to tell me; I think I know anyway. But listen, now. Listen: let an old man ask you this. Don't you think you're going to need that house anymore? I mean, if you give it up like you're proposing to do, just where in hell are you and these kids going to live afterwards?"

"That's my concern," she said. "Isn't it."

"Yes, of course it is, but —"

"And you agree it's legal, don't you?"

"Yes, as far as I can tell."

"So will you please give that piece of paper to the board? You can tell them we'll be out of the house by the first of May."

"But listen," he said. "Damn it, wait a minute now —"

Because Jessie had already stood up. She was already leaving. And Doyle Francis was still leaning toward the chair she had been sitting in. Those good intentions of his were still swimming undelivered in his head and his arms were still resting on that quitclaim deed on his desk. She walked out through the hallway and on outside.

In the scale room Bob Thomas watched her leave. When she had driven away he went in to see Doyle. "Well," he said, "she was here long enough. What'd she want?"

"What?"

"I said, 'What did she want?' Burdette's wife."

"Nothing. She didn't want anything."

"I don't believe that."

"I don't care what you believe. That woman doesn't want a goddamn thing from any one of us."

"What do you mean she doesn't want anything? She's a Burdette, isn't she?"

"I mean," Doyle Francis said, "get the hell out of here and leave me alone. Goddamn it, Bob, go find something else to do with yourself."

• • •

For some of us that was enough. I suppose we felt about it a little like Doyle Francis did, that she deserved the magnanimity of our good intentions. Privately, we understood that she was innocent, or at least we knew that she was ignorant — it wasn't her fault, we told ourselves; she wasn't involved. We could afford to be nice to her. Anyway, we could refrain from actually wishing her harm.

For others, though, who were more vocal and more active, it still wasn't sufficient. These people argued that the house didn't amount to enough. It didn't matter that it was all that she had, that it was the sum total of her collateral and disposable property. It was merely an old two-bedroom house in the middle of town. It needed tin siding and new shingles; it needed painting. Besides, there was still a fifteen-year lien against it when she signed it over, so that when the board of directors became the fee owners of the house and then sold it at public auction, it didn't even begin to make a dent in that $150,000 that Jack had taken. No, they weren't satisfied. A house wasn't alive and capable of bleeding, like a human was. It wasn't pregnant, like Jessie was.

Anyway, by the first of May she and the two boys had moved out of the house as Jessie said they would — they had begun to rent the downstairs apartment in the old Fenner place on Hawthorne Street at the west edge of town — and it was Doyle Francis who helped them move. They used his pickup. Jessie accepted that much assistance from him at least, although afterward she sent him a freshly baked chocolate cake on a platter, to square things, to keep that balance sheet of hers in the black.

Well, it was a nice enough apartment: they had five rooms — a kitchen, a living room, two small bedrooms, and a bathroom with a shower off the kitchen. They also had use of the front porch, a wide old-style porch with a wooden rail around it and with a swing suspended from hooks in the ceiling. From the porch, they could look west diagonally across the street toward open country, since that was where Holt ended then, at Hawthorne Street: there was just Harry Smith's pasture west of them, a half section of native grass in which Harry kept some horses. So it was a good place for her boys to grow up: they would have all that open space available to them across the street.

When they had settled in and after new curtains had been hung over the windows — heavier ones to block any view from the street —

Jessie began to take care of the money end of it as well. She began to earn a living. She took a job at the Holt Café on Main Street. Six days a week she worked as a waitress, rising each morning to feed TJ and Bobby and to play with them until just before noon when the sitter, an old neighbor lady — Mrs. Nyla Waters, a kindly woman, a widow — came to watch the boys while Jessie worked through the noon rush hour and the afternoon and the dinner hour, and then returned again each evening about seven o'clock to bathe and put the boys to bed and to read them stories. She often sang to them a little too, before they slept.

And working in this way — being pregnant and having to spend that many hours away from her children — was not the optimum solution to all her problems either, of course, but she didn't have many alternatives. She refused to consider welfare. Accepting Aid to Dependent Children, or even food stamps, was not a part of her schedule of payments — that local balance sheet of hers, I mean — since any public assistance of this kind came from taxes. A portion of that public tax money would have originated, at least theoretically, in Holt County. She knew that. And she didn't want anything from us. Not if she hadn't paid for it, she didn't. Doyle Francis was right about that.

But then, toward the end of spring that year, she discovered a way to make the final payment. She began to go out dancing at the Holt Legion on Saturday nights.

• • •

But no one would dance with her at first. She came down the stairs that first Saturday night early in May and walked over to the bar, lifted herself onto a bar stool, ordered a vodka Collins, and waited. And nothing happened. Maybe it got a little quieter for a moment, but not very much, so she couldn't be certain that she'd even been noticed. She looked lovely too: she had made herself up and had put on a deep blue dress that was loose enough that her stomach showed only a little, as if she were merely in the first months of pregnancy; she was wearing nylons and heels; her brown hair was pulled away from her face in a way that her eyes appeared to be even larger and darker than they were ordinarily. Sitting there, she waited; no one talked to her; nothing happened; finally she ordered another drink. On either side of her, men on bar stools were talking to one another, so she swung around to look at the couples in the nearby booths. They were laughing loudly and rising regularly from the booths to dance. Maybe they looked at her, maybe they didn't — she didn't know. So that first night she sat there at the bar, waiting, for almost two hours. Then she went home.

The second time, that second Saturday — this would have been about the middle of May now — she drank a small glass of straight vodka at home in the kitchen before she went out. Also, she was dressed differently this time. There was more blue makeup over her eyes and she was wearing a dark red dress with a low neckline that showed a good deal of her full breasts, a dress that made no pretense at disguising her pregnancy: it was stretched tight across her stomach and hips. Preparing to go out, she combed her hair close against her cheeks, partially obscuring her face, and then she entered the Legion again, walked down the steps into that noise and intense Saturday-night revelry a second time. And as before, she mounted a bar stool, ordered a drink, and then she turned around, with that short red dress hiked two inches above the knees of her crossed legs, with a look of expectation, of invitation almost, held permanently on her beautiful face.

Well, it was pathetic in its lack of subtlety. But subtlety and pathos are not qualities that are much appreciated at the Legion on Saturday nights, so she only had to sit there for an hour this second time before Vince Higgims, Jr., asked her to dance. Vince is one of our permanent Holt County bachelors, a lank, black-haired man, a man considered by many of us to be well educated in the ways of strong drink and ladies in tight dresses. "Come on, girl," Vince said. "They're playing my song."

They were playing Lefty Frizzell's "I Love You in a Thousand Ways," with its promise of change, the end of blue days — a song with a slow enough tempo to allow Vince, Jr., to work his customary magic. He led Jessie out onto the crowded floor and pulled her close against his belt buckle; then he began to pump her arm, to walk her backward in that rocking two-step while she held that permanent look of invitation on her face and he went on smiling past her hair in obvious satisfaction. They danced several dances that way, including a fast one or two so that Vince could demonstrate his skill at the jitterbug — he twirled her around and performed intricate movements with his hands — then they cooled off again with a slow song.

And that's how it began: innocently enough, I suppose, because unlike some of the others, at least Vince Higgims meant Jessie Burdette no harm. I doubt that Vince even had hopes of any post-dance payoff. It was merely that he was drunk and that he liked to dance. The same cannot be said about the others, however. These other men were still remembering the grain elevator.

They all began to dance with her. It was as if Vince had broken some taboo, some barrier of accepted behavior, so that now it was not only acceptable to dance with Jack Burdette's pregnant wife, it was required; it was a matter of community honor and retribution. And so, ten or fifteen men took their turns with her that night. They danced her hard around the floor. They swung her violently around; they held her clenched against themselves, forcing their own slack stomachs against her swollen hard one. From that point on they danced every song with her. And all that time Jessie seemed to welcome it, to smile and speak pleasantly to all the men who held her. When it was over, though, when the band finally stopped playing and the lights were turned on once again, she was very pale; she was sweating and her dress looked wrinkled, worn out, stained, as if it had been cheapened. She went home exhausted.

But the local routine was established now — that three-week-long Holt County system of payment was initiated and accepted. And so the third time, that third Saturday night in May, it was just the same — only it was worse. This time the men not only danced with her in the same fierce vindictive manner but they also insisted on buying her drinks. She was wearing that same red dress too, washed and pressed again but showing the additional week of pregnancy. If anything it looked tighter on her now, riper, as if the seams would burst at any moment, while above the deep neckline the blue veins in her full breasts showed clearly. Nevertheless, she danced with every man who asked her. They danced and danced — waltzes, jitterbugs, country two-steps, a kind of local hard-clenched fox-trot — anything and every-thing the men thought they knew how to do, regardless of the violence and energy it required. And this dancing, if you can call it that, this intense communal jig, stopped only when the band stopped. Then, during those ten minutes of brief rest between sets, the men bought her drinks. They sat her on a bar stool and three or four of them stood around her, telling jokes and buying drinks — taking turns with this too, ordering her double shots of Scotch or whiskey or vodka — it didn't matter what the combination or how unlikely the mix — they ordered liquor for her to drink and insisted that she drink it. And she did that too. She accepted it all, seemed to welcome it all, as if she were privately obliged to honor any demand.

Of course, by the evening's end she was even more exhausted this time than she had been the previous Saturday night. Also, she was very close to being drunk. When the lights came on at last, when the last man stopped dancing with her, she could barely walk off the dance floor. She was weak on her feet; there was a drunken waver in her step. She didn't say anything, though. Nothing in the way of complaint, I mean. And when that last man thought to ask her if she was coming back again the next week, she said: "You want me to, don't you?"

"Why course," he said. "Don't you know I'll be here? We'll all be here."

"Then I will too," she said.

And she was. Only, by this time, many of the women and at least some of the men were growing a little uneasy, a little uncomfortable with this particular form of weekly gambol and amusement. So not everyone showed up the following week, that last Saturday in May. Jessie did, though. It was the last time that she went to the Legion for a long time.

But again it was the same. She was wearing that same red dress, as if it were a uniform now, an essential part of the routine, and there was the same excessive amount of makeup on her face. She was drinking too — it was obvious that she'd been drinking heavily even before she arrived at the Legion. She entered the bar-and-dance room about nine o'clock and didn't even bother this time to lift herself onto a bar stool. She merely waited inside the door, with the music and smoke and laughter already at full strength around her. She didn't have to wait long: two or three men discovered her at the same moment and ushered her in.

"What are you drinking?" one of them said.

"Don't you want to dance first?"

"No, let's have a drink. I'm buying."

"All right," she said. "A whiskey sour then."

"Make it a double," he said.

She drank it fast, as if it were no more than water or lemonade, like she was no more conscious of what she drank than she was of the banter around her. When she had finished it, she set the glass down and said: "Now who's going to ask me to dance? I thought you boys knew how to dance."

"I'll show you how to dance," one of them said. "Come on."

This was Alden Haines, a man of forty-three who was only recently divorced and who farmed a couple of irrigated circles of corn east of town. He was not a bad man really, but he was still angry at the time about the divorce: his wife had been the one to initiate the legal proceedings. More to the point, he was a shareholder in the Farmers Co-op Elevator. "See if you can keep up with this," he said.

He took her out onto the dance floor. Pushing roughly through the other couples, he began immediately to swing her about the floor in circles and abrupt spins. Jessie kept up with him, moving back and forth or circling at the end of his outstretched arm. As we watched, she seemed almost feverish with intensity, as if she were resolved to test some private limits. When the dance ended, she and Haines were both sweating. The band played a slower song next and Haines pulled her close to himself, clenching his hands behind her back while she held tightly to his neck. He rocked her backward across the floor in time to the slow music. Neither of them talked. When the song ended, someone else cut in, and so it began again, with the same intensity, with the same feverish resolve. It went on in that way until the end of the set.

Then the band broke for ten minutes and the local men bought her drinks again at the bar. While they stood around her, not speaking to her very much but merely talking and joking among themselves while still paying close attention to the level of liquor in her glass, the rest of us in the Legion that night were also ordering fresh drinks. The two or three barmaids were kept busy carrying trays of glasses and bottles out to us in the booths. Across the room somebody started throwing ice cubes at one of the barmaids to get her attention. "Stop that," she called. "I see you — I'll be there in a minute."

Then the ten-minute break was over. The band resumed their places at the far end of the room and began to play. And Alden Haines led Jessie out onto the floor again. It was a fast song, the band's rendition of "That'll Be the Day." He swung her violently out at the end of his arm — and that was the end of it. Almost before it had begun, it was finished, completed. I suppose it was the ice cubes on the floor. Or perhaps during the break one of us had spilled beer or liquor in the dance area. We weren't certain what it was. In any case, her foot slipped on something wet and she went down. She tried to catch herself when she fell but she couldn't; she fell forward, hard, and didn't get up immediately. Afterward she lay there in her red dress while the rest of us around her stopped dancing. She turned onto her side, pulling her legs upward against herself. Haines leaned over her.

"You all right?" he said. "Can you get up?"

He lifted under her arm, helping her to stand. She was very pale. She was sweating again now, her face shining like wet chalk in the dim light. In the center of the dance floor she stood unsteadily on her feet while Alden Haines held her arm and people watched. "I think I need to go to the rest room," she said.

"You want me to walk you upstairs?"

"No. I want to be alone."

Later it was obvious to us that the pains had already begun while she was still on the dance floor — we remembered seeing her eyes focus peculiarly, a kind of brief intermittent stare — but she refused any assistance. She walked off the dance floor by herself, past the bar and up the stairs to the rest room near the front entrance. She went inside, into one of the toilet stalls, and sat down. We waited for her to come back. When she was still there ten minutes later, a couple of the women went in to check on her. She was still seated on the toilet, still conscious but quiet and very white. She was bent forward over her knees. There were clots of blood in the toilet. One of the women came outside into the hallway and told us to call the ambulance.

The ambulance got there in five or six minutes. The attendants went in and brought her back out in a wheelchair, tipping it backward to get down the front steps, and then they pushed the chair up a ramp into the ambulance and drove to the hospital. None of that took very long — the hospital is only three or four blocks east of the Legion — but it wouldn't have mattered if it had taken an hour.

When they arrived at the hospital, they wheeled her into the emergency room and Dr. Martin laid her down on a bed and examined her. He lifted her dress and noticed the blood. Then he listened for fetal heart tones. He couldn't hear anything, though: the little girl inside her was already dead. Afterward he said the placenta and uterine walls had separated. When she fell she had gone immediately into labor, and because its source of oxygen had been cut off, the baby had died within the first five minutes — probably during the time Jessie was still in the rest room. He didn't tell her that, though. He didn't want to upset her: she still had to deliver the baby.

They gave her Pitocin to help stimulate the contractions of the uterus. But she was in labor for nearly ten hours and there was additional loss of blood and she might have died. But finally she delivered the baby late on Sunday evening.

Afterward they held it up so she could look at it for a moment. The little girl was ashen but otherwise it looked quite normal. Jessie reached up and touched one of its feet. Then they took it away and one of the nurses said: "I'm so sorry, Mrs. Burdette."

So we thought she would cry then. We thought she would break down at last. I suppose we wanted her to do that. But she didn't. Perhaps she had gone past the point where human tears make any difference in such cases, because instead, she turned her face away and shut her eyes and after a while she went to sleep.

She stayed in the hospital for most of that next week. Mrs. Waters, her neighbor, took it upon herself to care for TJ and Bobby during that period. The old woman brought the boys in to see their mother as soon as she was able to have company, and Jessie talked to the little boys every day and held their hands and brushed the hair off their foreheads. She refused, however, to talk to any of the hospital staff about the little girl she had delivered and she refused absolutely to talk to a local minister when he came to her room to visit her. She preferred to lie quietly, looking out the window. When the week was over, they released her and she went home again, to the old Fenner House on Hawthorne Street. And then in another week she returned to work at the Holt Café. In the following months she continued to refill our cups with coffee and to bring us steaks and potatoes from the kitchen.

And so I don't know what monetary value people place on baby girls in other areas, but here we learned in May that year that $150,000 — less the resale value of a two-bedroom house in the middle of town — was a figure that seemed appropriate.

CLARE

James B. Hemesath

Feb. 14th. Valentine's Day. Clare and I made love late this afternoon. We both came away relaxed & pleased with ourselves and one another. David ate 2 lb. box of candy I got for Clare. David sick at supper & sent to bed. Clare saved box to keep photos in.

Feb. 16th. Return trip from Denver shopping. Blowing dirt turned day into night. Highway patrol shut down Interstate s. of Pueblo. 3 of us headed Bronco n.w. across mountains to Salida, next s. to Cibola City and home. Detour added 80 miles to trip. Stopped for coffee and donuts in Poncha Springs. David begged until he got pocketknife from tourist junk shop. Dirt, all that dirt, frightened & upset Clare. David read comic books.

Feb. 23d. Great Sand Dunes. Explored wooded bottom land along Medano Creek, encountering herd of mule deer. Young doe hesitantly approached David, licking his outstretched hand. Salt, I'd guess. 15–20 grazing deer all told, indifferent to us. We knelt beneath juniper tree and pulled cactus needles out of David's sneakers. House wren, tail cocked, flitted branch-to-branch foot or 2 above David's head. David wanted to walk out on sand. Clare said no. Dunes like small mountains. David said that Dunes changed colors from early AM to noon. Both Clare and I complimented him on being observant.

Feb. 24th. David & I drove n. of Cibola City to look at full moon thru binoculars. Vapor trail of jet plane bisected pie-like moon. Massive dark outline of 14,000 foot Mt. Blanca and Sangre de Cristo Mtns., Blood of Christ Mtns., viewed thru binoculars somehow unnerving, almost supernatural. Clare not up to ride she said.

Feb. 25th. Clare fixed spinach quiche for supper. David ate peanut butter sandwich. Peach melba for dessert. David and I washed & dried dishes while Clare studied her cookbooks.

March 9th. Up Mosca Pass Trail to Split Rock. Snow & mud made it slow climb, Clare complained she couldn't breathe, David claimed he saw bighorn sheep. On way down Clare kept stopping to look at animal droppings. See this, she said, see this. Finally I called her "turd-ologist." Turd-ologist Clare. She laughed 1st time I said it.

March 10th. Clare in bad shape. Blood clots on her legs. I yelled at David to clean his room. We ate supper at downtown cafe. Food terrible. We need to get Clare to doctor this week. We need to take care of her. How long you known about these? I asked Clare when she went to bed. I don't know, Clare said, couple of days, maybe longer.

March 14th. Clare to doctor, at last. Diagnosis, high blood pressure 150/120 and must slow down. Blood clots possible reaction to lack of oxygen at this altitude. Your doctor say that? I ask. Yes, Clare says, where else would I get it? Report on Clare's "white blood" cell count due next week.

March 17th. St. Patrick's Day. Leprechauns left trail of Hershey's kisses from hallway outside David's bedroom door to living room and wood stove. David's pot of gold — "Star Wars" t-shirt. Clare and I had our first date on St. Patrick's Day. Tinfoiled kisses shimmered in glow of crackling fire.

March 24th. Clare's doctor called 5:05 PM — "white blood" cell count haywire. Last night Clare had new bump on left leg just below knee. Doctor said to tell him if another bump appears. Clare didn't tell doctor when he called. Need to pick right time to talk to Clare about this.

March 27th. Forgot 1st day of Spring last week, but thought better late than never. David got Luke Skywalker action figure plus bag of candy corn from Spring Grizzly Bear. Clare thinks Spring Grizzly's a "hoot." Says I should contact Hallmark Cards about getting another holiday started. It's good to hear her laugh. David wants to know if Grizzly'll come again next year. Maybe, Clare says. She reminds him that Easter Bunny's coming in 3 days.

April 1st. April Fools' Day. At supper table, David recites endless string of April Fools' jokes he heard at school. Dad, your nose is bleeding. April Fool! Dad, your shoelaces are untied. April Fool! David, you can't watch Disney Channel rest of week. Dad!!!!!!!!!! April Fool!

April 5th. Yet another black lump on Clare's right knee.

April 10th. Failed to see Halley's Comet. Sky overcast, spitting snow. 2 or 3 weeks to go yet, then it's gone for 75+ years.

April 11th. Nurse told Clare doctor didn't need to see her. Hour or 2 later nurse called & said doctor'd call her. No call by 6, so we ate. Cuffed David at supper table. Clare said I was guilty of child abuse. I kept my mouth shut. David said he loved me.

April 13th. Great Wall of dirt just west of Cibola City. Wind gusts started at noon; our street turned into river of grit, junk & tumbleweeds. Still blowing at 10 PM. Bought David wiffle ball & plastic bat to help with his hitting for Little League this summer. Clare to bed after supper with pillow and covers pulled over her head. Clare says she hates Cibola City. Why did we move here? Why don't I quit Forest Service? I could teach high school biology. We could move back to Midwest — Minneapolis, Des Moines, Chicago.

April 19th. Clare determined that I see Halley's Comet. Drove 35 miles s.s.w. of Cibola City on county blacktop. We stopped on slight rise just couple of miles short of New Mexico. Clouds cleared approx. 10:25. Horizon & sky 95% free of ground light. No moon to speak of. Clare, excited, happy, pointed out constellations Crater and Hydra in 3-D firmament. Focus on Crater, she said, search above & below it, then backtrack along Hydra's tail. I did what Clare said. Look for big blur, blotch of dull light, Clare explained. Yes, yes, I said, peering thru binoculars. After 2, maybe 3 minutes, I saw something up there. I told Clare. God's thumbprint, I teased her, Almighty God's celestial thumbprint, that's what I see. Clare squeezed my arm. You see Halley's Comet, she said, ecstatic. She kissed me and I felt her hot breath against my cheek. When it returns, Clare said, David's children'll be grandparents. David slept in Bronco. Clare and I warmed our hands on truck hood. Cold night, Clare said, but I'd seen comet. I thanked Clare for it, holding her close to me.

April 22nd. Clare's legs worse. Clare joked that she'd tell doctor I kicked her. Blood test at clinic today. Doctor said that Clare may need to go to Pueblo for biopsy.

April 23d. No report on Clare's blood test. After supper dishes finished, 3 of us played Scrabble till David's bedtime. Clare and I watched TV news, then made love.

April 24th. No word yet on Clare's test.

April 25th. Received book on "good luck" that I ordered from BOMC. Read 1st chapter to Clare tonight in bed. We need to be positive. We need to position ourselves for opportunity. Clare said she might start going to church again.

April 26th. Rain 4:30 PM till now (8:30 PM) with great lightning and thunder. David asleep in our bed, cuddled next to Clare. Clare gave him "tiny piece" of Valium because he was afraid of storm. I don't know.

April 27th. Neighborhood dogs yappy tonight. Clare threatened to call police to complain. Asked her not to do that, it would cause more trouble than good. Clare & I got into fight. Clare still not heard from doctor.

April 28th. David butted out bedroom window with his head. When I asked him how it happened he said that he didn't know. Clare picked bits of glass out of his hair. No cuts. Reminded Clare that I had to go to Denver on business. Life goes on, Clare said.

April 29th. At last! Clare's appointment in Pueblo week from tomorrow for biopsy of hard lumps, blood clots. Doctor apologized for not getting back to Clare sooner. Clare calm, at least on surface, read to David at bedtime. Clare & I watched 10 o'clock news, then made love.

April 30th. Cold & windy tonight. Leave for Denver 6 AM sunrise to meet with Forest Service brass about project. Clare plans to clean house & bake cookies. Clare cheerful. Told David that he should help his mother.

May 1st. Long day. Scraped ice from windshield. Greasewood, rabbit brush on Valley floor coated, painted with frost. Couple inches of new snow in mountains. Sushi for lunch, then met for 3 hours about long-term effects of aspen blight. More meetings tomorrow. Denver 5 PM, overcast & rainy, clouds hang down distant mountains like great sacks of grey nothingness. Trees outside motel window, green & lush, dripping rain. Everything washed clean of winter dirt. Wish Clare were here. Bought David latest Berenstain Bears book. Called home 7 PM. We're fine, Clare said.

May 3d. Clare wrote $75 check for 8x10 enlargements of old vacation snapshots —Petrified Forest, cliff dwellings at Mesa Verde, narrow gauge train at Durango. Clare spent hour tonight trying to frame photo of David at Mesa Verde ruins. Clare got frame at K-Mart. Glass in picture frame's dirty, Clare said, squirting Windex, I want it clean, picture perfect. Clare giggled. Get it, she said. Picture perfect. Coaxed Clare into going to bed after she squirted photo with Windex. I'm sorry, Clare said, I just want things right. I know, I said. Clare said I should remarry if anything happens to her. Nothing's going to happen, I said. Clare sees specialist in 3 days.

May 7th. Clare cancelled her Pueblo appointment. Called Clare's doctor here in town and got his nurse. He called me later and said he'd talk to Clare. I must be careful not to yell at her, doctor said.

May 10th. Clare so damned stubborn at times that I want to hit her. Clare might have cancer, she might not. Clare secretive. Did or did not doctor call? How dare you talk to my doctor, Clare said. I have my privacy, I have my rights. I told Clare that I was sorry and that I loved her.

May 11th. Mother's Day. David brought card & gift home from school — gift, shadow picture of his head complete with rooster tails. Clare trimmed his hair this afternoon. Hit snake on road just before Uracca Cemetery. Looked for it on return trip, thought it might be rattler, but it wasn't there. David would like tail. Stopped in middle of nowhere, listened to wind & birds, talked to myself about Clare. I need to do something to help her, to get thru to her. I'm afraid for Clare, for David, for all of us. I would be lost without Clare.

May 13th. Beautiful day with light wind, lots of open sky and sun. Clare finished stripping her vanity, then rubbed it with tung oil. She's now at work on dining room table. She was outside nearly all day and looks years younger tonight. Told Clare at bedtime that I thought she knew what was best for her. Clare said she hoped so. Clare & I are close to talking to each other. Will wait day or 2, then mention Pueblo and need for Clare to make another appointment. We have to be careful about our health. We have to think about David. He needs us. That's what I will tell her.

May 15th. 3 million+ $$$ malpractice suit filed against Clare's doctor and Cibola City hospital. High school teacher checked into hospital for D&C, bled to death in recovery room. Clare claims she talked to dead woman at clinic. Told Clare she was mistaken because woman died 6 months ago. Clare asked if I thought she was worth that much.

May 19th. Dining room table pushed in corner of garage, half done, covered with sheet, trouble. Clare sews napkins and place mats. Nervous, inhaled too much stripper, she thinks. Backyard sprinkler hitting bedroom windows sounds like rain hitting tin roof of house Clare & I rented in Idaho.

May 20th. Clare won't listen to me, won't talk about Pueblo.

May 21st. Clare hides her legs. Blue jeans, granny nightgowns, my pajama bottoms. Pocket watch, gift from David last Father's Day, at jewelers after Clare knocked it out of my hand.

May 26th. Memorial Day. Trip to San Luis, Chama, San Francisco & San Pablo. Hamlets, villages, nestled s.e. corner of Valley, foothills of Sangre de Cristos. Adobe houses, I said. Real ones, Clare said. We took pictures. Fast-moving creeks lined with willows and cottonwoods. Horses out to pasture, cattle, much green grass, lots of wild flowers and magpies, field of dandelions shone like another sun. Cemeteries dotted with tiny American flags and plastic flowers. We stopped for pop and candy, more film, at "oldest store" in Colorado. David got Donald Duck comic book in Spanish. Good time, good trip.

May 27th. Clare dug thru shoe boxes of photos from 2, 3, 5 years ago and held up several pictures in bedroom mirror. She asked what I thought. How did she look? How did she compare? Would I always love her?

May 28th. Heavy rain tonight. Thick grey ceiling in Valley with Rio Grande close to flooding.

May 30th. David's last day of school + he received dog-eared story-book for being best reader in 2nd grade. Clare says she wants to go back home for visit. Told her that David's Little League started next week. Clare called her parents in Minneapolis.

May 31st. Clare & I not talking.

June 3d. Clare baked rhubarb pie.

June 5th. Clare promised she'd make another appointment in Pueblo once she returned.

June 7th. Clare & I made love before she left.

June 8th. Quiet Sunday at home, house damp, built fire in wood stove, heavy rain all day. Oiled, waxed, polished 12 pairs of shoes & boots. David spent most of day in his room. I must get grip on myself.

June 10th. Clare just called. She's arrived in Nebraska at her brother Tom's. All is well. She'll call again when she visits old college room-mate in Des Moines.

June 11th. David cried because Clare's gone. Another dreary day with cold rain tonight. Little League practice cancelled. David's base-ball glove made in Korea.

June 12th. Beautiful night once late-afternoon storm passed. Great puddles of standing water reflect blue sky. Rio Grande, wide, brown: endless flow of dark brown glass with ripples or imperfections. Valley springtime green to lower reaches of Sangre de Cristos. Mist, banks of mist, blood-red in sunset, float between snowy mountain peaks & Valley floor. Wish Clare were home to see this.

June 14th. Clare picked up for speeding in Iowa. Wrote check for $85 she explained. Clare wanted to know if I was mad at her. Told her that she was missed & that we wanted her back with us. David is here with me & I am glad. David will bring Clare home.

June 15th. Father's Day. David read to me tonight from dog-eared storybook. Remembered couple of stories from my school days.

June 17th. Clare called. Humidity in Twin Cities terrible. Her parents are fine, her legs are fine. She'll start back home in day or 2. David happy, Mom's coming home! We went to Dairy Queen to celebrate. David, hot fudge sundae; I had chocolate malt.

June 18th. Sheep huddled together in flooded field. Ceiling of bugs hangs, hovers like flying saucer over sheep. Sheep resemble human brain, storm cloud, surface of moon. Rivulets, valleys, ridges. Sheep in constant motion, alive with other life. Sheep off-white in color, color of dirty white car, tan in setting sun, soiled creatures, milling and suffering. Sheep on slight rise, knoll, one spot in field not underwater. No call from Clare. Dreamt last night that Clare had cancer, and that I couldn't find right doctor to save her.

June 19th. 1st baseball game tonight. David played 4 innings at 2nd. Caught little pop fly, ground ball, almost hit in head by line drive. David walked, struck out, and walked 3 times he came to bat. David hit 2 foul balls. We need to practice batting with wiffle ball in backyard.

June 20th. Clare called. She has office job in Minneapolis. She has rented apartment. Clare wanted to talk to David, but I said he was at Little League. Left phone off hook. Need time to think. Tried talking her into coming home, but Clare wouldn't talk. What can I do? I asked. Nothing, Clare said.

June 21st. Morning chill quickly replaced by oven-like heat and promise of late-afternoon thundershowers. Wall of black clouds lurked in west peeking above San Juan Mtns. Masses of cumulus clouds balanced like great airships on crest of Mt. Blanca and Sangre de Cristos to east. Return trip to Cibola City from Alamosa, sound of popcorn in red-hot popper, wave after wave of bugs hitting windshield & grill. Masturbated tonight.

June 24th. David received postcard from Clare with picture of beluga whale at Minneapolis zoo. Showed it to him, but didn't let him read it. Clare wants David to live with her in Minneapolis. Called Clare's doctor at home and got his answering machine. Doctor out-of-town. Called Clare's parents. Clare's dad said I should give her time. Her mom said I should get job back in civilization. Settle down! Stop moving! Wyoming, Arizona, Idaho, Colorado. Clare hasn't told them about her legs. Asked them for Clare's phone number. No phone yet.

June 25th. Twilight, dusk, early night in Valley, period of calm and sudden drop in temperature. Watchful hawks & eagles perch on utility poles, sharp-eyed & ready, search shadowy countryside for prey, hot flesh, rabbits, mice. Tourists hole up in adobe-front motels with Spanish-sounding names, stare at TV. Local people mow grass, swat mosquitoes, stare at TV. I must be going crazy. Thought I heard all TVs in town going at once. Told David turn TV off and get to bed. It's just 8, David said. Go to bed, I said, go to bed. Kept phone off hook, then put it back. Took it off again. No call from Clare. I know she loves me. We have been married 10 years. We waited to have David until I had job with Forest Service.

June 26th. Woke David at 5 and got going. Sunrise, explosion of reds & yellows, David burrowed like rabbit into truck seat. Herd of elk on highway near summit of La Veta Pass. Told David sit up and look. We honked and picked our way thru them. Isn't this great, I said. Counted 35–40 elk. Where are we going? David asked. What if Mom gets home and we're not there? She won't, I said. David started to cry. Breakfast at truck stop 10, 15 miles before Walsenburg and Interstate. David told waitress about elk. Waitress said he should try to get photo of elk, then send it to people who print picture postcards. Bought David sunglasses, comic books, also film for camera when we get home. Got road maps out of Bronco glove compartment. Told David to get back inside truck stop, to go bathroom again. I went bathroom again, then bought 2 more road maps and 6 candy bars. Dug out pocket watch and balanced it in ashtray. 7:45 AM. David & I started for Minneapolis to get Clare and bring her home. Mom wants us to come get her, I told David. That's good, he said.

JUMPING-OFF PLACE

Baine Kerr

Mack Brown was early. The airport bars at San Antonio International were not yet open. He wandered to the mezzanine and, sitting alone, passed the time before the flight in reflection. He freed his mind of small concerns. He compared himself with other men and to the way he used to be. Gazing out the plate window at the huge blue sky, he concentrated on the image he knew he struck: A man hitting his stride. A man for whom each moment could break open bright new worlds of adventure and delight. Confident, and resolute, he rose to obey the voice instructing him to board at Gate 16.

"Dallas or Denver?" the Braniff attendant asked him, hand extended for the ticket, fingers snapping silently, impatiently.

"I'm not particular," he smiled.

The attendant took the ticket, scanned it. "You're checked through to Denver, layover in Dallas twenty minutes. Smoking or non?"

"Smoking."

"Aisle or window?"

"Aisle, definitely the aisle," Mack Brown said, giving the attendant a confidential wink and a grin, his characteristic gesture, his trademark.

"Pleasant flight."

Mack Brown joined the ten or twelve other passengers in the waiting area — elegant Mexicans who would shop in Dallas, stetsoned Texans, a vaguely nervous-looking group of airmen, a mother and child. Home and family were on their minds, he observed. Home would not absorb his life and purpose again, and he marked his distance from them. Thirtyish (thirty-two in fact); styled, longish hair; neat mustache; engaging smile. This great suit; three piece but a bright wide plaid. The Burberry raincoat over his arm. And these new shoes. Divorce would not cripple him as it had so many men he knew, and so few women. Divorce would free him, and he would take advantage of his freedom.

His ambition was to do well and also to live well. The week in San
Antonio had been exhilarating, but incomplete. He'd worked hard to
win over the Lone Star Beer people and had secured the Denver
distributorship for their imported wine division. It would increase his
market 15, maybe 20 percent, and was his first big break. It had
required technique, the skillful execution of the first principle of sales
— to sell the product you must sell yourself — and it was an exacting
and worthy challenge. Trust, confidence, respect, these, like love and
grace, one had to earn. The rest was mere ingratiation and anyone
could do it.

It remained to turn his abilities to personal as well as business
advantage, and he was eager to do so. He was eager for departure, for
the trip itself. He had his book, *Fear of Flying,* an old book of his
ex-wife's, debris of the divorce, but in this situation the perfect touch.
And he had his aisle seat.

Little stood in the way of his ambition. He was his own boss,
mastering his own destiny. He lived by himself in the best condominium in Lakewood, with the best stocked private bar in Colorado. Life
and work blended like a well-mixed drink, as they had never, with
Betty, been able to before. He would roll back the walnut panels for
the Lone Star man, or the Brown-Foreman distillery people, and even
for the Hennessy rep when he came to Denver, revealing the hundreds
of neatly ranged, dusted, glistening bottles, lit from behind. The liquor
spoke for itself, spoke for *him:* Barbancourt rum, Dickel bourbon,
Dimple Haig, Rémy Martin "Louis XIII," a complete decade of Vosne-
Romanée wines, the 1946 Château Lafite he was saving — not for
another wedding night; for the last supper, a toast to a life lived to the
hilt, to possibilities seized and subjected to his fancy. "Occupational
hazard," he would say, with a wink and a grin, letting his liquor, the
finest blend of work and life, speak for him to his business guests.
"Occupational hazard," he would think also sometimes to himself,
alone in his Mission Viejo condominium, listening to the Jazz Crusad-
ers on Chrisman speakers, alone sipping thoughtfully his fourth Bom-
bay gin martini, feeling finally a little sleepy.

Little stood in the way of his ambition but the fact that, at five six,
he was a short man, and self-conscious about it. Yet many great men
were also short — Caesar, Napoleon, Alexander the Great — and all
men were equals sitting down. And these beautiful new shoes, tan
patent leather, buckled, platform shoes, purchased yesterday in San

Antonio, these shoes would be the first big step (he smiled) toward his success. They meant more than fashion. They meant personality.

The flight was boarding and its dozen passengers lined up at the security gate, some a bit irritated at the intrusion of X rays on handbags, others glumly filing through. But Mack Brown kept his humor. He walked with a wink and a grin under the metal doorway; back again at the lady guard's request; removed penknife, change, keys, full money clip; stepped through again, joking and confident — the high bouncing businessman, his own boss — and down the ramp toward the waiting entrance of the gaudy aquamarine Braniff jet. He had nothing to hide, nothing to fear. Mack Brown, with platform shoes, had reached the jumping-off place.

• • •

The plane ripped past runway, blurred weeds and wildflowers, a puzzled jackrabbit, nosed up and lost the earth. As it banked in a wide arc toward Dallas, the spare luxury of San Antonio spring lost features, tilted and leveled, telescoped into only a piece of a map. Old Texas was gone: cedar brakes, then blue-stem prairie, then the mesquite and acacia savanna — far away out the window a wide cambered land, annealed by sun and history, a region of missions and ranchos grandes from which long ago great adventures were launched. It was not a place Mack Brown knew except that it had been flowered and green, luminous, full of music, birds, and dark-eyed women, while Denver would be snowbound by yesterday's April storm. At the first bing and signal from the panel he lit a cigarette. At the second bing he unlatched his seat belt and turned from the window. The window did not interest him; the aisle did.

He opened his book. Only two stewardesses on this 727 ministered to the scattered passengers. One was quite pretty: blond, nicely built, almost glamorous; she'd smiled coolly at her charges, pointed to exits, and donned an oxygen mask with mannered gestures that Mack Brown found provocative. Of the other stewardess he wondered why they hired homely girls and he felt sorry for her.

Elbow propped on seat arm he held *Fear of Flying* at eye level, conspicuously angled to the aisle, as the pretty one made her way toward him. She interrupted his reading, asked if he cared for coffee and a roll. Mack Brown decided to begin by ordering a Bloody Mary.

"No cocktails on the morning flight."

He motioned with the book toward the forward cabin. A fat man in a western suit hunched over a tiny Smirnoff bottle on his tray table, unscrewing its tiny cap. "I guess I'm like that fellow," he said, winked and grinned. "Can't wake up without a Bloody Mary. Occupational hazard."

Next Mack Brown would explain. The occupation: independent wine and liquor distributor. Takes you all over the country. Might be going to France next year in fact, then the German wineries. Was just down with the Lone Star people, Texas importers, and locked up the Rocky Mountain region for their labels. It does mean a lot of traveling, of course, but he was learning to enjoy flying. She must too. By the way, he would then ask, had she seen this book? It doesn't have much to do with flying, he would smile.

But her professional courtesy had hardened into sullen resolve. "No cocktails," she said, "on the morning flight in coach."

Nothing ventured, nothing gained, so Mack Brown began explaining how to compose the perfect Bloody Mary (dill weed, stick of celery, Ro-tel tomato juice, Stolichnaya vodka).

"Excuse me, sir," she said, tight-lipped. "This is a forty-minute run to Dallas and I've got a planeload of people to see to. Can I get you coffee or a roll?"

He shook his head and she was gone, mincing down the aisle, offering the same to those who weren't dozing. Stuck up, he concluded moodily; he returned to the book. The book was getting good.

But reading didn't distract him from his preoccupation, his ambition. He considered how far he'd come. It seemed a lifetime, though not yet two years, since he had quit working for Fuelco, and the bitterness was not completely gone. He was bitter for having swallowed Fuelco's pitch: that the driver-salesman position was a stepping-stone to management, where the president himself had begun. Seven years he'd waited to get on the fast track, and at the end he was still bucking fifty-five-gallon drums, chasing orders, stacking quarts of oil on K-Mart shelves. A glorified truck driver, someone said near the end, and he'd wondered what that meant, glorified.

Their priorities had been dead wrong — home, security, their sacrifices for the company, the three-bedroom house they'd bought anticipating promotions and children that were never to exist. That was the root of their problems; it wasn't his fault and it wasn't her fault, though he'd turned away from her, then she from him, until he could hardly stand to be around her, and she could hardly stand his touch.

It wasn't as though she didn't fit into his plans, his new life, though that was true. It was as though she'd conspired in his failure, by preferring him in the company to him alone. Now his priorities had changed. Now he knew what he needed. Once he'd heard a girl say, "I'm a people person." It was nothing he'd ever say, but it was what he wanted to be.

He reflected on his reading, on Isadora Wing's dreams and adventures. What the world needs, he thought, is more women like her. And the world must be full of them: Dallas, Denver, and for sure Paris, France. The pretty one returned balancing a tray of cups and paper plates, the top two buttons of her Paisley Braniff blouse undone. She passed him, hips turning, the blue skirt tight across the tangent where her thighs met and the nylon crisped. The homely one followed up the aisle and stopped at his seat behind him. "Fun book," she said.

"What?" He was startled at being addressed. "Have you read it?"

"Couldn't put it down."

"It is interesting." Mack Brown was disarmed: a sparrowy little woman, clerical in glasses, black hair balled and pinned like a cook. "I find it interesting because it's written from a female point of view."

"That's not the only reason," she smiled. A pleasant smile. "We're about to land, and . . . "

"Well . . . " Mack Brown hesitated — the same hesitation (he was at once aware and chagrined) of stopping at the Safeway counter to deliberate whether a fifty-cents-off bone-in round steak would do for dinner alone that night. "Well," he winked and grinned. He suggested she sit across the aisle for the landing and continue the conversation.

"The seat belt sign is on," she said. He hadn't noticed the first bing. "Return your tray table to the back of your seat. Put your briefcase *under* your seat and," — bing — "please put out your cigarette." She smiled again, not unpleasantly. "Friend," she said. "Forget it." She staggered off, bracing herself in the choppy descent, and disappeared.

The view from the window was dismal: loops of cloverleafs and straight tapes of highway, endless unoccupied runways puttied over the drab prairie, the diagrammatic linked circles of the terminals. The Dallas–Ft. Worth Interregional, the world's largest airport, as the pilot announced. The airport of the future.

• • •

The boarding in Dallas had nothing of San Antonio's insouciance. Seats were quickly located and suit jackets stowed above; the *Dallas Morning News* fluttered open up and down the aisle like egrets taking wing. This was a conscientious, almost grim party of men. Home was not on their minds. Work was. Work had subsumed life, as is Dallas's nature. Mack Brown was glad he hadn't deboarded, hadn't had to hassle with security — his keys, knife, money clip — twice in a morning. Mack Brown no longer felt himself a debonair.

The plane was nearly full when a girl, tall, ungainly, bewildered, came stumbling into the aisle, stepping one direction then the other, swatting newspapers and shirt sleeves with the huge brimming-over laundry bag she lugged with great difficulty. After a half-dozen inquiries she was directed to Mack Brown. She struggled across his knees, squirmed securely into the window seat beside him.

"Is this *my* seat?" she asked.

"I have no idea," he said. She handed him her boarding pass. It was.

"Oh thank you," she said. She thrust furiously at the laundry bag, Mack helped, and they managed to fit it partially under the seat, mostly between her legs.

"Thank you so much," she said, her bony kneecap jabbing at his. "This is my first plane ride and I'm *so excited*. My name's Melanie Jones. What's yours?"

"Mack Brown." Just his luck that day, he thought. Melanie Jones — a big, skinny, unhealthy-looking kid (a good five nine: taller than he even in new shoes), no older than sixteen, seventeen tops — Melanie Jones was excited, and Mack Brown only wanted his book.

"Have you been in Denver before?" she asked urgently, suddenly looking absolutely anguished.

"Oh yes."

"I've got to get a bus in Denver and I just *know* I'll get lost. I'll *never* find it by myself. Will you help me when we get there?"

"Where are you going?"

The worry vanished, her eyes widened, she whispered close to him, Vail. She pronounced it Vayul and she squealed happily.

"No problem." Mack said. The bus, he knew, left directly from the airport. He prepared to resume *Fear of Flying*, but the plane had taxied to the runway and Melanie Jones required his help with her seat belt.

Melanie Jones had done a lot of exciting things in her life but nothing quite like taking off in an airplane. She couldn't believe it: the power pulling at her cheeks, the whole world surging past. Then she pressed her face to the cold double window and saw the vast prairie sink and turn and the scattered shocks of cloud falling beneath them. She wheeled to Mack Brown and grabbed his arm.

"Scared?" he asked.

"Oh no! It's so *fun.*"

She beamed. Texas was gone. She was sick of Texas and when she'd seen the story on Vail she knew that was the place. "Do you go to Colorado a lot?"

He closed the book. "I live there."

"You *live* there? I'd die to live in Colorado. Where do you live, in Denver?"

"Lakewood."

"Is that in the mountains?"

"No. It's near Denver."

"Denver's not in the mountains?"

"No."

She was crestfallen. The poor unattractive kid, Mack thought. A lurid excess of makeup, a wild bush of bleached hair. A massive dose of Clearasil masoned in pink lumps about her face, like the first phase of giant hives. "It's only two hours to Vail, though," he said.

Melanie Jones proceeded to tell him about her plans. She came into a lot of money, $850, and just up and left. Left her aunt's house in Abilene — her parents were dead, had been dead awhile. Car wreck. She'd already quit running orders at the Dairy Queen a couple weeks now. And when you think, if she'd been working she'd never been driving that morning west of town — Abilene got so *dull;* nothing to do but *drive* — when she spun off the road. But if she hadn't spun off the road she'd never have got the $850 (about twice what the durn Dodge Dad left was worth), the $850 settlement from insurance and still be down, right down there in the flatlands. Not up here, headed to Vayul, and the mountains, and the parties.

The jet passed through a brilliant sky across the panhandle south of Amarillo, directly over the Palo Duro canyon. The patchwork of perfectly level irrigated plains reached abruptly the ragged rim of the canyon, graven into the view below in fine layers of purple and gold. Beyond lay the red beds of the Comanchería, where the great herds, the longhorn and bison, had been chivied and driven and finally destroyed. This, the Palo Duro, was the jumping-off place to the West, and from her new height Melanie Jones turned against it, a dark scar, turned from the window toward Mack Brown. Melanie Jones had taken off. She was *flying* to Colorado to *ski.*

. . .

"How does it work?" she asked Mack Brown. She strained, pulling at the bottom of her tray table.

"Hmmm?" He'd been reading again, half-absorbed in his book, half-fantasizing. The stewardesses were marching back and forth serving lunch, and the pretty one had stooped two seats ahead to retrieve a fumbled cup and napkin. He'd watched rapt, agape, and she had caught him. She had drilled him with a look of unequivocal unpitying annoyance and contempt, and he had gone back to reading.

"They said," Melanie Jones continued, referring to the intercom, "to put your tray table down if you want lunch and I can't get it to work." Mack Brown reached over to twist the catch at the top and lower the tray for her. It rested precariously on her laundry bag.

"Oh thank you," she smiled. "Aren't you having any?"

"No. Dieting."

"Dieting? What do you *mean?*" she said. "You have a wonderful physique for a man."

"Well thank you." He winked and grinned.

The homely one handed him Melanie's lunch — Salisbury steak, limas, mashed potatoes, roll and butter, an agglutinated cherry cobbler — and he handed it on. The homely one looked from Melanie to Mack, shook her head. Mack ordered a martini.

"I'm a vegetarian," Melanie confided to him. "I've only been one a month but it's working wonders. Of course it is hard." She scraped her Salisbury steak onto a coffee saucer. "But you really feel healthy, you really do." She reached across, awkwardly holding the saucer with its little patty — smothered, as they say, in gluey gravy — in front of Mack.

"Oh no," he said.

"You should eat *some*thing," Melanie said, poking it at him.

"No. No thanks."

"O.K." She sighed and began spooning in the cherry cobbler. "Know what my biggest problem is?" she asked.

"No idea."

"These." She fetched a pack of Parliaments from her purse. "What's the good of giving up meat if you can't quit smoking?"

"Absolutely right." Mack Brown was amused, enjoying her.

"But I've smoked for *years*," she said. "I smoke like a *fish*."

"A fish?"

"Oh *no* . . . " She covered her mouth, dropped a spoonload of cobbler. "I mean *chimney.*"

Mack Brown guffawed.

The homely one appeared with two tiny bottles, glass and ice. He chided her about the price, the lack of olive or Gibson onion. He emptied the little test tube of Gordon's gin over the ice and expressed a dollop of vermouth on top. He sipped and smiled, reached across, and held it unsteadily for Melanie Jones.

"Oooh!" She wrinkled her nose. "How can you *stand* it?"

"Occupational hazard," Mack Brown said. He proceeded to tell her what he did. His work, his travel, his private bar, his stereo, the important people he knew. How well he was doing; how well he lived. That he was his own boss and wouldn't have it any other way. Melanie Jones was impressed and urged him on. He talked, enjoying himself, and watched her, stroking the cool beaded plastic glass, and watched her legs, blue jeans spread so artlessly, and felt her kneecap against his.

She shrieked.

"What is it?"

"LOOK!"

The plane had banked slightly and out the window they could see immediately below two small round cones, spattered with snow — odd incipient Rockies at the northern corner of Texas, like lighthouses designating land's end. Behind these, still distant against the pale afternoon, the horizon was frothed with snowcaps, and Melanie Jones could not speak. The plane bore on in an empty sky, on a north northwest azimuth tracking the Goodnight Loving Trail, and the mountains gathered definition. The great weaving cordillera of the Sangre de Cristos, then the glistening ranks of the Colorado Rockies — the terrible, the wonderful, the unknown places that meant to Melanie adventure and delight — the frozen fastnesses where no one dwelled, not a soul.

"Oh Lord save me," she almost whispered; she chewed her lip. "Just *look.*"

• • •

He'd have nothing to do when they arrived, 2 P.M., Mountain Time ("Their time?" Melanie had said when she asked him. "Our time," he'd corrected her). No boss to report to at work, and no one at home. That's how he wanted it, of course, but the days could get empty, living alone.

He decided that after they landed he would drive her downtown toward the main Greyhound station. He'd caution her about Vail Pass, that Eisenhower Tunnel was probably snowpacked, convince her to catch a morning bus. Then he'd show her around downtown, maybe stop at the Mint. Or they might go straight to Mission Viejo. Tonight he'd take her out, to the Quorum, no, to the Magic Pan: crepes — less expensive, and she'd surely never had them. The poor kid, he thought, watching her stare at the window. Skinny, scatterbrained, friendless, absolutely alone. She'd stay with him in Lakewood (No, he'd say, it's not *in* the mountains, but it's *toward* them). Then go to Vail, go home, whatever.

The jet droned north, skirting the mountains up a corridor just east of the Front Range, then almost squarely over the beautifully riven hulk of Pikes Peak, he informed her to her amazement.

"What are the dark parts?" she asked.

"Trees."

Soon the plane veered sharply away from the mountains, dipped a wing, and began a precipitous downward spiral. "Mack," she said, upset, "I'll just be *lost*. I just know it. You will find the right bus for me?"

He nodded, smiled, and winked. "Don't worry." He explained that she would have to leave from the downtown station; said he had nothing better to do, he'd drive her over in his car. Maybe see a little of Denver before she had to go.

"You *angel*. I'm so glad I sat by you."

"Here," he said. "Let's get that seat belt fastened." She watched as the ailerons lowered, the wing seeming to break in half. Sun struck the window and blanched the view with glare. She turned to Mack Brown and smiled, trembled her lip a bit, raised an arm on the support next to his. The landing gear clanked loudly down beneath her feet, as though the floor were giving way. "Mack," she said. "I think I'm scared." He took her hand and held it firmly through the landing and until the plane had stopped at the terminal gate.

Mack Brown shouldered Melanie Jones's laundry bag, led her by the elbow to baggage claim, retrieved his hanging bag and her tiny overnight case. He told her to wait there with the bags, he'd be back in a minute in the car.

She watched him go, stepping jauntily in his funny high-heeled shoes, in his bright plaid suit in the bright sun. Snow sparkled on roofs and in troughs along curbs. A veil of water dripped like rain from the eave above the glass door he'd pushed through. Inside, next to the door, a line had formed at the Colorado Bus Company counter. The marquee above the counter announced an immediate departure for Idaho Springs — Frisco — Vail — Glenwood Springs — Aspen. "Vayul," she murmured, and looked again through the door as Mack Brown disappeared among vast glittering levels of parked cars. "The little guy lied to me."

He turned the car in between two cabs near the bus and found her waiting to board in a noisy crowd of kids in cowboy hats and orange or blue down parkas, bearing skis, with poles and shiny plastic-cased ski boots swinging from hands. She mounted the steps behind a Robert Redford type, his sunburned face white around the eyes. She noticed Mack Brown and waved, pointed to his luggage on the sidewalk, pointed to herself, then pointed to the bus, mouthed something — see y'all later — waved again and vanished.

Mack Brown walked with his briefcase and hanging bag through the baggage area, milling with impatient Denverites anxious to pluck up their suitcases from the metal carousels and clap spurs for home. He entered a room marked cocktails; he ordered a martini. No point in going home yet, not yet. There would be nothing to do there, no one there at all. He opened his book, held it close to his face in the dim light at the little table. He read, absorbed, not noticing the two Braniff stewardesses at the bar (the pretty one with a steward, the homely one with a captain), not noticing the fat-thighed, hot-pantsed waitress, not noticing a soul.

MATTER AND ENERGY
Russell Martin

The dark air that hung over Denver in winter like the lid of a heavy pot had been washed clean by summer rain; from the running path I could see the thin swirls of snowfields that still hugged the peaks of the Front Range, and beneath the mountains the city sprawled across the sloping prairie. I had spent the night in a dreary motel on South Colorado Boulevard, eating Fritos, drinking beer, watching three former Playmates on the Playboy Channel discuss whether orgasm was always essential. I woke up early, drove to Washington Park, and started to run. The morning was cool and still, and it felt surprisingly good to be back in Denver — a place where I had never actually lived, but the one large city where I nonetheless felt I might belong. I had gone to school twenty miles away, in Boulder; Peggy had grown up here; I had had a variety of friends who were based in Denver at least briefly; and in recent years I had made a steady series of trips up from Houston to the Martin Marietta plant, first to test and comment on the prototype manned maneuvering units, then to train for our mission on the MMU simulator — a machine that really did have an uncanny ability to convince you that you were flying a rocket backpack through the empty sea of space.

Running at the edges of the park's small and glassy lakes, I kept trying to convince myself that the abrupt end to my visit with my parents in Durango was nothing to brood over. But I knew from three decades of experience that I would have to harbor my familiar filial guilt until Dad's tone on the telephone told me I had been forgiven. Maybe Mike and I could call them together; surely that would please both of them. My penance for standing up my father, the Episcopal priest, in front of his entire parish simply would be to make contact with my brother, my brother the crazy, to have an honest talk with him, to let him know I really did love him, and to give Dad some glimpse of my continuing concern.

But I didn't want to go to St. Andrew's and to see all the blank-eyed old boys who lived in heavy, ragged coats in the hot weather of summer, who stood in line at the kitchen as if they had already given up the ghost, their lives so hideously quiet. I wasn't one of those people who could serve them stew, or work at the Goodwill once a week, and feel invigorated by the experience. People like Mike or the derelict men at the mission somehow seemed like cruel and uncomfortable challenges to my success and my material ease. They were capable of making me feel even more guilty than my father was, and the questions they inevitably raised about why I had not suffered the same fates as they had were questions I couldn't confront. I was dazed by their desperate conditions, by their crumbling hopes, and never did any more in response to them than to write modest, occasional checks at my desk in the calm seclusion of the family room.

But for once, perhaps, I could do a bit more. Maybe Mike and I could go watch the Zephyrs play, or climb the Flatirons; maybe have dinner and a few beers at the Brewery Bar and reminisce about the days when we conspired to build an invincible raft we would launch into the languid waters of the lower Animas and that would take us on to the silty San Juan, to the boiling brown Colorado, and at last to the shimmering Sea of Cortez. Maybe it would be good for both of us just to remember those secret plans and pacts, the boyhood hopes that bound us together until Mike began to torment himself and I pulled away, afraid.

The commuter traffic began to get thick before long and the number of runners increased, their sweating faces flushed and serious as they nodded when we met. The sun rose high enough to begin to be hot, and I ran for just thirty minutes or so before I got back into the car. At the motel again, I showered and dressed, putting on a tie for the first time since I'd come to Colorado. But when I studied myself in the mirror I realized that it probably made more sense to meet Mike without one, so I took the tie off and zipped it inside my bag. I wasn't sure where I would spend the next few nights, but I knew I didn't want to keep staying out on that commercial strip with all the red-nosed traveling sales reps, so I checked out of the motel and eased my wheezing Honda — its injectors tuned for the soupy, sultry air of Houston — into the traffic on the Valley Highway.

• • •

The air seemed damp in the shade of the small, spireless Gothic church, and I rubbed my hand against its smooth brick, darkened by age and the city's soot, as I walked toward the door of the two-story rectory that was connected to the church by a breezeway. I pushed

open the massive wooden door and walked into a room that was empty
except for a long, low, threadbare couch and a lovely old Navajo rug
that lay on the polished terrazzo. A wooden crucifix hung on one white
wall; on another was a framed poster — a photograph of a chalice and
a loaf of bread with the words JESUS OF NAZARETH REQUESTS THE
HONOR OF YOUR PRESENCE AT A DINNER TO BE GIVEN IN HIS
HONOR. I could see down the dark hallway toward the doors to two
rooms where the lights were on, and as I started toward them, a man
in a black cassock emerged. He wore leather sandals and a clerical
collar; his close-cropped hair stuck out in every direction, and his short,
narrow beard did not conceal the sharp cleft in his chin. He smiled
when he said, "Hi. Can I help you?"

"Yes. I'm looking for Michael Healy."

"I'm sure he's down in the kitchen right now. I'll show you the
stairs. Are you . . . ?"

"I'm his brother."

"Well, then you must be Jack," he said. His eyes brightened as
he put out his hand. "John Long. I think we met here several years
ago."

"I think we did briefly. Good to see you again."

"How are your folks?" he asked.

"They're well, thanks. I was just down there."

"Your dad's one of my favorites. I always look forward to the
clergy conferences so he and I can catch up. We're bridge partners —
not very good, I'm afraid. But I've spent several memorable evenings
at the bridge table with him, drinking sherry and laughing, no doubt
annoying our more serious competitors. Say, we've heard a lot about
you lately. We don't have a TV here, but from what I read in the paper,
I guess your — what? flight or mission? — went very well. Congratulations."

"Yes it did," I said. "Thank you. It went real well. And how are
things here?"

"Hectic. With our ongoing projects; some new things we're trying
to get started. We get tired, but we know this is what the Holy Spirit
would have us do, and we try to do it joyfully. Michael gives us a lot of
help."

"How is Mike?"

"Well, you'll see for yourself, but I think he's doing quite well.
There's no question that he still has some of what the doctor calls
psychotic episodes. He may always have them. But I think he feels he

has a home here, a niche, and Michael's faith is very important to him. Come on. Let's go find him. Cup of coffee?"

I followed Father Long down the hall to the head of the stairs. He didn't look as though he could be any older than I was, but there was something in his manner, in the way he spoke, that made him seem like one of my dad's contemporaries, and it was easy to see why they were friends. Although no one ever considered Dad to be any sort of radical priest, he did have a reputation for being more readily sympathetic with what you might call the socially conscious wing of the church than with those who considered "street ministries" rather seamy and ill-advised. At the foot of the carpeted stairway, John Long stopped at an enormous stainless-steel coffee machine, filled a Styrofoam cup, and handed it to me. "He's back in the kitchen," he said, pointing across the long, empty tables that were covered with butcher paper. "I'll let you make your own introduction. By the way, you're welcome to stay here while you're in town. We have a guest room, a guest cubicle really. Michael can show you where it is."

"Thanks," I said. "I'm not sure yet what my plans are. And . . . I know my dad appreciates all you've done for Mike. They don't worry about him here."

"They shouldn't. Stop by my office later." He put his hand on my shoulder before he turned to go up the stairs.

I wound my way across the concrete floor, between the low wooden benches covered with peeling red paint, tucked under the tables' edges. The swinging door that led into the kitchen was propped open with a number-ten can of corn, and I stood in the doorway before I entered. A plump man in a white uniform stirred a large kettle on top of the Monarch range; a young woman was slicing heads of iceberg lettuce with a chef's knife, a scarf pulled low on her black forehead and tied at the nape of her neck. Michael stood at the deep commercial sink, rinsing baking pans, stacking them on the counter. He wore jeans and a white sleeveless T-shirt. The dark hair that he had worn long for more than a decade was pulled back and held in a single braid. I had forgotten how handsome he was — tall and muscular, his face smooth and pale, his square jaw as sharply defined as Dad's. "Mike," I said, and he turned to look at me. He didn't smile; he put down the pan he held and dried his hands on a towel as he came toward me.

"Well, Jack," he said, as if he had been expecting me. "So here you are." He looked at my hand for an instant before he took it. I started to hug him, then stopped.

"So here I am. It's good to see you, Mike. Did you know I was coming?"

"You told me, didn't you? You must have told me the other day when you were floating around out there."

"Oh . . . " I said. "Well, good. I'm glad it worked out so our paths could cross. It's been a long time. When was the last time we saw each other?"

"I guess it was at home. You and Peggy brought the kids up from Texas."

"Three years ago, I guess." I took a sip of coffee, then awkwardly fingered the white cup. "Listen. Am I interrupting you right now? Maybe I ought to come back after lunch; we could take off for a while."

"I should help Wendell and Lucy get everything ready." He turned to them. "Wendell, Lucy, this is Jack, my brother, Jack." Wendell nodded; Lucy smiled and said hello.

"I'll let him get back to work," I said.

"You can eat lunch here," Mike said in his familiar monotone. "Then we can go for a walk. I used to work here in the afternoon, but that was when I worked at the bakery in the morning. But they were way too jealous of me at the bakery. Especially that girl who was pregnant, so I stopped going."

"Why were they jealous of you?"

"I don't know. I guess she wanted me to be her baby; it was still inside her and she tried to get me to be it. I wouldn't though. I don't want to be a child all over again."

"No. I don't blame you," I said. "I'll come back down after a while." I set the Styrofoam cup on the counter; Mike picked up the cup, drank the last of the coffee in a single gulp, then threw the cup in a trash can.

"Good, Jack," he said.

· · ·

In the hot early hours of the afternoon, Michael and I walked east on 20th Avenue, past rows of neglected brownstones, their windows shielded by heavy, drooping curtains and fading cotton blankets, their screen doors standing ajar. Old men in pairs sat on the shaded porches; children with crayons drew pictures on the steaming sidewalks and dug into the squares of dirt that surrounded the trunks of elm trees. Mike said hello to everyone we met; he didn't know the people, I was sure, but he offered his flat, almost unfriendly, greeting to each of them as we passed.

Mike asked me about the kids as we angled our way through the parking lots at St. Luke's Hospital, the car windshields reflecting the searing sunlight into our eyes. I remembered the summers when Michael and I would hold a plastic magnifying glass above each other's forearms until the pinpoint of pain, the small solar burn, was too unbearable and we would pull our arms away, laughing, sometimes with tears in our eyes. He knew that Peggy had gone to Austin, but he seemed surprised to hear that Matt and Sarah had gone with her. "You live in that house all by yourself?" he asked.

"Me and the cat," I said. "And the cat's giving serious consideration to making a permanent move next door."

"You should get some roommates," he said, seemingly troubled by the image of empty rooms.

The tall trees on Pennsylvania Street gave us some shade, and I could smell the sprinklers on the small lawns that sloped down to the sidewalk. At Colfax, we turned left onto the stained cement where people with satchels and paper sacks walked slowly, aimlessly, stood curled over parking meters, or sat with their knees pulled up, their backs bent against the hot brick of the buildings. The traffic was steady, noisy, and we wound through clumps of young men who asked for money in quiet voices, or offered us lids of marijuana and grams of uncut coke. "No, thank you," Michael would say to each request for charity, to each offer to buy. He pointed across the street to the bakery where he had worked, then stopped in front of the open door of a sex shop, its racks of magazines visible on a red pegboard wall, seemingly every cover a photograph of a woman with an enormous penis in her mouth.

"Have you ever seen the quarter movies in here?" he asked.

"Not here. But I've seen some quarter movies."

"You have? Where?" He seemed intrigued.

"Oh, I don't know. Other places."

"I go in here sometimes," he said. "But when I do, then I'm ashamed that people see me walking out."

"Nothing to be ashamed about, as far as I'm concerned. They're usually kind of grim places though." We started to walk again.

"But that kind of thing is sinful, Jack. You can't be proud of it."

"I didn't say I was proud of it. I said I didn't think you need to be ashamed of it. As far as sin goes . . . I don't know what I think about sin, Mike."

"I didn't think you were a very sinful person, Jack. It's hard to imagine you going into those little booths to watch all that fucking."

"Well . . . I've done it. Most people probably have. You shouldn't be so surprised. People are people. You want to get a Coke or something?"

I held open the glass door for him at the Wendy's, but Mike reached behind me for the door and insisted that I go first. He studied the brightly lit menu board as though it were an examination, then finally told the teenager in the checkered cap he wanted a large Dr. Pepper. I paid for the drinks, and we sat at a small square table near the salad bar. Mike asked me how long I would be in town.

"Just a day or two. I've got to get back to Houston, but it was a good chance to come up for a short visit. I probably should stop by to see Peggy's folks, but . . . I don't know. I don't really want to explain anything to them. She said they both have been pretty upset by everything. They might just as soon not see me."

"They called me when I got to St. Andrew's," Mike said. "Well, she called. She said to let them know if there was anything they could do for me, but I wouldn't call them back. I could tell they just wanted to spy. You must have told them to watch me."

"Mike. I didn't even tell them you were here. I haven't talked to them since before you came. I don't know how they knew. Mom, maybe."

"Don't lie to me, Jack. I'm aware of a few things, you know." Mike stiffened. I could see small beads of sweat standing on his upper lip.

I took a deep breath. "They live way down by DU. They couldn't spy on you."

"They could if you told them to. The thing that worries me . . . now that you've been up in orbit, there's no place I can go where you can't watch me." He seemed to speak to the table. "You . . . you could try to grab me no matter where I was in the whole world. I don't know why you think I'm so terrible that you can't leave me alone."

I remember rubbing my eyes with my fingers, my fingers cold from cradling the cup, trying to come up with something to say. "I doubt I can convince you, Mike, but I don't think you're terrible. I think you're a hell of a good guy, as a matter of fact. I have never wanted to change you, never wanted to control you, never caused you any kind of trouble."

"You tried to keep me in the hospital," he said, his voice rising, his words coming in quakes. "Then you got together with Father John to make me get a job where they could watch me. He finally figured out what you were doing, but you still wouldn't stop. You just keep talking. Telling me this, telling me that, every single day. But you're not so perfect, Jack. You're just as bad as I am."

I waited before I spoke again. I looked at Mike, but he had turned his head away, his eyes held on the far wall. He seemed to suck in air, and his chest heaved with each big breath. "Mike," I said slowly, "I'm probably about ten times worse than you are, and I am not your goddamn problem! You can't lay all of this shit on me."

Mike stood, tipping his chair backward; it rocked on two legs for an instant before it came to rest, upright. "I can't stand liars!" he shouted, raking his strong, bare arm across the table, driving the paper cups of Dr. Pepper into the couple seated next to us, soaking their table and their pants legs, before he ran out of the restaurant.

The thin young man and his girlfriend were shocked for a second, then angry. "What the fuck is — ?"

"God, I'm sorry," I said. "I'm really sorry." By the time I got out to the sidewalk, Mike was already half a block ahead of me. I tried to catch up, dodging a car as I crossed the street, shouting "Excuse me" as I ran through the parade of people, running as fast as I could until Michael slipped out of sight. I slowed to a walk, shuddering, then turned the corner, trying to catch my breath, searching the shaded street for Michael.

• • •

Mike wasn't at St. Andrew's when I got back; I wasn't really worried about him, but Jesus, I wanted to finish the conversation. I had never known before that I played such a role in his demented nightmares, in his bizarre conception of the way things were. I was mad, and I was hurt — wounded enough by Michael's accusations that I decided I very much wanted to see my in-laws. Now that Peggy and I had separated, my relationship with them would have to be a bit abnormal too, but even if they held me completely responsible for what had happened, at least they wouldn't think I had done it with some kind of mind control. Michael made me feel alienated from so much that had once been vital to me, and I didn't want to think that because of the separation, or the divorce, or whatever was in store for us, Peggy's parents would have to slip away from me as well.

Marge was surprised to hear my voice, but said they would love to see me. She said Buddy usually got home from the cleaners at about five, and I said I would see them then. I drove to Argonaut Liquors, a converted supermarket on Colfax a block away from the Wendy's, and ambled through the aisles, looking for a bottle of wine to take to Buddy and Marge. I found one, and also bought a tall can of beer, drinking it as I drove down Washington Street in the tangle of traffic and the steady hold of the heat. I thought I heard the word "Canaveral" as I turned the radio dial; I scanned back for the station, found it, and heard the end of a report about the successful test firing of *Discovery*'s main engines. I had seen *Challenger*'s final pre-flight test a year and a half before, and I remembered what an astounding sight it was — the pale blue fire suddenly spewing from the three exhaust bells, the billow and swirl of steam and rocket smoke as the heat boiled the thousands of gallons of water that were dumped at the base of the pad to dampen the vibration, the orbiter swaying and straining against its bolts like a captive bird struggling to free itself. Congratulations, *Challenger,* I thought as I watched. You'll be a spectacular ship.

I could see that Buddy's small white truck with QUALITY DRY CLEANERS emblazoned in blue on the door was already in the driveway when I turned onto Pearl Street. I pulled in behind the truck, twisted the paper around the neck of the wine bottle and took it with me to the door. The screen door was closed, but the wide wooden door was open and Marge called, "Hello, hello," as she crossed the living room to greet me. She had gained some weight, which suited her, in the more than a year since I had seen her; her hair had been permed, and she looked tanned and happy. She wore a blue skirt and gold sandals and I noticed that her toenails were painted a surprising shade of orange. She gave me a big hug, kissed me, and said, "Isn't this a treat?" then said, "Oh, you shouldn't have," when I handed her the wine.

Our wedding photograph — Peggy looking lovely and me looking young and ugly and uncomfortable — hung with others in the entryway, and as we walked into the living room, Buddy came in from the hall, rubbing his cheeks with his hands as if they were wet with aftershave. His yellow sport shirt was tucked into brown trousers and he wore a pair of tan running shoes — not the kind of footwear I would first associate with Buddy. "Son of a gun," he said as he shook my hand, both his broad palms in a firm and friendly grasp of my hand. "So. Do you feel any different?"

"Not a bit," I said. "I grew an inch while we were in orbit — everybody does — but unfortunately I lost it as soon as we landed."

"Well, you look great," Marge said. "Doesn't he, Frank? He'd probably like something to drink, though."

"I got a bottle of Chianti open, or beer, or what else? Probably some bourbon back there."

"Beer, thanks."

"And a glass of wine for the landlady," he said as he went to the kitchen. Marge sat down with me on the sofa; she smiled — that tearful smile of hers that was so sudden and so much a part of her — and she squeezed my hand. "Frank and I are so proud of you, Jack. We always have been, of course, but this is just great."

"I appreciate that. Especially coming from you. I was afraid I might not be terribly welcome this time."

"Shhh, that's silly," she said, big tears now running down her ruddy cheeks. "You're family. You're always welcome here. If you hadn't called, then we would have been upset, wouldn't we, Frank?"

"I think he's probably a pretty busy man," Buddy said as he handed me a bottle of beer. Marge set a cardboard coaster with a picture of the shuttle on the table in front of me, whispering, "I got those in Houston that time," while Buddy asked, "When they going to let you go up again?"

"I wish I knew. The earliest would be at least two years or so. Could be a lot longer though. There are a lot of people waiting to fly."

"I made a scrapbook," Marge said, "with all the newspaper articles, and the things in *Time*, and all those photographs that you very nicely sent us, by the way."

"I was sorry that you couldn't come to the launch."

"Well . . . so were we," she said. "But . . . since Peggy decided not to go, we felt it probably would be best to just stay right here and watch it on TV. And it sure was something to see. Frank took the morning off from work, and his brother and his wife came over to watch with us. I fixed a big ham omelet and a nice fruit salad."

On the first page of the scrapbook was an article cut out of the Denver *Post,* headlined COLORADO ASTRONAUT FLIES ROCKET PACK TO RETRIEVE STRANDED SATELLITE. A *Post* reporter had called me in Houston on the day after we landed. He was friendly, and seemed well informed, but he kept calling me John, as if we were friends, and as if that were the name I was known by. A few pages later, I noticed my official NASA portrait, the one that the astronaut office mails to every kid from Colorado who writes in hoping to find an astronaut for a pen pal. In the photograph, I am wearing a space suit with an American flag on the shoulder and emergency evacuation instructions stitched onto the sleeve. I had written on it in bold ink: "To Buddy and Marge, who let me fly away with their darling daughter. Love, Jack." Marge could tell that something about reading those words really got to me. I closed the scrapbook and stood up to say good-bye.

• • •

I could hear the clear, quiescent sound of plainsong as I locked the car in the small parking lot across the street from the church. The last band of orange light hung on the western horizon, silhouetting the ridges and peaks of the mountains, reflecting off the smooth steel-and-glass facades of the buildings downtown. The church's stained-glass windows, long rectangles of radiant color, seemed to stand out from the dark surface of the brick, and the sound of the single chanting voice grew sharp as I walked up the steps to the open doors.

Only a few people stood in the long rows of walnut pews; John Long was at the side of the altar, a long white surplice covering his cassock, a heavy brass Celtic cross hanging from his neck. Michael faced Father Long from the opposite side of the altar, dressed like the priest except that he wore no cross. Only two of the altar's tall beeswax candles were lit, their flames fluttering in the breeze that curled in from an open window.

Father Long began the *Magnificat* as I stepped into a pew at the back, and after the first versicle, the rest of the people joined him, chanting the evensong canticle that flooded me with memories, its lilting and lovely melody sharply etched in my mind, my father's voice suddenly coming to me, his steady baritone so full of emotion and strength. I watched Michael as he chanted, crisply enunciating each word, singing with an assurance that was also reminiscent of my father. I thought I could make out his voice among the other voices:

> *... And his mercy is on them that fear him, throughout all generations.*
> *He hath showed strength with his arm; he hath scattered the proud in the imagination of their hearts.*
> *He hath put down the mighty from their seat, and hath exalted the humble and meek.*
> *He hath filled the hungry with good things; and the rich he hath sent empty away ...*

Following the *Magnificat,* everyone sat while Michael read the New Testament lesson, the Genesis account from St. John. Michael's voice was loud, his monotone broken by the unusual words he chose to accent: " . . . and the Word was with God, and the Word was *God. The same* was in the beginning with God. *All* things were made by *him;* and without him was not *any thing* made that was made . . . " I watched Father Long casually scan the church as he listened, and when he caught my eye, he smiled.

I stood with the others for the Creed, but did not recite it; and for the first time in at least three years, I knelt when the priest began the collects, chanting each short prayer in simple plainsong. I could see that Michael's eyes were closed; I saw Lucy, the woman I had met in the kitchen that morning, in a pew near the front, a boy about Matt's age beside her. Just before the Thanksgiving, I could see John Long turning the pages of his missal to find another prayer. When he found it, he read it in his speaking voice: "O most glorious God, whom the heaven of heavens cannot contain; whose mercy is over all thy works; we praise thy holy name that thou hast been pleased to conduct in safety, through the perils of space, thy servant Jack and his fellow crew members. May they be duly sensible of thy merciful providence toward them and ever express their thankfulness by a holy trust in thee; through Jesus Christ our Lord. Amen."

After Father Long gave the blessing, Michael genuflected in front of the altar and followed him down the chancel steps to the communion rail and out through an arch at the side of the church. As the scattered congregation began to go, I waited for Michael outside, near the breezeway that connected the church to the rectory, assuming that he and Father Long would walk by on their way back from the sacristy. I felt like having a drink and considered whether I ought to try to get Mike to walk down to the Broadway Grill with me. But we couldn't even make it through a soft drink at a Wendy's, for God's sake. What made me think we ought to try our luck at a trendier establishment? And I knew too that the last thing Mike would be interested in would be sitting in a bar with the boozy professional set, keeping a practiced eye on the tables of talkative, unescorted women, or the inevitable woman in a silk dress who would be sitting alone at the bar, drinking a wine spritzer and smoking a cigarette.

I waited there in the darkness, the night air cool and moist, the scattered sounds of the city seeming like a steady assurance that everything was in order, then I finally decided to try to find my brother. I checked his room and the kitchen and John Long's office before I found him at the back end of the basement, near the small rooms that had once been used for Sunday school classes and that now had become sleeping rooms for people who came in off the street.

An outside door was open and I could see a line of people on the cement steps that led up to the alley. Michael and two young men I hadn't seen before were busy in an alcove near the door, Mike collecting quarters from each person in the line, the others handing each man and woman a canvas pad and a green army blanket. I watched a grizzled man in a gray coat, his head shaved, his beard growing down into his shirt, carry his pad into the large, linoleum-tiled room. He put his nylon athletic bag against a wall and curled the top of a paper sack to close it. He laid his pad perpendicularly to the wall, then slowly tucked the blanket beneath it before he took off his coat, folded it, and placed it carefully on the pad for a pillow. Several more men soon followed him into the room, placing their narrow pads in rows, each sleeping with his head against the wall, leaving a big, bare patch of linoleum in the center of the room. I only saw three women, each of them surely under thirty, carry pads and blankets down the short hallway and through the swinging door to the small, secluded room where they slept.

Mike closed the coins inside a metal box, and one of the men he worked with closed the door to the closet where a high stack of pads still stood. I heard the other man say, "Okay, guys, lights out if you're all set," as I said hello to Mike.

"Jack," he said. "You're back."

"I'm back. I saw Buddy and Marge. I decided I really should see them. Are you finished now?"

"Finished. I'm never on duty all night. Just Benny and Jim do that. I just help them check people in. It's easy in the summer. We only have crowds in the cold weather."

"Why do they have to pay?"

"I don't know. I guess just so it's not free. Just a quarter, though. I always loan them a quarter if somebody doesn't have one."

"Do you think we could find someplace to sit and talk for a while?" I asked. "I kind of think I'd better head home tomorrow."

"We can sit outside here," he said.

I followed Mike out the door and up to the top of the steps. He sat on the steel rail that surrounded the stairwell, his shoulders hunched, his hands gripping the rail at his hips. I sat on the top step; I could smell the sweet rot of the food scraps in the dumpster across the alley, and I dimly saw a white cat bound up to the dumpster's lip, then disappear inside it. "I heard you read at evensong," I said. "I've always liked that, the 'in the beginning was the Word.'" Mike was silent. "I used to imagine that that's how the Big Bang began — that at the point when the whole universe was just a pinpoint of matter and energy, it began its expansion with a spoken word. Course, from a physicist's point of view, that's a little crazy, but I still think it's an appealing thought."

"What would the word have been?" Mike asked. I was surprised he was really listening.

"I don't know. I don't know what it could have been; and even if you figure that God was the one who spoke it, where was God when He spoke? Outside the pinpoint that made up the whole cosmos? Or was He the pinpoint? Maybe the word was . . . *now.*"

"I saw something on TV at the hospital about the universe," Mike said; he turned to look at me. "They said that some of the stars you look at, maybe even some of the ones everybody knows about, may have already been dead for thousands of years, but there's no way we can find out except wait. That really seemed strange to me. It made me feel kind of weird, like you never know. Maybe so, maybe not."

"You just put your finger on the essence of modern astronomy. Those are the words we live by. Listen . . . I'm sorry about this afternoon. I sure wasn't trying to badger you. But . . . it's important to me that you try to understand that I'm not telling you how to live your life."

"I don't want to talk about it. Maybe you don't know it when you do it. Just like that light from the stars."

"No. There's a difference. That light is real; you can measure it, study it. The voices, or those feelings you have that you get from other people, are imaginary. They're imaginary."

Michael was silent, and I didn't say anything again until he slid off the rail and sat on the step below me. The light from the doorway gave a glancing illumination to the side of his face that I saw, and his dark braid seemed to split his white shirt in half. "Do you remember watching Apollo 13 through my old Celestron back when we lived in Boulder?" I asked. "I'm not sure what year it was; I think Peggy and I had just gotten married, I know I was still in grad school. You must have just been roaming around that spring. We were watching from the yard of that little carriage house we lived in at the edge of Chautauqua Park."

"You mean when you saw the explosion?"

"I had tracked enough flights that I thought it would be easy to show you guys. I remember I got the command module sighted — just a bright speck of light — and then all of a sudden it flared for an instant, much brighter, like old light bulbs would do before they burned out. I couldn't figure out what it was, the flare, but it seemed pretty strange. Then Peggy went to get the transistor and we heard about twenty minutes later that the LOX tank had blown. The radio made it sound like Lovell and Haise and Swigert were goners. The Denver stations were all trying to get Swigert's mother to tell them how it felt to have her son be a sitting duck. I think I stayed out in the yard all night, watching the light reflecting off the module, whenever I could find it, listening to the reporters in Houston who all sounded a little shaken. Peggy went to bed finally, but I think you stayed up with me, didn't you? There wasn't a thing in the world we could do but sit out there with our sleeping bags pulled up to our armpits, but there we sat till the sun came up."

"It was called the *Odyssey*. That was the name they had given to the module."

"Yeah, I think it was, wasn't it? I guess the reason I even remembered that night is that I end up feeling that same way with you sometimes. It's like you're two hundred thousand miles away. We can see you and we can tell that something's bothering you, but there's not a damn thing anybody can do except just sort of keep the night watch. That probably sounds dumb, but I don't know what else to say — just that I'm not the one that's causing the explosions. I'm just one of lots of people who are pulling for you. Does that make any sense?"

"They called the other thing, the lunar landing thing, *Aquarius,* I think. They all crawled inside it on the way back to the earth. It kept them alive, but then they had to pitch it so they could do their reentry."

"Mike, do you see what I . . . what I'm . . . " I stopped. Mike was running the fingers of both hands through his hair. I leaned forward to try to catch his eye. "I'm . . . I'm just trying to say that I'm on your side."

"Oh, I'm with you astronauts a hundred percent," he said. "You're the new explorers. You're at the head of the line."

I didn't know what to say. It probably didn't make any sense to keep at it, and I didn't want to let things slide into another fruitless fight. I tugged at his braid and put my palm on the back of his neck. "Thanks," I said, "I appreciate it." And I did appreciate it; I appreciated the fact that he could still be civil with me, that he still seemed to count me as a brother, when all I could ever offer him was a handshake or a hug and a couple of hours a year. "Can you show me where that room is?" I asked. "I don't have to leave too early. Let's go get some breakfast before I go."

We both stood up, and I followed Mike down the concrete steps. "It's a nice room," he said. "It's right by the room where I sleep. They're tiny, but from the window you can see the skyscrapers. Sometimes I watch, and you can see the lights go out, one by one. When I see one, I wonder, you know, who it is that's leaving and where they live and how long it will be before they get home."

At Mike's suggestion, and after he had left me alone in the little room, I watched the lights in the Republic Tower for a time, but none of them ever seemed to go out. I wondered if Mike was watching, and if he was, I hoped he wouldn't worry about those people who couldn't yet go home.

MUD SEASON

Antonya Nelson

That first night in the city where her daughter had died, Lois dreamt she was standing in the English countryside. Though she'd never been to England, everything looked just as it should. Green hills dipped back on themselves as far as she could see, stilled waves in a grassy ocean. In this dream, Lois could fly, and she sailed above the ground, taking in the hills and the fine yellow light of sunset, which was so bright she couldn't look at it directly; rather, she had to watch covertly, staring ahead of her while noting it in the periphery.

Suddenly she began rocketing skyward, fast enough to see the world changing below her, slow enough to appreciate the expanding color of the blue sky. Soon she saw a new world, England turning from a borderless countryside into an island all its own. Marvelous. Still, there was that intense light to the west. Perhaps it was not the sun after all, she thought. Perhaps that was the atomic explosion that would end the world. But, no — its light was yellow and white, painful to the eye but restorative to the skin. Lois knew that if she didn't waken she would continue upward, shooting into some other, dark galaxy. She hesitated, atmosphere thinning around her, before she fought her way from sleep.

• • •

She and her husband Alan were staying at a bed and breakfast place in Durango, Colorado. Their youngest daughter, Gwen, had been killed on a mountain pass outside town — not more than a ten-minute drive from where they were — five months earlier. Lois and Alan had come to see the site, at last.

Lois looked out their window into the muddy landscape. A boy on a bicycle came slowly meandering down the street, twisting the handlebars from one side to the other, seemingly in order to maintain the slowest speed possible, stalling. He wore bright primary colors, red shirt, yellow cycling pants, blue plastic boots. He wobbled lazily through a puddle while Lois watched, and thereafter left an endless dreamy curve of S's after him.

"What's his name?" Alan shouted to Lois from the shower. "I've forgotten this S.O.B.'s name."

"Pittman," Lois said, dropping the curtain. She spoke only loud enough for her husband to hear her voice and not the word.

"What's it?"

Lois walked into the steam of the bathroom putting an earring in. She pulled the shower curtain completely open and enunciated quite clearly. "Pitt man." She gave her husband's body a thoughtful appraisal. Do I love you? she wondered. He was small as a preteenage boy, skin still almost tight over muscle, but not attractive. The sense of promising vitality beneath the surface was gone. Lois's own body had relaxed into its years. Lois hadn't really felt comfortable with herself until she'd had children; since then, somehow, her joints and flesh had suited her better. Men's bodies, she thought now, looking at Alan's flaccid penis, never got the chance to ripen — just to age. It was her theory that this was the reason he'd had affairs in the last few years.

Later, over breakfast, Lois confessed that she wasn't sure she wanted to see the site. Her heart had begun beating audibly in her ears, louder as the hour drew near. "Maybe you could go without me."

Alan was pretending to read the paper. He wrote a syndicated column and this paper was open to his small picture and byline. *About Which,* Lois read, upside down. They were running his old pieces while he was away. A little flare of impatience went up in her; Lois thought it would have been more honest to simply let the column go for a week.

"Going will make you feel as if it's done with," Alan said. Maybe he didn't realize he was mimicking their counselor. Or maybe he didn't think Lois would know, since their sessions were separate. Could he possibly believe Dr. Frank came up with completely fresh advice for each of them?

"Actually, I think I'll have this vivid mental image," Lois said, slowly, pinning the feeling. "I think I'll be better able to imagine Gwen flying off the mountain . . . "

Alan turned sharply away. He was contemptuous, staring angrily out the window at the falling snow. What was it, this time? Her word choice? He felt bad for her, for both of them, but he could barely stand to be around her anymore. It sometimes seemed hopeless, their marriage. It had seemed that way before Gwen's death, but now it was fated to continue for a while longer, on a different path.

"I'll be okay," she said, waiting until he turned back to the paper before she opened her own section.

Lois believed in human-interest stories in the newspaper the way she believed in dreams. She was susceptible to both, drawn to their messages, which she took almost entirely at face value. What did a dream of flying over England mean? It meant she wished to fly over England, to see the earth from a distance. As for the newspaper, her husband's column included stories about his youth, things he saw in a passing car or while standing in the grocery line. He liked to make a point, shaping the tidbits he witnessed into an emotional essay. But over the years, Lois realized those columns were awfully overwritten. All the daily pieces were. No one seemed capable of controlling tone. Everything was so unmanageable it all rang false. She believed in straight facts. They spoke for themselves.

These stories sought her out. When she sat in the sunroom in the morning, paper spread on the glass table before her, she had only to slowly turn the pages. Soon, the boldface proclamations would rivet her. *Three Sailors Wed Lottery Winner.* Little stories from out of state, stories that might get far too much attention if they were local but which only received a cursory paragraph or two of lucid facts if they happened elsewhere. *Baby found alive under El tracks.* The baby was abandoned, then found after surviving on its own for at least twelve hours. Amazing. Heart-stirring, and without any pomp. *Nurse playing hero may have killed 10.* A nurse injected patients with lethal drugs, then revived them in order to be a hero. What could be clearer? Why comment further?

Her husband made use of these stories, but only to elucidate some point more specific to himself. Lois imagined if he'd read about the nurse injecting patients, he would write about a culture that required heroics and heroes to garner attention. The everyday heroism of nursing was not enough; lifesaving was now necessary in order to receive commendation. That would be the first part of his column — Lois could see it as if it were before her on the page — the next part would be about something comparable in himself. Lois tried to think what. How had he made himself perversely important in his life?

She admired that he seemed completely able to confess his flaws. All of the nation knew his failures and shortcomings, his sins against himself and others. What bothered her was that, in confessing them, good Catholic he'd once been, he somehow felt absolved.

"Alan," she said. "Did you read about this male nurse?"

He had finished reading the paper and was now working the puzzles, his bifocals balanced on his nose. He looked at her through the top part of the lenses expectantly, if a little impatiently, which meant he hadn't. After she'd told him about it, he grunted.

"What does that make you think?" she asked.

"It makes me wonder how the hospital explained away those deaths." He licked his pencil tip and went back to work.

Lois nodded to herself.

But in a moment, Alan looked up once more. "It also reminds me of that report that said most serial killers, when asked what profession they'd most like to pursue, answered cop. Remember the ambulance driver who was a mass murderer? Killed prostitutes and then picked the bodies up later the same night?"

Lois did. Alan had speculated on the desire to be a policeman, a surgeon, any occupation that involved day-in, day-out exposure to carnage. He wrote about soaking a cat in gasoline when he was younger, setting it on fire. He'd won an award for that column. It was a brave essay, Lois knew, though it had made their children cry to read it.

"I had the strangest dream," she began. "I took off like a rocket. Usually when I dream of flying I go horizontally, like an airplane. But this morning I was heading up, up and away." Alan was working another puzzle. This one was the one where a sentence was given in code. Each letter stood for another. "Why do you like that puzzle, do you think?" she asked him.

"Couldn't tell you," Alan answered, without raising his eyes. He had been whistling the rhythm of the missing words and discovered the solution in the process. Rapidly, he filled in the last blanks and swung the paper in Lois's direction so she could read the nonsense sentence. *Life of crime can oftentime pay overtime.*

"And then I saw a boy on a bicycle," Lois said to herself.

"That whatshisname is going to be here soon," Alan said, rising and running his thumbs between belt and trim tummy. "I believe I'll brush my teeth."

• • •

Sheriff Pittman met them in the bed and breakfast house foyer. He was kind and slow with them, which made Lois a bit awkward. He had children of his own, she understood. They drove out of town, up the winding mountain road, listening to police static and sudden bursts of dispatched, sputtering numbers on the radio. Lois tried to guess what the numbers stood for, which ones meant robberies, which ones meant fatalities. The sheriff clicked his end of the radio after each one, answering in his own code. The scenery — snow filling the deep and high crevices of granite peaks and turning them somehow more than three-dimensional — made Lois feel unbalanced and she noticed she was holding on to the vinyl of Sheriff Pittman's back seat. Their waiter at breakfast had told them this snow was unusual, as it was mud season: the end of the ski season, and before the summer tourists arrived. He did not know why they were there, and Lois was grateful for his obvious disdain of people so out of touch as to visit Durango during mud season. She basked in it, the normality of his smugness.

Riding along, she was tempted to tell Alan about something else she'd read at breakfast. A woman had written Dr. Lamb to say she was sick of her husband's habit of eating his own hair. Except she phrased it like this: he finds the coarse hair on his body, pulls it out, chews it up and swallows it. Lois wondered if anyone she knew had a habit as shocking. The atavism of it thrilled her. What would Alan make of it?

But Sheriff Pittman was pulling over, very cautiously, next to a yellow diamond warning sign. The sign showed a black arrow bent at a forty-five-degree angle. Underneath, it read 25 m.p.h. Alan, who was sitting in the front seat, had stared out the passenger window the whole trip, not noticing the sheriff's glances now and then in his direction. Lois had tried smiling into the rearview mirror to let Pittman know they appreciated his taking care with them, but she had never quite caught his eye; after all, she told herself, he was a man, and he was identifying more with Alan than with her. Now, Alan remained for a moment in the car as the other two got out.

Lois had prepared herself to draw in breath, to have her equilibrium abandon her entirely, her heartbeat become so furious her body pulsed, but nothing happened. It was a beautiful place, and she stepped right into it. She was not frightened as she walked over to the edge and looked down. What had she expected? Gwen's body was in Missouri, buried in the same cemetery with her grandparents and great aunts. There was gravel and then the drop, which Lois saw was gentler than she'd pictured. A squirrel hustled by, holding a nut in its mouth. At the bottom was no black void where the world had reclaimed Gwen; up here, no white cross.

She could see how it pained Sheriff Pittman to show them the spot. He cleared his throat. "There were skid marks," he said, swiping his cowboy boot heel across the crumbly asphalt. "Torn brush and the bent aspen saplings."

Gwen had toppled like a toy the thousand feet. It was Pittman's pain that touched Lois; he certainly must have children of his own. He must have seen every one of them, in his mind, make the same horrifying miscalculation, slide and fall. For herself, Lois had been imagining that fall for months now; it seemed she had been anticipating such a fall since the day she'd brought her first baby home from the hospital. She'd looked at the world from then on as a place full of forty-five-degree angles and cliffs. It surprised her that seeing the actual spot — *here,* she told herself, *right here* — somehow lessened its power. Even the gray sky and wet snow failed to make the turn ominous. An Airstreamer in the far lane rounded it like a ponderous metal elephant. And behind it was the boy on the bicycle. She recognized his yellow pants. Now he bent forward, pedaling hard, a smile — or, more probably, a grimace from the hard work — on his face. Lois lifted her hand in a wave, and felt her whole self lift just a bit. She wished she knew his name to call out.

Alan turned to look behind him at what she was waving at. He scowled at her. "I've seen enough," he said. He hadn't even come to the edge. Pittman, between them, stood with his arms dangling, as if he might draw, also watching Lois. She resisted, the way she had in the car, asking Alan why he didn't want to look over. Their states of mind were at such odds these days that she did not trust his understanding her — something that, once, she would have taken for granted — and she did not want him to turn away from her, as he had at breakfast. So she allowed herself another private glance down. Wildflowers would grow. More squirrels would appear. She hadn't wanted to come, it was true, but now she was glad she had. There was nothing — not the skid marks, not the broken aspen, not the crumpled machine — to indicate what had occurred. This place had healed.

. . .

Gwen had missed weeks of class in Boulder, her parents discovered later. They received notes of condolence from several of her professors. The man who taught her Social Problems and American Values course had called one afternoon (teacher's hours, Lois had thought, long-distance in the afternoon). He introduced himself and then seemed at a loss. Lois heard, in his silence, the things that could have been between him and Gwen. If Lois had learned nothing else in her life, she had learned to trust what was not said.

"When did you last see her?" she asked him, quiet Peter Somebody or Other, desperate that he not hang up.

"Let me think."

Lois could hear him breathing. He remembered, she could tell, and was trying to put it some way that was presentable to Gwen's mother. They'd been lovers, Lois understood. She wanted to tell him it wasn't his fault. He was tangling with all the little parts — his loyalty to Gwen, his loss, his not knowing Lois at all.

"I saw her at the Union," he chose to say. "She was getting a salad and paying a parking ticket." And then he was silent again. "I don't really know why I called," he said after a moment.

"Thank you, anyway," Lois said. "Even if you don't know, I appreciate it." She was crying, but she thought she could sit for a long time saying nothing with this man.

"It's useless," he finally said, "but what I feel like is that if I could take some of your pain, I would."

"You probably have enough already," she said. "Thank you, though."

Lois did not tell Alan. She could have secrets, could she not? Alan, fortunately, was gone all day; otherwise, he would have answered the call. She imagined him wanting to reach through the telephone receiver, across all those miles of cable, and strangle Peter Whoever. He would have demanded answers: Why was she in Durango? Where had she gotten a motorcycle, for God's sake? Alan had kept up an annual vigilant campaign against motorcycles, writing column after column about their dangers. They were second only to handguns on his list of consumer evils. It was registered in Gwen's name; she'd owned it for over a year without ever having told them. Alan wanted someone to blame, and Peter, sad and silent, would have sufficed.

Lois had come to admire her daughter's life, secret from the family. She imagined Peter as a kind and older man. Gwen's belongings had been carefully packaged and sent to them, two large boxes that arrived UPS one day when Alan was away. Lois had read the return address, Gwen's dorm, and felt for an instant that she'd been offered a reprieve. Packages from her daughter.

The boxes were full of both familiar and unfamiliar items. Lois picked them up one by one to investigate. She couldn't tell which hurt her more to see: those things that were the past, or those that were the present? The ceramic rabbit Gwen had had since she was little, cotton balls for a tail? Or the mysterious sky-blue case that snapped open to reveal a diaphragm?

It was not long after Gwen's belongings had come back that Lois stopped wanting to leave the house. Maybe she was waiting for another phone call? She had started any number of days with the intention of going somewhere — the Nelson, the plaza — and had made it through all the preparatory stages, but once she opened the front door she was lost. The world wowed her; leafless trees appeared somehow to be sapping her of energy. It took all her willpower to shut the door behind her and walk to the garage — there was no spark left to actually make her drive away.

Instead, she'd allow herself to be drawn back inside, where she'd gather all the linen napkins in the house to launder them. Their size and texture made for perfect ironing and folding. She was in love with the starchy warmth of these napkins fresh from the dryer. Countless times she comforted herself by sorting them, folding them into perfect squares, her hands flattening, smoothing, stacking, making order out of chaos.

Lois told Dr. Frank about it. It was an "am I crazy?" kind of question. Dr. Frank had pointed to the enormous potted begonia in her window. "That's its third pot," she said. "Every time it gets root-bound, it throws itself to the floor and breaks its pot. When that happens, I just have to get it another one. Bigger, of course."

"You think I'm outgrowing my house?" Lois asked. "Like a hermit crab?"

Dr. Frank laughed. "Really, kind of the reverse. You're turning back toward that smaller world. It's healthy, I think. The point is, you seem to be helping yourself by doing what feels right. Warm napkins? They sound lovely."

"They are lovely," Lois said.

If Peter had called again, she would have had something to tell him.

• • •

Sheriff Pittman invited them to his house for supper. His wife, he informed them, had been very sorry to hear of their tragedy.

"Quaintly small town, isn't it?" Alan said to Lois, after they'd declined (at Alan's insistence) and Pittman had driven off. Briefly, Lois pictured a column for *About Which,* eating supper with Durango's sheriff and his wife. The tone would be flat, affectless, but affecting nonetheless.

"He's a good person," Lois said, though she, too, was relieved they were eating alone. She enjoyed the thought of oblivious strangers, like the boy at breakfast, serving her.

They stood at the inn's entrance and looked up and down the street. It would have been a good time to nap, to pass the two hours before dinner with mindlessness, but they could not sleep. Instead, they walked.

It was Alan who had wanted to come here. Lois had never believed it necessary to see where Gwen had died. She hadn't wanted to see the body either. Alan tried, without success, to make her agree to an open casket ceremony, sure, Lois knew, that he was acting in her best interest. He'd had just enough counseling to know there were things, unpleasant, resistible, one had to do to recover. This trip was in the same vein. He considered traveling, by any means, a dangerous business and he avoided it whenever possible, so Lois knew he felt he had to be here, had to do this. They'd driven to avoid flying, taking a southern route to miss the highest passes. He'd been very nervous (that is, short-tempered) the whole way. Though he'd thought this trip essential, Lois had agreed only because she wanted him, them, to be cured, to be strong enough to overcome such tremendous odds. The counselor had told Lois that most marriages did not survive the death of a child. Dr. Frank also suggested that Gwen might have committed suicide. She said this as if she were offering consolation instead of complication. Lois had made her promise not to tell Alan either thing, believing that she could successfully circumvent them, but that he could not.

The two of them wandered the older section of town, Lois peeking into shop windows out of habit. Soon she realized she didn't even know what she was looking at, could not remember whether the place they'd just passed sold antiques or car parts. She put her arm through Alan's for balance, smiling but scared.

He did not pat her hand, as he once would have. His love was confused, she knew. It tore him this way, that way, distracted him. His latest affair had been longer and more serious than the previous ones, ending only a year ago. He and Lois had still been mending the terrible wounds their marriage had suffered when Gwen was killed. It was like stepping from the foreignness of another country into the alienness of another world. Their grief took hold of them like a merciless wild animal.

And Lois understood that he felt responsible somehow, that he'd pulled his love from the structure of their family and let the edifice slide. His ego allowed him that feeling; he considered himself a cornerstone. He had yet to write about it, and perhaps he never would. It cheered her to think there were some things, however rare, he could not purge.

Now, Lois felt they were riding some wheel together, that on the far rungs of this wheel they could not touch, could not even know one another. They could only suffer. Eventually she hoped they would work their way toward the center, toward love, where they could be together once more. Alan's affair had created the wheel; Gwen's death enlarged it. They had more distance to come, it seemed, though she believed, finally, that there was no way off for either of them.

Alan stopped suddenly and somehow made Lois drop her arm from his. "I don't think it's too much to want to know why," he said, irritably. "Do you?" He looked hard into her eyes. He was looking to see if she was sane.

"Yes," she told him. It was far too much. That was the whole point. "Look there!" she said suddenly. "That's the third time today I've seen that boy on the bicycle. See his yellow pants? He's like some friendly poltergeist . . . " No, that wasn't it. "Or something."

Alan glanced where she indicated, then slowly turned back to her, his eyebrows and forehead drawn downward in a V. But Lois barely noticed, she was so happy to see the boy again.

• • •

They sat on opposite sides of a plastic booth in a fast-food restaurant eating chili from Styrofoam cups. Of course this was better than being at Sheriff Pittman's, where the only thing everyone had in common was a death. Better to be here, which could have been downtown Kansas City in winter, snow turning into slush as night fell, headlights and muddy cars passing outside the window, where large cheerful pictures of hamburgers, french fries and chocolate ice cream hung.

"You think Durango carries the *Times?*" Alan asked her. They hadn't spoken for a long time and Lois's thoughts were far away from the newspaper business. Sometimes, when she and Alan were close, they seemed to think along the same lines and when one of them spoke, it was precisely what the other had been thinking, two minds in a winding relay race, passing the baton. Not so, today.

"Surely," she said, shifting her thoughts to match his. Reading the paper, she knew, was his way of coping with empty time, idle hands.

She wondered what sort of story the Durango paper had run about Gwen. It had never occurred to her before that there would have been a story, but of course there must. The story in the *Star* had been front-page news, since Alan worked for them. They'd run a photo of Gwen from one of the awards dinners her father had been honored at several years earlier. She'd been clapping, big teeth exposed in a beautiful smile, her sister and brother flanking her at the table. The editor had wanted to run a column Alan had written about Gwen, and asked Alan to choose one, but, in looking them over, Alan had realized how many of them were about her foibles as a safe driver. The story ran alone.

But what had been in this paper, Lois wondered? Perhaps a two-paragraph piece, facts only.

"This was a good idea," Alan proclaimed suddenly, their thoughts having gone different ways once more.

Lois considered it. "I don't think we'll know for a while," she offered, disagreeing.

He scowled, standing with his plastic brown tray full of trash. "I meant dinner," he said. On the way out, he threw everything in his hands away, tray and all.

. . .

At the inn, which had once been the home of a Durango doctor during mining times, Lois and Alan sat on their twin beds staring at the fireplace as if there were a fire in it. There was wood in the grate, newspaper beneath it, long matches in a cup on the mantel. Still, neither of them moved toward lighting it. Lois was thinking of Alan's mistress again, imagining their making love. She was tired and these images came to her when she was too exhausted to fight them. Her friends had rallied round her when Alan was discovered, but then had fallen away when he'd come home again, happier, Lois supposed, to believe him irretrievable. To put Alan and his mistress from her mind, she tried to remember flying from the night before, the light and the freedom and the frightening unknown. It had been exhilarating, but now there was no fuel left in the memory.

Eventually they turned out the lamp, both in their own beds. It was only nine o'clock. The snow had stopped and they could hear a dog, barking in an otherwise still night. Lois attempted to put a good image before her, Gwen walking to class, one of the other children hanging Christmas tree ornaments, the table set for a formal dinner — crystal, linen — their own dog, barking in their own yard, a colorful, simple boy on a bicycle, but superimposed over them all were those other awful images.

By morning both she and Alan were in her bed, wrapped together among the sheets and blankets as if they'd wrestled all night for leverage.

• • •

They left town before sunrise, taking a different route, at Lois's request, than the one they'd arrived on. This one would lead them over Monarch Pass. It felt good to Lois to be leaving Durango. Somehow, in the clear melted light of morning, she was comforted in having seen the place, in no longer having to hang on to her imagined site. She couldn't really even recall the accident she had played over and over in her mind. It had disappeared, and a new one, one that included the place Sheriff Pittman had shown them, had yet to come to her. She would fight against its arrival, she decided, sitting beside Alan in the granite-blue of this Colorado morning. If she fought the image hard enough, all day long every day, it would not be able to come in. For a second she could see Gwen's throat, twisted unnaturally, exposed, her youngest, most difficult daughter tumbling down a hillside, new aspens crushed beneath her . . . but she stopped herself, made herself remember only color, blue and red and yellow, and then focus on the scenery outside the car. A fence, the gateposts of a ranch, cows — steam coming from their mouths — clustering at a barn entrance.

• • •

When they hit the deer, Lois saw only fur and a single eye before the windshield broke. Its glass rained down on them like pebbles. The deer slid off the hood, leaving a broad smear of blood.

"Is it a mother deer?" Lois whispered to her husband. In a flash she thought of fawns and of full udders, the terrible ache of needing warm milk and needing to provide it.

Her husband remained in his seat, staring straight ahead of him, his hands bouncing lightly on the steering wheel, then harder, until the dashboard rocked. He turned on her, his face a horror, red, monstrous. Through his clenched teeth he spat, "Didn't you see antlers? Are you so blind and *stupid* not to have seen antlers? *Mother* deer do not have points. That's *father* deer."

And just as suddenly he fell against her. He cried without tears, male crying. She did not know what to do at first, his head against her chest, butting into her again and again, the hard guttural sobbing. It would have been easier to handle in the dark. Even the day they'd heard of Gwen's death, he'd been late at work and she had sat on the back steps waiting for him, her arm around the dog, unwilling to enter the house. When he'd come home, they'd sat there together until it grew dark and then they'd been able to comfort one another.

She tried to soothe him now, running her hand through his hair. The worst had to be over. This would be the last bad thing. She imagined the deer, which she could not see, in front of their car. Perhaps it was alive? But she had no resources; she could not make herself leave her husband to go find out. She pictured its fur as she smoothed her palm over Alan's head. The fur would be sprouting in whorls at its haunches and throat. Its underbelly would be white. There was only so much you could do with one pair of hands, she justified.

"There can't be any more bad luck," she told Alan, in a firm whisper, using a tone of voice she'd once used to promise her children their house would not be robbed, their parents would not die. "We've reached our limits." Alan nodded adamantly into her breasts. "This trip is the end of it," she went on. "*Fin.* Goodbye."

Not a single car passed. What odds, Lois thought, Alan finally quiet on her lap. The only car on this highway and this deer could not avoid getting hit. Alan would see a column in it, but to her it seemed like a mathematical problem, the kind she used to try to help her children with. In a landscape with only two moving objects in it, how long will it take for them to collide?

Forest rangers on their way to work found them ten minutes later. One of them was young and impatient, shaking his head at their out-of-state license plate, angry with them for having hit the deer. Lois found herself nodding in agreement with his assessment. Careless of them, yes, traveling too fast. They should have known to expect wildlife at sunrise, in the spring, indeed. The other ranger was like Sheriff Pittman, a man who saw them through eyes screened with sympathy and recognition. Perhaps he saw that more than this accident had claimed these two people, both of whom still sat in their broken car, unable to go on.

WINTER ASCENT

Kent Nelson

A t ten o'clock at night it was snowing hard at nine thousand feet. The wind blew across the ridge from the northwest, driving the snow into the corners of the windows and against the thin walls of the A-frame. Bill Tyms was asleep on the top bunk under the eave, and between the rushes of the wind Jack could hear his snoring.

"What's it doing outside?" Werner asked from across the room. He was a darkly tanned German, thirty years old, with experience in the Alps. In winter he taught skiing, but his love was to climb mountains. He looked up from his game of solitaire and smiled at his own joke. "Want to play some gin?"

Jack shook his head and continued to stare out the window. Twenty feet from the cabin the stand of spruce was hidden by the snow.

"It'll take your mind off the weather," Werner said.

"I don't want my mind off the weather."

Jack was glad Marcy had not come with them. She had wanted to climb to the A-frame and send them off, but they had been there two days already, waiting for the weather to break. In truth, she had wanted to make the ascent herself. "It has nothing to do with you," Jack had explained. "It has to do with me."

He turned away from his own shadowed reflection in the glass and crossed the wooden floor to his pack. He had checked the equipment in town, and again when they had arrived at the A-frame, but he wanted to be sure. Stoppers, pitons for rock and screws for ice, crampons, rope, hard hat, waterproofed matches, Primus stove, down gear, mini-flares.

"We're all on edge," Werner said.

"Not Tyms."

"Tyms is on edge in his own way."

Just then the tin roof, warmed from the inside, shed its burden of snow. The roar woke Tyms.

"Fucking snow," said Tyms. "I was just dreaming I was on a beach in Antigua."

Werner laughed, and Tyms stretched his lanky body and dangled his legs over the edge of the bunk.

"With three women," Tyms went on, "and one of them was Marcy."

Jack nodded. "That proves it was a dream."

A gust of wind hit, and the kerosene lamp swung back and forth, throwing garish shadows across the room. Tyms rubbed his eyes and put on his rimless glasses. "What time is it?"

"Past ten."

"Outside temp?"

Jack leaned closer to the kitchen window. "Sixteen degrees."

Tyms jumped down from the bunk. He was the best of them on ice, a master skater in total control. But on the wooden floor in his long underwear, he looked ghostlike. "How's Jack holding up?" he asked Werner.

"Great," Jack said.

"Really?"

"He misses Marcy."

"Fuck Marcy."

"My sentiments exactly," said Tyms, leering. He smiled ambiguously, showing the space of a missing tooth.

The wind suddenly dropped, and the silence tightened the small room. Tyms went to the stove and put in two pieces of dry spruce. "If the clouds lift in the morning," he said, "it'll be cold as a nun's mammary up there."

• • •

From town the Needle looked more like a steeply rising jet than a mountain. From the valley it soared eight thousand feet, and among the other peaks of the Divide it seemed out of place. That was why the mountain fascinated Jack. The land sloped upward from the town, then jutted into a high plateau. Above the plateau, the dry foothills broke into a hundred canyons and gullies. But it was the high peaks beyond the foothills — the Continental Divide, the range of the Sangre de Cristo — that caused Jack to spend hours at his bedroom window.

In high school, he had run from the trailhead to the ridge without stopping, his thin legs dancing up the zigzags and his breath coming in waves. His fingers were so strong he could scale a thirty-foot cinder block wall by holding himself like a spider in the niches of cement. He spent nearly all his free time with Tyms in the mountains.

And at night, when he should have been sleeping, he pressed his face to the cold, cracked glass of his bedroom window. In all seasons, the Needle was etched in white because the sun never reached the crevasses on the north face. In winter that face was dark, its wind-whipped granite too steep to hold snow. A cornice hung over the jagged summit, and a thin white ridge of snow outlined its flank. Jack liked the clean line of snow, broken by the crack in his windowpane: he saw two horizons, one higher and one lower, and each with the dead night beyond.

And in time he had come to know the Needle better than anyone else alive. When he met Marcy three summers before, he was twenty-seven and had already climbed the mountain eight times.

• • •

"I'm going out," Jack said. He opened the door and pushed his way into the wind. He fastened the leather latch and moved off several paces to urinate. The frail light from the A-frame faded in the gauze of snow, and the heavy flakes nicked his face.

When he finished, he walked up the ridge into the immense web of darkness. He liked the feeling of the clouds around him, the snow, the sensation that he was suspended with no mountain above him, no town below, no edge to the ridge upon which he stood. The bottomless space soothed him, yet, at the same time, made him restless.

He had done the Needle in winter only once, going up the backside with Tyms. That day it had been clear and crisp: the first day of January. Cold. The sun had burned them on the snowfield on top.

Now waiting: he hated waiting. That was the trouble with his mood. Or was it Marcy?

Just three nights before — it seemed to him longer ago than that — she had been lying on her side, facing him in the half-darkness of the bedroom. The smooth curve of her hip was raised beneath the white sheet. He could not quite see her eyes. "Jack," she had asked, "why are you so afraid?"

"Am I afraid?"

"It's not what you say," she said calmly. "It's the way you hesitate when you do things, the way you look . . . "

He had felt anger burn. "Then don't watch me."

"But that won't change anything." She had turned onto her back and had stared at the ceiling. "Tyms said . . . " She paused. "It worries me that you'll never get beyond where you are now."

"Tyms said what?" he asked.

"He's your friend," she had said, and then she had added, "He thinks about you, too."

The snow let up, and above him the stars drifted in the blackness. Clearing, he thought. Snow still blew over the ridge, spindrift, and a cold mist wet his skin. Marcy would see.

He turned and started down toward the A-frame.

"How is it?" Werner asked, when Jack came inside.

"Lovely."

The warmth of the room swarmed into Jack's face, and he went to the stove and turned his hands over the barrel.

"You okay, really?" Tyms asked.

"It's breaking," Jack said. "We can start in the morning."

• • •

Marcy was a tall woman with long, straight brown hair and a wide-lipped mouth that turned ambiguously whenever she asked a question. He had liked her right away: that much had been simple. When she had walked into his mountaineering store for information about the Needle, he had offered to take her up.

She had smiled and answered, "No, thank you. I want to go alone."

Still, he had spent time with her going over maps and photographs. He cautioned her about false routes, about the places where the objective dangers — falling rocks, ice — were the worst. All the time he spoke to her of the mountain, he was feeling something else. Yet she listened carefully. She absorbed everything he said, as if his own words and not his tenderness toward her were all she wanted to know.

When she was ready, he had hiked with her to the base to watch her start. She seemed in control of herself, certain. On the first pitch of the strange mountain, she seemed to know the fluting of the rock; each crack. She never lacked the strength to pull herself to the perfect position.

In their three years together, she had left him many times to climb other mountains; twice she had left him for good. The trouble between them was never drawn in clear terms, never discussed. Marcy planned her own life, and sometimes she invited him to join her, sometimes not. For months they lived well, day to day, and then suddenly she would say she was leaving the next morning for Wyoming, or California, or South America.

"You could give me warning," he told her.

She shook her head. "No, I can't."

"When are you coming back?"

"I'll have to see."

He tried to find some humor in her tone, but at that moment she was always serious. Her hair was pulled back and her wide lips were set in a line. Her eyes looked tired.

"What is it you don't want to come back to?" he asked.

"I didn't say that."

"We're easy."

She nodded. "Yes. That's part of it. We get along so well."

She did come back. She was gone a month, maybe two, and then one day, again without warning, she would be back in town collecting her mail, saying hello to friends as if she hadn't been away. God, he loved her. He tried not to think that she would do the same thing again.

• • •

Jack led through the scraggly trees near timberline, though he could not see the trees themselves until he was a few feet away from them. The beam of his lantern caromed from the rough shapes of rocks and gnarled branches. The wind had blown the ridge clean of snow, and for the first mile and a half they hiked easily. Tyms kept pace with his fluid stride; Werner moved doggedly in the rear.

Orion had slid wide to the edge of the morning sky, the belt tilted at an angle to the horizon. A few clouds moved fast across the stars, as if the wind were sweeping the sky clean. Tyms had been right: it was cold. Jack's feet were already tinged with pain, and as he walked he curled his fingers into fists inside his gloves.

At the boulder field at the base of the mountain, they rested a few minutes. A pale blue light spread through the air.

"We're behind schedule," Tyms said. "It'll be light before we can get up the first pitch."

"Who was sleeping late?" Werner asked. "Jack, who was so anxious last night."

Jack looked past the boulder field. It would be slow going on the snow-slick rock. He felt tired, as if the sleep he'd had hadn't done any good. He watched Tyms and Werner start out across the snow, the colors of the parkas — Werner's orange and Tyms's red — separating from the gray dawn.

He had never understood how his own crisis had begun. He could point to no particular time, no incident. On the rock the summer before he had begun to feel shaky; he sweated profusely even when the climb was easy. The strength in his legs had diminished through no fault of his own. His fingers ached.

"Old Jack," Werner had said. "That's what happens when you get married."

"It's not that."

"A batting slump," Tyms said. "You have to keep taking your swings."

Jack had trained even harder. He had run the pass — six miles up, six back — before he opened the store in the morning. He kept weights in the back room so when business was slow he could exercise. In the afternoons, he made short, technical climbs near town.

"Maybe you should take a rest," Marcy had said.

When he had asked Tyms about it, Tyms had said, "What does she know?"

• • •

Jack climbed free on the first pitch, then belayed for Werner and Tyms. The early morning sky had deepened, cold as blue ice. Only Venus was left in the east; Orion was gone. Clouds were strung along the Divide to the north.

Jack angled to his left, skirted a buttress of cold stone, then wedged a stopper into a crack. His planned route led across the pitch, then into a couloir over ice, and up a ridge into the center of the face. The route was burned into his mind, fixed in drawings he carried in his pack. In the late summer, he had done the same route in shirtsleeves.

Tyms ran the couloir in crampons, setting some ice screws and leapfrogging. Jack hesitated before starting onto the ice.

"You'll do it," Tyms said. "We've got the net below you."

Jack smiled grimly and started across; he made it easily.

Then Werner had trouble. He began happily, with a shout, but the noise brought down a wash of snow that swept him off his feet. Tyms laughed when Werner bounced on the belay, but Werner seemed hurt when he righted himself. He moved his arm in a circle and winced.

"Shoulder," Werner said, when he had climbed back to the others. "We'll take a rest."

They sat in the lee of the ridge and watched the sun's halo beyond the low hills to the east. Jack ate a granola bar and passed around cups of hot chocolate from the Primus. "We'll all drop back," he said, "if Werner's hurt."

But when they resumed, Werner still complained. After the first fifty feet, he still wasn't able to pull with his arm. "It's no use," he said. "I'm going down."

Jack and Tyms looked at each other. They had planned the climb, had trained and believed in it for a long time.

"I'll be okay," Werner said. "You two go up."

But they took Werner back across the couloir and belayed for his rappel to the boulder field before they could retrace their steps. The sun was already up on the peaks of the Divide.

In an hour they were back across the couloir and climbing toward the center. They stopped once and saw, far below, Werner's orange parka stalking the ridge toward the A-frame. He waved.

At the center of the face a long fault slashed a scar, a two-hundred-foot chimney that led upward and to the right. The sun glanced from the planes of rock, from the patches of snow. Jack felt his body move with the old ease, the muscles lifting, grasping, pulling. The physical skill was there, he thought: the sprints, the ice work on waterfalls, the isometrics. It was the mind that was difficult to train.

Fatigue.

Cold.

Height.

Fear.

Death.

Marcy said that when she climbed she never thought of falling. She had been in an automobile accident once, a head-on at fifty miles an hour, and as the cars collided, she said she had not thought about the end of her life. The same with falling: on a climb in the Dolomites she had been struck by a rock and had fallen five hundred feet. She had tucked her head and held onto her ice ax. Her pack twice kept her off the rocks, and then she had rolled. She claimed she had only thought about being alive.

When he had started to climb, Jack had never thought about death either. Even now he did not consciously worry about it. But he felt the possibility. It could happen. It was not a dream. Death was in every second around him, sifting into his brain the way oxygen was absorbed by the lungs.

"I've never seen anyone take care of details the way you do," Marcy said.

"Is that bad?"

"No, symptomatic."

"Nothing to chance," Jack said.

"The only thing — it leaves you so little time for other things."

"I'm solving the problem as best I can."

"You think it's about winning?" she asked.

"Don't you?"

She had smiled wistfully. "No."

• • •

To the northwest the clouds bubbled like a boiling sea. Tyms sat on a crag and ate a piece of chocolate. "It hasn't cleared," he said.

"It will."

"Static," Tyms said. "It looks like a new front."

The sun was warming the rock, and snow had started to melt from the few places it had reached the face.

"We ought to move, then," Jack said.

From the top of the chimney they kept right, dipped ten feet onto a spacious ledge, then started a sun-and-shade traverse which would take them to a long pitch toward the snowfield.

Tyms tested the conditions on the traverse. Jack belayed. Jack had climbed so often with Tyms that he knew what he was thinking; he knew his moves. He could tell Tyms did not like the cold breeze that had begun swirling down from the top.

A small piece of snow snapped off above Tyms, and when the snow hit the rock, powder exploded over Tyms as he was trying to secure a piton. Tyms swore, took off his hard hat, and wiped his goggles. Another drift broke. Tyms ducked, losing his hat and goggles. The hat struck a rock, bounced thirty feet out, and disappeared.

"You okay?" Jack called.

Tyms did not turn back. "I want to get the fuck off of here." He moved upward, out of the shadow.

After the traverse they struggled with an icy overhang. Normally Tyms would have done the ice logically, precisely, but he was cold, and in hurrying he made mistakes which cost more time. Jack kept silent.

The clouds did not help Tyms's frame of mind. Tyms had been right again: a new front was moving in, blocking the sun. The snow turned crusty, and the water from the short melt had frozen into verglas. Everything took minutes instead of seconds.

Tyms was visibly shaken when they reached the long pitch that would take them to the snowfield. His face was red, the skin raw from the cold. He smiled, then released the smile quickly.

"Maybe we should head back," Jack said. "We can take the backside."

"No." Tyms's voice was too loud. "It's a simple shot. We're fine. Go."

Jack made the free climb to the snowfield, belayed, pulled Tyms up the last few feet. "It's all snow now to the top," Jack said. "We won't stay long." Jack checked his watch. "One-twenty. At three we go back."

"Plenty of time," Tyms said.

Jack resisted the temptation to argue.

• • •

He had never got used to Marcy's way of thinking. Her beauty, he knew, was not in her appearance, but in the way she left him uncertain about himself. She challenged him with a few small phrases which, days afterward, came back to haunt him. She answered his questions with terrible equivocation.

"Do you love me?" he had asked once.

"Yes and no."

"You came back."

"What does that mean?"

"Well, coming back means you wanted to be here."

She replied with silence.

"Isn't that true?"

She had stared out the window at the mountains. "What do you think, Jack, about loneliness?"

"I try not to think about it at all."

"Do you get lonely when you're alone?"

"Without you."

"Do you ever know what it's like, deep down?"

He had tried to understand what she meant, but before he could ask her, Marcy had slipped through the door and out of reach.

Later he had thought about it without wishing to. The notion of being lonely came to him when he was arranging a display in the window of the shop, or again, as he emerged from a restaurant and happened to glance at the Needle. Marcy never seemed lonely. She had such friendly eyes, and an enthusiasm to do many things. Yet, why did she insist upon being alone?

• • •

The last half-mile to the summit was a mindless exercise in pain. Jack led for a while, breaking the trail. Most of the time, the crust held; but when he broke through, he sank into waist-deep powder. When Jack tired, Tyms went first. The snow consumed them. To their left, the cornice of white angled sharply against heavy gray clouds. The wind stiffened, and the afternoon turned colder.

Tyms did not lead for long; he tired and fell back. Jack slowed his own pace, though they were no longer roped. His feet had become cold again, and the wind sliced across the skin of his face. But he knew Tyms was worse than he. Tyms's usual gait was gone; his face looked haggard. Jack stopped and gave Tyms his goggles.

But they persisted to the top. The view was not the familiar panorama that Jack knew from memory; no view of his parents' house, no colored blocks of town buildings, no highways, no farms with yellow or green fields, no Divide running into the distance, no peaks, valleys, outcroppings of rock. Instead the wind kept them low. The gray clouds swirled around them, misty, heavy, opaque.

They shook hands and barely smiled. Then they turned and started down.

• • •

"Relax, Jack."

"I am relaxed."

Marcy kneaded the muscle of his upper arm between her hands.

"I can feel the tension in your muscle," she said. "It's not relaxed. You have to get the mind to control the body."

"I see." He had smiled at the innuendo. "And how does one practice this art?"

"You're old enough to know."

• • •

They moved more quickly on the broken trail on the downhill. The mist had closed away even the cornice now, and a gray airless space surrounded them. Off the windline they stopped.

"Shall we get something hot?" Jack asked.

Tyms shook his head. "I'm all right — I'm cold. But so far it's just clouds."

Jack nodded, knowing more. He skirted a drift and found a spot where they could rappel from the rock just beneath the snowline. He knew the way down: fast. They had left most of their technical aids in place, but downclimbing took too long. They needed to get out.

Tyms belayed while Jack worked down the traverse.

With the cold, the mountain was more treacherous. Ice had formed a film over the rock, and they used their crampons all the time. Jack knew he should not try to make Tyms go faster than he could. When he watched Tyms on the rope, Tyms had the tentative movements of a sleepwalker feeling his way along. He did not let go, fall, catch himself on the rappel, but rather he slid the rope a step at a time, groping for places to put his feet. The bravado was gone, and the new reserve was a further burden.

Tyms was pale when he finished the first rappel. "Do you know the way?"

"Yes," Jack said. "Everything."

"I'm sorry about myself."

"Werner knows when to expect us and where we're going. So does Marcy."

Tyms looked up, his eyes large beneath the yellow plastic of the goggles. "Marcy," he said. "Forget her."

Jack felt Tyms's weak voice like a sliver under the skin. "Forget her? Why?"

Tyms did not answer.

• • •

The storm hit them in the middle of the descent. Wind, snow: the whiteout was terrible. They could barely see the rock beneath their feet. Tyms seemed to lose heart completely, and Jack had to double the rope and help Tyms on the rappel. Jack talked to him, exhorted him, yelled.

"We're almost down," Jack said.

"Down."

"I'm cold, too."

"It's not the cold."

Jack felt Tyms's hands. Ice. He made Tyms rest on a ledge, and Jack got out the Primus.

"Move before dark," Tyms said.

But the darkness had already begun, settling over them like a darker cloud. Light gray shifted to blue, then deeper blue. The snow became invisible in the air.

Jack made Tyms warm his hands around the blue gas flame as the water heated. When they had drunk their tea, they did another rappel. Tyms went first, with Jack following. Jack knew the place. At the bottom of this stretch of glazed rock there was, he remembered, a short ridge which petered out into an overhang. They would swing west again to cross the couloir.

But they made bad time along the ridge. Tyms's steps were slow, teetering. The snow let up, then came harder. It took an hour to make their way down the ridge.

"Can you belay?" Jack asked.

Tyms nodded.

"I'll use the light. When I get part way across the couloir, I'll fix a rope and bring you to me." Jack shined the light into Tyms's eyes through the goggles. Tyms seemed to understand.

Jack edged out into snowy space. He moved in a rhythm of small steps, downward and outward. He drove an ice screw, moved, drove another. Snow whirled in the cold wind. In the beam of his miner's light, he could see white slithering beneath him down the couloir. Yet he did not panic. He worked smoothly, took deep breaths, gauged his speed. When he had gone about halfway, he stopped and looked back along the yellow length of rope which stretched into the darkness. Snow sliced through the beam of his light. "Tyms?"

No answer.

Jack waited, then began to put in some insurance. He set another ice screw.

Then, without warning, he was jerked backward, straight out from the mountain. He grabbed his ax with two hands, flailed at the ice, bounced once, then fell through space.

As the rope reached its length, there was a wrenching. It caught. Tyms had got him. Jack bounced at the end of the rope, hit the ice again with his shoulder and his face, then scrambled to dig in with the ax. He struggled for position, footing, afraid that something else might happen. But he was alive.

"Tyms!"

He took a breath of air and snow. Twenty feet away, he made out Tyms's body hanging free on the other end of the rope.

. . .

Marcy was so clinical. "It happens," she said. "What difference does it make whether you're hit by a train or fall off a mountain or die peacefully in your sleep?"

"It makes a difference to me," Jack said.

"Jack, we're so small anyway. Compared to millennia, we've got seconds. The difference between twenty-seven and ninety-seven is nothing."

"It's seventy years."

Marcy smiled. "I mean . . . "

"I know what you mean," Jack said. "You're right, too, I guess. Unless . . . "

"No unless." Marcy paused a moment, staring at him. "Ah," she said, "so you *believe*."

. . .

It took the better part of a half-hour to reach Tyms. Each small step had to be protected. His shoulder and his right arm were barely useful. Small snowslides washed the couloir, and wisps of powder covered him. Going so slowly and carefully exhausted him. The cold was endless.

Jack brushed away snow and drove two new pitons into a crack with his left hand. He ran a short piece of security rope through the pitons and tied himself on. He had to work with a pocket light, painstakingly testing every step. Tyms's red parka was the only color he saw.

When Jack reached him, Tyms was still alive. One of his gloves had come off, and his head was bloodied beneath a knit cap. His legs were dangling. Tyms must have passed out and fallen head first, without a sound, into the couloir. The ice screws Jack had fixed had held them both.

The sweat froze on Jack's face. His leg muscles were gone; the tension eased from him. He could fasten Tyms to the mountain and take the extra rope for a long rappel, but to leave now . . . no, not when he was so tired.

He lit a flare, but in the falling snow it could never be seen.

He set himself on the ice, close to Tyms, touching him. To operate at a sixty-degree angle to the mountain suddenly became funny. His laughter was brittle, monstrous. Then he became angry: they had been stupid. They should have turned back with Werner, or when they had seen the change in the weather, or when Tyms first showed symptoms of hypothermia. Weak. His own training had made so little difference. His anger diffused against the mountain, against Tyms for falling, against Marcy. "Now," he shouted wildly at no one, "now, see?"

His anger vanished like a spirit into the cold. He bent his knees and knelt against the ice.

It was easy to love things in someone else that you wished were in you. Marcy was so distant, so ready to disappear, while he was afraid. He had always been afraid, and yet his fear was better than Marcy's lack. Making love she was so silent he never knew where she was. Sometimes she would move her lips in a silent embrace, as if speaking, but at the same time, she closed her eyes. She would never look at him. The closer he got to her, the more she backed away, so that he was forever guessing what she needed.

He wanted more than that.

He drifted. Cold seeped through hands, feet, even through the pain in his shoulder. The snow soothed him, danced white in the air.

· · ·

When he woke, the stars had jumped into the sky. Orion was rising. Beneath him and far away, the small blinking lights of the town burned his eyes. He could feel nothing in his hands or feet, and his knees were frozen into the ice.

Werner's voice came from the edge of the ridge, almost in a whisper.

Jack slid into and out of consciousness. Someone was chopping at the ice around his knees, someone was lifting him. He felt his body float free, gliding beneath the stars.

"Easy, now, Jack."

"Tyms?" Jack asked.

"No pain."

Jack tried to moisten his lips. The sky opened out into a black space, bordered by a ridge of white. He breathed deeply. Cold. He was being lowered along the face of the mountain. He tried to say her name, but the word would not come.

HIS MOTHER'S IMAGE
Manuel Ramos

Tony de la Vida died in Vietnam when he was twenty. A bullet from a high-powered automatic weapon tore out most of his intestines and stomach. At the instant of his death, as his blood flowed into the dark, damp earth of the jungle, the ghost of his grandfather walked up to him, cradled his head and whispered in Spanish. The apparition had tears in its eyes but Tony noticed that it was smiling too. He remembered the toothy grin. For Tony, dying confirmed that he had seen *la llorona* one summer night twelve years before.

Tony's death was one of many that day, uncomplicated by terror or prolonged suffering. It went unnoticed except by the remnants of Tony's family, spread across the Southwest, and by his friends back home in Florence.

Florence was, and still is, a small town of three thousand people. It sits near the Arkansas River, twenty minutes from Canon City. The people of Florence described where they lived in relation to other places like Canon City, or thirty miles from Pueblo or, when the listener knew little of Colorado, "a couple of hundred miles south of Denver." That is how it was in Florence. Life was compared to something else, some other way.

Tony was raised by the people he called his grandparents in a large stone house. It had two stories, a dilapidated garage, a chicken coop, two doghouses and an apple tree. Chickens and dogs roamed in the back. The grandmother, Jesusita, was boss as she gathered eggs and threw feed to the hens. Kids trailed after her or chased the animals. There were always kids.

Jesusita and her husband Adolfo raised more than a dozen children. Some were their own but the others, Tony never learned how many, were given to the couple to care for without any formal adoption process or the interference of a social services agency. These children were castoffs. Orphans and abandoned children like Tony found a family at the house of Jesusita and Adolfo Gonzales.

Tony's *abuelito* was a storyteller, a man who related his history and the history of his family in long talking sessions that fascinated the children.

Adolfo liked for the kids to sit with him at the table at night while he drank Jim Beam and Coca-Cola. He talked of his life or the lives of his brothers in Mexico and the States since he had come north looking for work after Villa stopped fighting. Adolfo's voice boomed across the room in a rhapsodic mixture of Spanish and English that flowed with poetry, curses, songs and other sounds the children did not understand but which always fit into the story at the right time. Adolfo told a different story each time or added to one he had told before. The updates changed the meaning completely but they made absolute sense to the kids.

Tony would sit with a glass of Coke listening to Adolfo. The boy took a drink from his glass each time the grandfather sipped the bourbon. In this way Tony learned of the Mexican revolution, of working on the farms and of the spirits of the men who had died in the mines of Chandler on the outskirts of Florence.

The stories continued through the years. Adolfo died when Tony was fourteen, surrounded by his children, in the hospital that was a converted chicken farm. On his last night he began the story of a card game with the devil but he did not finish.

When Tony was eight he went for the first time to the river with his brother Johnny and some of his buddies.

It was a hot, dry summer. Jesusita allowed him to go with Johnny to the river to escape the heat. The boys swam in the river where a pool had formed that was deep and still. Trees kept the place hidden from anyone on the highway that followed the river for a short span outside the town. The river was wide and fast and perfect for tubing and fishing. The boys swam most of the time or shot at the birds with their BB guns.

Tony floated for hours in the water almost forgotten by the older ones. The water was cool and Tony soaked away thoughts of his missing mother. He wondered who she was, why she had left him. He imagined what she looked like.

On one of the days that stretched for miles across the cloudless sky, Tony first encountered *la llorona*. He was at the river, floating in the water listening to the *chicharras*. Johnny and Paco were by the bank, smoking and talking about Linda Garcia and her dark, almost black nipples.

Tony was drifting, half asleep, when he noticed the change. The *chicharras* quit their humming. Birds suddenly flew from the trees in squawking bunches. Tony opened his eyes to see what was causing the commotion but the brightness of the sun blinded him and he saw only a glare from the water.

Then there was silence. It covered the woods like a thick, heavy blanket. Tony swam to the shore.

He quickly put on his clothes. The sun was still out, the day hot, but Tony shivered in the silence. He did not hear Johnny or Paco. No wind stirred the wild grass. The roar of the river was different. It was muffled and seemed to come from far away.

Suddenly there was a moan from the river, a noise Tony would remember for the rest of his life. The sad, melancholy cry surrounded him. It created feelings that he did not understand. Tony's eyes watered, filled with tears, and he was forced to wipe them. The sound was of a woman crying. She wanted something so bad it was killing her not to have it. Tony looked up and down the river but saw nothing.

Johnny and Paco found him at the river's edge, crying softly that he wanted to help her. They had heard the sound too. Johnny said it was *la llorona,* the woman who cries, and it was time to go home.

As they walked away, Tony looked back at the river and saw a woman dressed in black wandering along the bank.

That night Adolfo told Tony the story of *la llorona.* "*Hijo,*" he began, "*la llorona* is a woman condemned by God himself to roam the earth searching for her children, children she threw away years ago."

He held his glass of liquor with small, bony hands. The veins in his arms popped out of his skin. Their gray color deepened to blue as he drank more Jim Beam. His hair was thin and white, his moustache full and gray. Two gold teeth glistened from the corner of a smile that stretched from his black moist eyes to the wrinkled, grizzled chin.

Jesusita hollered at him from the kitchen where she stirred a pot of beans. "*Viejo, déjalo.* These things are not for children. *Mira, no más.* You will make him afraid to go to sleep, afraid of his own shadow."

Her words were wasted. Both the boy and the old man were determined that the story would be told.

The woman was a young Mexican from South Texas. Adolfo was not sure if she was rich or poor but he was positive that she was beautiful with Indian looks framed by long, rich black hair. She was desired by every man in her *pueblo,* but she wanted only one — Don Antonio Perez, a rancher and a *vaquero.* She snared him, of course, and they were said to be more in love than two people have a right to expect. They prospered in wealth, influence and happiness. After a few years of marriage the woman gave birth to three children in rapid succession, two boys and a girl that mirrored her beautiful mother.

That was where the love story went awry. Don Antonio loved the children with a generosity that bordered on the hysterical. He showered the babies with gifts they could not use for years. Toy horses, guns, clothes and money piled up in their rooms. He watched over them with a single-mindedness that caused him to neglect his business. He gave them so much love that he had little left for his wife. He loved her, but not with the same intensity of his love for the children.

Jealousy replaced the feelings of affection the wife held for her family. She blamed the children for the lack of fire in her husband's lovemaking. She saw them as rivals for his attention. When she remembered the love from the early days of her marriage to Don Antonio she hated the children more for taking it away.

She made a plan to do away with the children so that Don Antonio would love her again. She turned to the devil and his ways for help.

"*Pues, tú sabes, 'jito,* that in those days it was much easier to deal with the devil than it is now. *Brujas* were everywhere. A person only had to ask the right one to get what he wanted. That's what a person had to do." The old man whispered the word *bruja* each time he said it, making it sound sinister and threatening.

"The woman sought the help of one of the bad *brujas.* The *bruja* told her to take the children to the river where the devil would trade Don Antonio's love for the little ones. On the night of the exchange, driven by hatred, she threw them into the rushing water."

Tony drank the last of his Coca-Cola and tried not to think of drowning babies.

"Then, son, she learned the lesson all who deal with the devil must learn sooner or later. He doesn't keep his part of the bargain. Don Antonio never loved her again, *por razón. Se murió de sentimiento por sus niños.* His last words were that he hated her and would see her in hell soon. She wasn't that lucky. She tried to undo her evil but that was impossible. The *bruja* had disappeared and none other would talk to her, much less give her any help. Priests avoided her. Church doors were slammed in her face. *La mujer se volvió loca.*"

Tony heard the words as if they were coming from God directly. His mind burned with the imagery of the story.

"She convinced herself that the children were not dead. She said they floated down the river and were waiting for her to find them and take them home. She searched all over *Tejas, Nuevo México, Arizona, California, Colorado* and *México*. She followed rivers to their end, crying for the children, but she never found them. To this day she wanders earth looking for the children, crying for them."

Tony understood. In the middle of the story he lost his fear of the woman. She was a mother looking for her lost children, a woman like his own mother who regretted giving him away and who now wanted him back. Adolfo's description of *la llorona* matched Tony's idealized vision of his mother. She was sorry. He was ready to go with her.

Tony kept his conclusions about the woman to himself. He knew no one would believe it was his mother and Jesusita would not let him go to the woods to find her. He spent hours thinking of ways to bring her to him, or to let her know where he was. He knew he could not confide in his brothers, sisters or cousins. He withdrew from them. He was quiet, subdued and surly.

The opportunity to go to the river again was provided by Johnny. The older boys treated the story of *la llorona* as a joke. They made *la llorona* faces at the young ones. They laughed at the articles in the newspaper. Johnny wanted to show everyone that *la llorona* was just another fairy story, another fantasy of old Mexicans. He decided to search the river until he found what was making the sounds and then expose it.

Johnny's idea was simple. He and his friends would go to the river around midnight, split up into pairs and search the riverbank. When the sounds started the boys would converge on its source from different directions and surround whatever it was. They would have gunnysacks, knives and baseball bats. Johnny stashed one of his grandfather's rifles in the trunk of his car as a precaution.

The night of the search Johnny wore his best pair of khakis. His hair was brushed into a ducktail. A gold crucifix hung from his neck. He put a card of the Virgin Mary in his wallet. He told Jesusita he was going to a movie in Canon City and would spend the night at Paco's.

Tony decided this was his chance to be reunited with his mother. He had to keep Johnny from her. He moped around the house waiting for everyone to go to bed.

When the house was quiet he left, sneaking out the back door. He grabbed a bicycle and rode through the dark town to the river.

The heat of the day lingered on. There was a heavy, stuffy feeling in the night. Tony rode under long, dark shadows from the trees in the moonlight. The air was clean and still. Details stood out. He saw numbers on houses, hopscotch patterns on the sidewalks. Fireflies flitted around the bushes near the library where he turned onto Pikes Peak Avenue towards the river. A few bats circled the trees but he tried to ignore them. He concentrated on the woman he was going to find. He conjured up the face of his mother. She was sorrowful, loving, eager for him.

Tony parked the bicycle on the edge of the woods and walked into the darkness of the trees. He went through thick clumps of bushes and weeds on the way to the swimming hole.

The sound of the rushing water relaxed Tony. He was aware of its patterns, the consistency of its changes.

He did not see nor hear Johnny and the others. He walked along a rocky stretch of river beach illuminated by the moon. Bright stars hung over the hills beyond the edge of the highway. A dog or coyote howled in the darkness. Owls hooted sadly.

He stared at the river, the moon and the trees. He saw nothing. He waited and worried that she had gone. He threw flat rocks into the river, frustrated with his bad luck. He began to walk back towards the bicycle.

The crying came with a suddenness that made him jump. It started low and soft, slowly increasing in intensity. A wind stirred the trees. Their shadows danced on the ground. Tony felt as though the earth was moving. The moaning was loud, vibrant. He thought he saw shooting stars fall behind the hills. The moon passed behind a cloud and Tony was in darkness.

He heard footsteps behind him. He turned fast but there was nothing. He heard other sounds from other directions. Things seemed to move in the bushes. The moaning covered the sound of the river. The wind whipped dust around Tony in small whirlpools.

Tony realized he had made a mistake. He did not belong out there near the river looking for a woman who had drowned her children. He tried to calm himself with thoughts of his lost mother but they were not the good ones he needed. He wanted to be home with his grandmother, with the woman he loved like his own mother, with the flesh and blood person who loved him and cared for him better than any imaginary mother could. He wanted to run but he forgot where he left the bicycle. Sobs came out of his throat in hiccups.

Then he saw her. The woman in black walked towards him with her arms open. She was beautiful. Coal black eyes pierced into his, asking him to come to her. *"Hijo, . . . niño. Vente conmigo, tu mamá . . . niñooooo, . . . niñooooo."* The voice was like the sound of the whistle Tony heard late at night as the train approached Florence, miles away, letting all the dogs know it was coming.

Dark red lips pursed into the kiss she blew to Tony. *"Niño, . . . corazón niñooooo."* Her hands signaled for him to come to her. Tony stepped in her direction driven by a need to know his mother.

"Run, Tony, run!" Johnny hollered at his brother from a hundred yards away. Tony saw him running, holding a long stick in his hands. He started to tell Johnny it was no sweat, man, this was his mother, his old lady.

A loud hiss stopped him. His beautiful, beckoning mother had become an ugly, grotesque creature. Her skin was lumps and oozing pustules. Ragged teeth grinned evilly at him. Patches of scalp gleamed beneath strands of wispy hair. The eyes were red-orange balls.

She lunged at him.

"Run, Tony, run. Get out of there!"

He felt fingernails scrape his back. He dodged her by twisting back and forth as he ran to Johnny who stood on a rise pointing the stick at the woman.

"Move you little shit. Run! Run!"

Something grabbed Tony from behind. He felt a warm slimy arm wrap around his waist. He looked into the horrible face and smelled the sweet, putrid odor he remembered from the time he found a dead chicken in the coop. He screamed. "Johnny, help! Help!" He kicked at the thing that had him. He saw a light flash, felt a thud in his back, fell to the ground and threw up. He sobbed into the earth until Johnny picked him up and carried him to the car.

Tony was in bed for a week. Old doctor Davis gave him shots of penicillin and prescribed juices but could not explain the fever, nor the long scratches on Tony's back.

He was delirious. He mumbled about his mother. He hollered for Johnny. When the fever left him he refused to talk about that night, even with Johnny.

The sounds at the river stopped. A few days after Johnny saved Tony the body of a huge bird was found on the shore of the river. The newspaper said it was a rare crane or heron that had strayed from its normal nesting place. The story speculated that the bird had been driven to the waters of the Arkansas by the unusual heat. Its long beak and spindly legs made it an object of curiosity at the fire station where it was displayed. When it decayed the firemen burned it.

Johnny tried to convince his friends that he shot *la llorona* just as she was flying off with Tony. Paco said it was no use trying to bullshit him. He was there and he had not seen anything except Tony getting sick. Paco figured Tony was out to scare his brother and his brother's friends, but had managed to scare himself instead. "Serves the little asshole right," he told Linda Garcia the night he got her drunk up on Union Mill Hill and tried to make it with her in the back of her father's Plymouth.

Adolfo knew the truth. Years later, in a place he had not known existed, he told Tony he believed him as Tony again lay in the dirt crying from fear.

"Hijo, you saw your mother for what she really was. The evil in her made her ugly. You came back home then, come with us again."

THE BLACK CANYON

Dan Schoenholz

Whenever Don comes down from Duluth to visit me and do a little fishing, I always take him to the San Miguel River. It's only 20 minutes from my cabin, and he practically always catches his limit of good-sized German Brown trout. Of course I don't tell Don that the only time I fish the San Miguel is when he's in town. He'd be crushed if I told him the trout in the San Miguel are just too stupid to keep me interested. For me it's no more fun to fish there than at one of those ponds on Highway 27 where they guarantee you'll catch your limit. Why, I feel more of a sense of accomplishment when I get salmon under $5.00 a pound at the A&P; at least there's some uncertainty, a little thrill when I look at the price tag.

No, when I fish I head straight for the Black Canyon of the Gunnison. Ever since I saw the Big Guy, I've fished the Gunnison once a week, regular as church. There's some huge old brownies in there, the Big Guy included, and they aren't old and fat by accident. Those fish have seen a lot of stuff floating past their noses, and if it doesn't look just right, they won't so much as twitch. Whenever I manage to pull one of them out of the water I feel proud but kinda foolish, too; they're so beautiful, all silver streaks and brown speckles and bright red circles, it just doesn't seem right yanking 'em into the shallow edges of the river and making 'em sit there humiliated while I pull the hook outta their lip. When I finally turn 'em loose, they don't look thankful, like a San Miguel trout; they look pissed off, like I had a lot of nerve ruining their morning.

I've been living in Colorado for three years now, ever since my divorce. I've come to like it all right, although it isn't as wonderful as Don might think. Of course he loves it here; any place seems like heaven when there's pink Alpine glow on the peaks after the sun sets and you're catching fish and you can go home after a week and tell your wife all about it. When you live by yourself in a rickety old cabin, though, with furniture from the 1950's and plumbing from the 1850's, some of the glamour seems to seep out the cracks with the heat. My cabin is cold in the winter, especially in the morning before I get some coals going in the cast-iron woodstove that sits in the middle of my bedroom. At least in Duluth when it was 30 degrees below zero I could turn on the heater. I've gotten used to the bitter cold on winter mornings in my cabin, though; I can't afford anything better, and it's amazing what you can get used to when you got no choice. Even being alone.

It was hard at first, though. When I left Duluth, after Carrie finally left me for good, I didn't know what to do with myself. Every day was like a deep canyon, where the bottom is so far down below you can't see it. All I did my first few months in Colorado was drink and fish, fish and drink. I even drank *while* I was fishing, which I was very ashamed of. I knew how horrified my Dad would have been if he ever found out. Not that my drinking kept me from catching fish; I was fishing the San Miguel in those early days in Colorado, and you gotta be half-dead to get skunked on that river. In fact, one time I *was* half-dead and still caught a lunker; I passed out on a sandbar while my line was out in a riffle, and when I woke up a couple hours later and picked up my pole, it felt awful heavy. I reeled in my line, and sure enough there was a 16-inch brownie sitting there looking embarrassed. It was like bringing in a brick; the damn thing must have worn itself out fighting while I was snoring away in the sand. I let it go, of course — even back then, I never kept any of the fish I caught — but I'm sure that fella ended up in a frying pan. He was stupid even by San Miguel standards.

Looking back, I guess I was pretty stupid myself. When Carrie and I first started going out, it was the first time in my life when I didn't see how things could be any better. My old life just sort of melted away. Carrie was so smart and so pretty, and she made me want to tell her things I'd never told anybody, things I never even knew I wanted to say. I told her how much I loved fishing with my Dad, sitting with him in a canoe at dusk, pulling in Northern Pike while the cries of the loons echoed across the water. I told her how she looked when she came into the bedroom at night in her silky robe, like an impressionist painting in the moonlight. And I told her how I always thought love happened to other people, until I met her.

Carrie told me things, too, like how her parents split when she was ten years old, and how she always felt she was to blame. She explained how she still had a hard time trusting anyone, especially men.

"I trust you, though, Andy," she said, as she kissed me first on the corner of the mouth, then smack on the lips. "You're the most stable man I've ever been with, and yet I feel as if you need me. I know you'll never walk out, so it's safe for me to love you."

Somewhere along the way though, somewhere between the time when we were deep in love and got married and the time when we started to have problems, I stopped making her feel that way. It wasn't that I stopped caring for her, but I guess I felt like I'd put a lot of things aside for a while, and I just naturally started drifting back to the way I'd been before, the way a bobber floats downstream in a slow current. Carrie noticed it right away and tried to tell me things weren't right. She said that I wasn't putting enough time and effort into our marriage, that we needed to work on some things.

"Just because we're married doesn't mean we can relax and take each other for granted," she said. "Marriage isn't easy. We need to work at communicating better."

All that talk about working on a marriage made me uneasy; my parents never seemed to work on their marriage. They were just married, no questions, no arguments, and I guess deep down that's how I expected my marriage to be.

I tried to go against the current though, I really did. There'd be stretches where I'd come home right after work almost every night and we'd eat dinner together and talk about nothing in particular. If it were winter, I'd build a fire and Carrie would read a book while I tied flies. In the summer, we'd sit on the porch, me with a Pabst Blue Ribbon and Carrie with a Diet Coke, watching the sun set over Lake Superior and listening to the Twins game on the radio. But after a while I'd get antsy and start finding excuses for going out after work with my buddies. Then I'd plan a weekend fishing with Don or a skiing trip with my Dad. Carrie wouldn't say anything at first, but eventually, just when I thought maybe we'd reached a middle ground that was acceptable to both of us, she'd explode.

"You've got to choose, Andy," she'd say angrily. "Who's more important? Your wife or your buddies?"

"For Christ's sake, honey, it's not like I'm running off with another woman! You know how much my friends mean to me!"

"I know, Andy," she'd say, relenting a little. "It's just that I used to be the most important person in your life."

"You still are, Carrie, you still are," I'd assure her. "I guess I just need to try harder to show it, that's all."

So I'd bring her flowers, or cook up a nice dinner, and everything would be OK for a little while. But the talking was the hard part; after a while, everything I said to her sounded a lot like things I'd said before. "You don't tell me how you feel anymore," Carrie complained, and I knew she was right. But I also knew I was tired of having to think about how I felt all the time; sometimes I just wanted to coast.

The night Carrie left was a Tuesday, bowling night, and I'd just rolled a 246, my all-time high. Don and another friend Eric took me over to Grandma's Saloon to celebrate; that was our deal, bowl your high game, drinks were on the other guys. We had a couple of pitchers and did a round of tequila shots, so I was pretty hammered when I walked into the house. Carrie met me in the entryway.

"You're drunk," she said.

"I bowled a 246, honey!" I told her.

"Andy, we gotta talk," she said.

"About what?"

"I'm not happy," she said. Her voice cracked a little bit. "Living with you makes me feel like I can't breathe."

"Allergies," I said. "Call Dr. Lundstrom."

I was just kidding, but my timing was poor, and Carrie started to cry real loud. Usually when she cried it was in muffled little sobs, but this time it was in great, gulping bursts. For some reason I remember that the tears were pouring down in little streams from each corner of her eyes and meeting on her cheeks. "I'm your lowest priority!" she sobbed. "I've been trying to tell you that I'm unhappy! I've been trying to tell you that you're taking me for granted, but it's like talking to a wall!"

"You've got no reason to be unhappy, honey," I said. Even three years later, I wince when I remember saying those words, because they really set her off.

"No reason!" she screamed. "No reason! I'll give you a reason! I'm married to someone who'd rather put worms on a fishhook than spend a morning with me! I've had it, Andy, do you hear me?" Then all of a sudden she stopped screaming and crying and just sat there sniffling for a minute. "I tried to tell you, but you wouldn't listen," she said softly. "I tried so hard!" And that was it. That was the last time she ever showed any passion toward me, the last time she treated me much different from other people she knew. She packed up that night and went over to her Mom's house, and nothing I did or said after that mattered. She wasn't angry with me; she was unemotional, which was a thousand times worse. She explained to me over and over, patient as an angler, that she realized now that she couldn't expect me to change, that she had to take responsibility for her own happiness. I'd get mad at her sometimes, scream that there was no way a woman's feelings could change in the space of two minutes on a Tuesday night, but she never lost her composure. Her feelings hadn't changed in one night, she assured me; it had been a long and painful process for her. "Finally I had to accept the fact that our expectations were different, Andy," she said matter-of-factly. "You wanted someone to be around without disrupting your life too much, and I wanted someone to build a life with. I guess love is blind, huh?"

Well, there's something about having the person you love most in the world talking to you like you're a houseplant that makes you want to run away, and that's what I did. My boss at the U heard about a temporary job to install and maintain a computer network for a ski resort in Southwest Colorado. He even had a friend with an old cabin in Montrose who'd let me stay there for free if I kept it up, so I said goodbye to Don and my folks, packed up the Suburban and drove south, hoping to leave my old life behind. When I found out my memories had climbed up on the passenger seat and made the trip to Colorado with me, I tried to saturate 'em in whiskey, but every day, when I woke up with a headache and a tongue like sandpaper, my first thought was of Carrie.

I called her regularly at first, which she said she liked. "How are you doing?" she'd ask. "Are you OK?"

"I'm OK," I'd tell her, even though I wasn't. We would only talk a few minutes; or rather, she would talk, chattering on about her new furniture or a class she was taking, while I would sit on the rough wood floor of my cabin, watching the spiders on the ceiling and taking an occasional swallow of Jack Daniels. Finally I would interrupt her. "How can you be so blasé about this?" I'd ask. "Don't you love me anymore?"

"It's hard to explain, Andy. I still care about you, but all my life I've been so worried about pleasing other people that I haven't worried about myself. Being on my own is what I need right now." After we'd hang up, I'd just sit there with my bottle, remembering good times with Carrie, and further back, with my parents and friends. I wondered if I could keep living like this; if the past were always better than the present, what did that say about my future? I didn't think I could stand it if things kept getting worse.

Yeah, I was in a pretty sorry state for my first few months in Colorado. I spent more time at the bars in Montrose and Telluride than I did at work. Otto, the bartender at Leimgruber's in Telluride, he worried about me a little, and when he found out I liked to fish he told me we were going on an expedition. One spring afternoon we drove out to the Black Canyon. The place we parked was way above the river. "It's a six mile hike down," Otto informed me. "Not too many people are willing to go to the trouble when there's so much other good fishing that's so much easier to get to." It was like hiking down through the steepest garden you ever saw; the hillside was dotted with columbine and lupine in patterns so pretty it was like they hired someone to arrange 'em. We made camp by the river, and I remember looking up that night at the band of sky that showed between the canyon walls like a river of stars, and thinking how strange it was that this time a year before I'd been at home with my wife in our little house in Duluth.

Otto and I got up at first light and crept up to the river's edge. I was just setting up my pole when a fish came roaring out of the deep pool not five feet from where I was sitting. He was the biggest brown trout I'd ever seen, musta been five or six pounds, and I got a good look at him before he went crashing back into the dark water like a breaching whale. I looked over at Otto and he nodded to let me know he'd seen it. We both tried everything we could think of to tempt the trout to bite, but neither one of us had any luck. "That was a big guy," Otto said in his slightly accented English as we were packing up our gear, and after that the fish had a name.

Not long after I first saw the Big Guy, I started to get my life together. The first thing I did was call Carrie. "We can't talk for a while," I told her. "It's too hard on me."

She was understanding. "I hope we can be friends eventually, Andy," she said. "If it takes six weeks or six months or six years, that's OK."

"I'll call you when I'm ready," I said.

I stopped drinking so much and started working more. A couple of middle-sized companies moved down here and needed some help with their computers, so I had some work after my contract with the ski resort ran out. In between jobs I drove a taxi in Telluride.

But I never worked Sundays. Every Sunday for the next three fishing seasons, I hiked down that mountainside to the pool where Otto and I saw the fish. I went from late April, when snow still covered the trail, until October, when the aspen were so red and orange and yellow it was like hiking through a wildfire. I tried everything: spinners, dry flies, wet flies, live bait. I tried different types of line, different leaders, every possible combination I could think of. I hooked and landed some trophy trout, but none of 'em was the Big Guy. It was OK with me; chasing that fish was like chasing a woman, the thrill was in the pursuit. Success would be a letdown, I was sure.

'Course I still thought about Carrie a lot; she popped up at all sorts of weird times. Usually there was some reason: a song on the radio; a cat running across Colorado Avenue that looked just like our old tabby; there was even a 1981 Pinto in Montrose that had a dent in the door, just like Carrie's. Other times, though, she'd just show up uninvited, usually in my dreams, when my defenses were down. "I changed my mind," she'd say apologetically. "I want you back." We might go for a walk or talk for a while; a few times we even made love. But then the alarm would go off and she'd disappear. I never felt as lonely as when I woke up and realized she wasn't there.

• • •

Last summer when Don was on the last night of his annual visit to Colorado, I drove him up to Telluride to catch his flight home. We were early, so we stopped off at Leimgruber's. It was busy for a weeknight; the waitresses were rushing around, dresses swirling, and you could barely hear the German drinking songs over the noise of the crowd. Otto saw us push open the big wooden door and he had two mugs of Spaten waiting for us by the time we worked our way to the bar. Don handed me my beer and rammed it with his own. "Cheers," he shouted. "Here's to the best fishing in the world."

I took a drink, then I sniffed the mug where Don had held it. "Everything you touch smells like a trout," I told him.

"The mark of a great fisherman. Probably be a few days before it wears off," he said happily. Don was as pleased with himself as I'd ever seen him; he'd dragged ten more unsuspecting brown trout out of the San Miguel that day, and they were crammed into his ice chest with about 20 of their buddies for the flight to Duluth.

Otto walked over and handed me a bowl of pretzels. He reached over the bar to shake Don's hand. "You're leaving tonight?" he asked. Before Don could answer, Otto lifted his hand to his nose. "Tuna fish for lunch?" he asked.

"Ten more brownies today," Don told Otto, who had turned on the water at the little sink behind the bar and was madly scrubbing his hands.

"Don't believe him, Otto. He caught an eight-incher the first day and he's been carrying it around in his pocket all week, like a rabbit's foot."

Otto laughed and turned off the faucet. He sniffed his hands, then wiped them dry on his apron. "Next time I'll just wave," he said. "Don, have a good trip home."

"See you next year, Otto," said Don.

Don took a deep swig from his beer and turned to face me. "You decide about Carrie?" he asked through the foam that lined the bottom of his mustache. It was the third or fourth time he'd asked me that week.

"Why do you keep asking me that? We're divorced, Don. I think we already did all the deciding we need to."

"I ran into her a few weeks ago. She still looks great, and she's still single," Don said.

"So you told me."

"You should call her," Don said. "Not that I want you to come back to Duluth; you're much more useful here where I can freeload off of you. But I get tired of watching you walk around in a trance. Maybe she's realized that there's guys even worse than you that she could get stuck with."

I looked around the bar; every available ledge had some piece of German paraphernalia; a beer stein, or a little blue porcelain plate with a picture of the Alps, or a plaque with old-fashioned German writing on it. Otto had told me that the owner was a Bavarian woman who hadn't been back to Germany since the fifties.

"I think about her all the time, and a few times I've almost called her, but something always stops me," I said. "I got this bad habit of remembering things better than they were when they happened."

"You gotta do something, Andy. Even if she doesn't want to talk to you, at least you'll know. Then maybe you can pull your head outta your ass and see what a great gig you got down here."

Don was right, I knew. I had to talk to her. Maybe she was willing to give me another chance; after all, it had been a long time. I knew now that I was happiest when I was with her; maybe she could be happy with me now, too, now that she'd learned to be happy on her own. When I climbed into bed that night I couldn't sleep, imagining myself phoning her and convincing her that we should get back together. When I got up the next morning the first thing I did was fix some coffee; the second thing I did was call Carrie's Mom's house. Carrie answered.

"It's me," I said.

"Andy," she said. We hadn't spoken in more than two years, but she didn't sound angry or even excited. She sounded polite and cheerful.

"How you doin'?" I asked.

She was doing fine as it turned out; she'd enrolled in a nursing program and liked it a lot. She caught me up on her family and on some gossip regarding mutual acquaintances. Then she asked me how I was, and she seemed genuinely pleased when I told her I was starting to enjoy Colorado.

"Are you seeing anybody?" I asked her abruptly, even though I already knew the answer.

"I go out sometimes, but nothing serious," she said.

"I'm not seeing anyone either," I said. I had rehearsed a few things to say next, but suddenly I couldn't think straight. My heart was still pounding, like it had been since I woke up. "Carrie, I think we ought to try again," I blurted. I wondered if fiber-optic technology had betrayed me and revealed the desperation in my voice.

Carrie didn't reply for a minute. "Andy, people don't change," she finally said. "You shouldn't feel bad. You're a nice man and someone will be happy to have you. You and I just shouldn't be together, that's all."

"I still think about you a lot," I said.

"I'll always have a special place for you in my heart, Andy. That's why I want to stay friends. But people don't change." Her words hurt bad enough, but it was the tone of voice she used that knocked the hope outta me like a blow to the stomach. She sounded patient and a little exasperated, like when she used to have to repeat her pizza order at Domino's two or three times before the guy got it straight. She couldn't have used that tone if she had any romantic feelings left toward me.

We hung up a few minutes later, and I went straight over to the cupboard and pulled out the bottle of Jack Daniels that had been sitting there untouched for months. I didn't get drunk; I just took a couple of slugs to slow my mind down a bit. Around 4:00 P.M. I loaded my fishing gear and my pack in the Suburban and drove up to the Black Canyon. By 7:00 I was crawling on my hands and knees to a spot just above the pool where the Big Guy lived. I'd caught a few grasshoppers on the hike down and I put one on my hook in a way that allowed it to keep flapping its wings. I dropped it right where I wanted it, right into the main part of the whitewater that spilled into the pool.

Now, I'd tried hoppers in that pool plenty of times with little success, but this time on the second or third cast I felt a tremendous yank on my pole a split second before I saw the brilliant flash of silver in the vicinity of my hook. My fishing rod bent almost in half and the reel was screaming as the line went racing out. I knew this was the Big Guy; I'd never hooked a trout this big in my life. I kept the line taut, reeling in when the Big Guy sat still, and letting him have some running room when he got restless. One time I got him where I could see him, sitting not 20 feet away, huge and unconcerned. Then he went swimming over to the far side of the pool and hovered in an eddy. He sat quietly for a minute or two; then suddenly he started swimming as fast as he could straight toward me. I managed to get my drag as loose as it would go before he veered off, so the line didn't snap. He tried the same maneuver a couple more times, but he never managed to break my line, and after about a half hour he started to run outta steam. I finally got him close enough so I could net him. He was as big as I remembered him, six pounds easy, between two and three feet long. He flapped a little in the net; he was tired, but dignified and proud, and he seemed confident, like he knew I'd send him back out into the river.

That's when I lost it. I pulled the net out of the water and lugged him up onto the shore. I found a good-sized rock and started beating the Big Guy on the head, methodically smashing his face in 'til the bright red blood ran from his gills. I kept going long after he quit wiggling and gasping for air. Finally I stopped and looked at that big beautiful fish, lying there dead in the grass, and me with its blood all over my hands and the sleeves of my jacket. I suddenly felt nauseated, and I almost got sick right there. For a while afterward all I did was stare at my hands, watching the blood get hard and sticky under my fingernails and thinking how things always turned out different from what I intended.

It was starting to get dark, but I sat for a while, taking occasional swallows from the bottle of Jack Daniels in my vest pocket. Finally I got up, walked over to the Big Guy and picked him up by the gills using both hands. I lugged him over to the Gunnison, and gently as I could I laid him in the water. I righted him and give him a little shove so that he drifted off into the current. In the dim light of dusk it was hard to make out his shape; and for a second I could pretend he was swimming downstream under his own power, as if the cold black water had washed away what I'd done.

BACKTRACKING

Gladys Swan

S alida, Colorado. He stepped down from the Greyhound on stiff legs and looked around raw-eyed from a night of broken sleep. He was there. Home: on the concrete of its bus station, in the very exhaust fumes and restaurant smells and fluorescent glare of it. Welcome home, Jason. Bring out the brass band, folks — here I am. But first tell me where the restroom is. . . .

He combed his hair in front of the mirror, picked up his satchel, gathered himself together, moving parts still intact, and outside the bus station took a scan of the street to get his bearings. Where to first? Not to the house. Save that for the last. What he wanted to do was look, wander around loose, get the feel of the place fresh coming back to it, before he got hooked into some new situation and the focus shifted and things darkened perhaps, threw up walls, turned strange. He started off along the main street with an open eye, tracing around cornices and taking in signs and studying the fronts of stores, not even trying to catch hold of anything, connect himself — if there were anything left to catch hold of. . . . Strangers, he thought, glancing into faces — like everywhere. Yet an impression gathered, despite store-fronts having been remodeled, things coming in and going out — a hardware store where he remembered a grocery, the theater he used to go to on Saturday afternoons closed up, cage boarded: the scratch house, as the kids used to call it. The town had kept a certain flavor. Nor had everything been carried off in the flow of change. He found himself opposite his father's place — still a bar. Whose place now? he wondered. They'd kept the same name: The Spur. The spur you wore or the spur of the moment or the spur of the taste for drink? He decided to go in. The spur of curiosity — at least nothing so definite as desire nor so vague as impulse. He crossed the street.

Inside: a heavy-set fellow tending bar. Widow's peak, tight face, narrow eyes, as though whatever they looked at, it was all the same to him — somebody Jason didn't recognize. He ordered a draft and looked around. They'd pulled out all the old wooden booths and put in tables with formica tops and a jukebox and a t.v. But they'd kept all the old woodwork around the bar, curlicues and all, and the chandeliers with the colored glass shades. The two sets of things drew up sides and let you have it in the crossfire. He'd liked the old booths.

"Who runs this place now?" he asked the bartender.

"You're looking at him. Own it and run it."

"Used to be a guy named Avery."

"So they tell me."

"You don't happen to know what became of him?"

He looked at Jason as though he were trying to get a rundown on whoever the answer was going to, why he might be wanting it and what he might be going to do with it — all in a glance.

"Drank himself to death."

"It figures. Broke the first rule —"

"You knew him?"

"A little."

"Got his liver finally. They said he used to chug down a quart a day."

Poor bastard. Ironical. He thought of how his father had lost the place to Avery in the poker game. It had been Avery's luck — and his fate. "How long's it been?"

The bartender seemed to loosen up a little, let through a sort of low-grade affability: "I've had the place seven, eight years now. Closed it up for a while after he went bankrupt. Had to get the lawyers to quit hassling over it. You always got to pry them loose of a thing. You live here?"

"Just visiting," he said, drained the glass, and left.

He had to cross the river to get over to Victor Street, where the house was. He paused on the bridge to contemplate the Arkansas. The old river. It had never been a big town, but it had the river. Cross plain and mountain in a wagon and there it is: precious water. You don't let go of it — you plant a town down on it every chance you get, even a little town. Every boy growing up will go fishing in it, as he had done, and, grown up and gone, carry the river along with him, running through memory, always there. The river was still there, always the same and always different. But looking at it, he felt somehow disembodied, the ghost of whoever he had been. Some few still had a memory of him — unfortunately. That thought alone had prevented him from coming back for his mother's funeral. He'd have had to stand there among them, their eyes on him.

Well, better get there and get it over with, he thought, leaving the river and turning down the street. Nearly fifteen years. God Almighty, where had the time gone? He'd walked down that street so often, he fell back into the old frame of mind, seemed to fall back into the time when it had all been familiar. But when he came to the old neighborhood, the mood collapsed. He scarcely recognized it. It had cut leading strings with the past and gone off on its own. Nearly all the other houses had been torn out. Gone without a trace, leaving not so much as a shell of the life that had gone on in them. Old Miss Pennuel, his fifth grade teacher, who spent nearly all her life indoors pumping out hymns on her organ. Vern Grider, who'd put the cat up into the canary cage one morning for the sake of experiment. . . . A filling station took up part of the block, next to that a hamburger stand. Only the white frame house on the corner stood like a relic. The moment he saw it, something collared him: he'd done it, all right, and just let him walk in the door and the roof would land on his head.

He walked past the house and on to the end of the next block, crossed to the other side of the street, and came back. One of the pillars was gone, he noticed, and the porch, a clutter of tricycles and broken rockers and crates, had weakened to the point of collapse. The rest was all of a piece with it, the white paint a dirty dull, chipping, bare boards showing through. So that was what he owned half of. . . .

Not that he gave a rat turd for it, he thought, crossing the street. Callie could have it and welcome to it. No doubt she'd earned it, nursing the old woman through her last bout of illness. God knows he'd done nothing for her, hadn't even come back to see her. So he couldn't figure out all the pestering, the letters that kept following him around for months, from his sister and from some lawyer named Jackson — Curtis Jackson, or Jackson Curtis, whatever the hell it was — the envelopes bearing a freight of postmarks and cancellations and addresses crossed out and smudges and creases from fingers clean and dirty. Every letter seemed to come to him with a weight of unknown humanity impressed upon it — a transaction with an anonymous fellowship — as he turned it over and tried to figure out how many hands it had passed through. He'd written letters back and signed papers — asserted and sworn and disclaimed — but the outcome of it was his being stuck with half a house that Callie and her kids were living in, and which, by all rights, ought to be hers. They were going to have to settle it one way or another, Callie wrote him: he owed her that much. Opening the last letter as he stood in the lobby of the flea-trap transient hotel in Albuquerque, he wondered at the faith or desperation that would make a woman suppose he'd come back there a second time. Inside he found a bus ticket home. So from a sense of some obscure obligation he'd come back — it was a matter of inheritance.

He rang the doorbell. A little girl of about six opened the door and stood there staring at him. Dinah, was it? He felt a sudden impulse to sweep her up and whirl her around, but thought better of it. It might scare her and, besides, Callie might not approve.

"Hello, honey, is your mother home?"

She left him standing in the doorway and disappeared. It was dark within, and on the blaring t.v. dark shapes jumped on the light patch of screen. As he adjusted his vision, a woman appeared in the darkened interior, tall, rather gaunt, and for a moment he saw his mother.

"Hello, Callie," he said, a tightness in his chest.

She looked at him, much as his mother would have done, sharply, as though nothing she saw made things any better or worse than she already expected. "Come in, Jason."

He went into the living room among the shapes of furniture. The child had returned, and now he saw another in front of the t.v. "This Dinah?" he said, bending down on a knee so that he could look at her.

"Diane," she said, giggling. "My name's not Dinah — that's a funny name."

He was sure that went over big. He put his hand into his pocket and pulled out some chocolate.

"Don't spoil her with candy," Callie said. "I got enough to worry over without trips to the dentist."

"Just this once," the little girl pleaded. "Please."

"All right," Callie said, wearily, "but go play somewhere out of here and take Billy with you. Billy," she said, "you go on with Diane."

"I wanna watch."

"Look what I got, Billy. Come on, you can have a piece."

"Go on, get on out," Callie said. "She'll give you some. Give him half, you hear. And no fighting, or I'll paddle you both."

When the children were gone, Callie turned off the television and pulled open the shade.

The same wallpaper, Jason noticed, surprised to recognize it. It had been a silver-grey in an ivory background, but aged now to the color of yellowed parchment, it trapped the light, made the room dim.

"Sit down," she said to Jason.

There was an uncomfortable silence after he had done so. He found himself staring at her and shifted his gaze to a spot on the wall. She was only three years older than he, but the years had not been kind — she looked forty. She'd been a pretty girl, he remembered, though in a rather severe way, and even now you catch something of what had faded out, like the design of a piece of goods that had gone through the wash too often.

"Well, you're back," she said.

"Got your letter just the other day. How are you getting on?"

"Much as it's been a concern of yours all these years," she said, with half a smile. "Well, never mind that. I didn't send that letter or ask you back for old time's sake — it's a matter of business and a matter of money, and right now that's all I care about."

He didn't say anything.

"You know the will. Half the house is yours —"

"I thought we got all that straightened out," he said. "Take it, it's all yours. I don't want any of it."

"That'd make you feel good, wouldn't it? Big and easy brother. Well, don't think I wouldn't take it. If Mother had wanted me to have it, I'd have taken it all. God knows I earned it. What do you think it was like these last years with her on my hands? And the kids. And Sam running off. Why they haven't carted me off is the wonder of it."

"I'm sorry," he said.

"Yes, that's a good word. Covers a multitude of sins. You think it does any good?" she demanded. "You think it makes up for anything?"

She waited, apparently for him to think it over.

"Anyway," she continued, "she made me promise. 'It's his and he's got to have it' — she was that pig-headed about it. Or maybe senile. Or maybe, Gene being dead, she didn't want to write off the men in this family as a total loss." She gave him a straight look. "I wasn't to take it and you had to come back and settle it."

He shrugged. "I'm willing."

"All right. I'll give you five thousand dollars for your share of the property."

"Whatever you say."

"Yes, Jason the big-hearted. It'll be a satisfaction to me to cheat you. They've offered me thirty thousand for the land, to put in a supermarket. And I'm going to get the kids out of this hole and go to California and start over."

He said nothing.

"And you wouldn't stand up to me, would you? Not even insist on what's yours by rights — half after it's sold. No, you'll come home, your head all down in sorriness, wanting me to say, 'Welcome home.' But you won't stand up to me, will you?"

"Goddam you, Callie," he said. "Don't push me too far. You got what you want. And you don't know what I want. Push me far enough and I'll change my mind."

She laughed. "So I got a rise out of you after all. I just wanted to see how long it would take you to get down off your high horse and start acting like other people." She looked at him with contempt. "Oh, yes, I see I got to be nice to you, don't I? I was forgetting how you got to coax and wheedle a man, though maybe he'll run off anyway and leave you high and dry." She sat back, her face a blank.

"Good Lord, Callie," he said, his anger gone. "Don't let it all get you whipped."

"I've suffered, Jason," she said, quietly, "all my life. You could get out — you got out and didn't look behind you. I been here all the time."

She held that against him — all his greener pastures. He went over and sat on the arm of her chair and took her hand. It was like ice. For a moment she let him hold it and smooth it and try to put some warmth back into it, but then she pulled free. "No," she said. "I don't want any of that any more. All I care about is the money."

"Isn't there anything . . . " he began, thinking of the children, " . . . to look forward to?"

"It's too late," she said. "I know what I know. All I want from everybody is to be left alone. And all I want from you is your signature."

"That's fine with me," he said, standing up. "The sooner we settle it the sooner I can leave, the better I'll like it."

"That's your style, isn't it?" she said. "We can start tomorrow. I'll call up the lawyer. The grocery chain's just waiting till they hear from me." She seemed almost to come to life. "You'll be wanting to spend the night. You can sleep on the couch."

"You sure you don't want me to sleep out on the porch or back in the shed?"

She ignored him. "Supper's at five and it don't wait."

"I won't be needing any, thanks," he said, thinking . . . might not even be back . . . and left the house. He had half a mind right then to hitch a ride out of town and leave her in whatever legal tangle she'd find herself in. He might as well prove to her — what? That he was one more man to leave her in the lurch; that the world was exactly the way she thought it was? At least he could prove to her that she should have thought twice about getting him riled. But it was not just what she alone was doing to him. He wasn't even sure what all it was down there making all the boiling and bubbling now that she'd lifted the lid off the cauldron. Why had she made him come back, his mother? To humiliate him even from beyond the grave? Half the house — wanted him to have it. His inheritance . . . more stately mansions. . . . He hadn't built anything better. Not by a long shot.

He'd left his gear at the house, but there was nothing he was unwilling to part with; he was free to go on if he felt like going. He started walking out toward the edge of town, though that didn't seem like what he wanted to do either. Then it occurred to him that if he went far enough, he'd find the cemetery. He wanted to see where she was buried. And old Avery too. He wasn't sure why. For the living to exult over the fallen dead?

It was good to walk, after the night on the bus and the half hour in the house, which had seemed far longer; good to be out in the late March weather. It was still cold, though the sky was bright and deep blue, and spring was somewhere whispering to the blood. Old snow still kept the ground, small drifts of it among the gravestones and patches of ice frozen in with brown matted grass, as though the cemetery would hold on to winter till the last.

He knew the cemetery, had sneaked off there as a boy with his buddies to smoke cigarettes, sneak a drink of whiskey. It seemed a little strange to him now that here in that fearsome privacy had begun the flirtations with the forbidden. And lovers, too, he had spied now and again, snatching at passion among the cold stones.

He entered the gate, as though into the dead center of things. No hurry. Nothing was going anywhere — all things had been delivered of their motion. And he found himself yielding to a stillness, an absence that called him beyond himself. No hurry: he wasn't going anywhere either. Everything pushed aside, suspended, he walked, without thinking about it, back to the old part of the cemetery, where the markers were so worn the names had all but disappeared into the stone. Some of his mother's people, Wagoners and Sewells, were buried there, including the one infant his grandmother had happened to bear in Salida. Her other twelve children had been born in nearly a dozen different towns around the state, while her husband had worked at one thing and another, bought and sold land, hauled rails by wagon for the D & RG. She'd scattered her children like so many seeds to the wind.

She herself was buried out in California. Hadn't spent much time in any one place. Runs in the family, he thought. I come by it naturally.

A lot of little ones, he noticed. He'd read the name of a woman dead in the prime of life and there clustered around her would be the graves of four or five of her children, infants mostly. Few of them had made it past the age of five. It must have been rough, the life on the frontier — and for some reason he thought of Callie. Hard on the women and the kids. Sickness and hunger and danger. Hard to keep the fires lit. Fodder for graves. Whatever had brought them to the West must have been pretty heady stuff. Only the strong had made it. The hardiest — or maybe the hardest. It was a question.

The dates became more recent, the old part of the cemetery merging into the new, in the continuousness of death. He found Avery first, right in his path. Ten years dead. He'd hated Avery and he'd tried to get even with him. . . . Yes, and destroyed him, a voice spoke within him. That's what his mother would have said. "There's no defense, is there?" he said. In his mind, Avery merely laughed, gave him a drunken leer. And his mother turned her back on him. He stood looking down at her grave. No explanation and no understanding . . . and no forgiveness either. How to put into words what had had no words then, what had seemed too powerful or too confused for human speech? How to speak to the dead? The power they exerted when living seemed to have grown beyond all bounds now that they were beyond him. Perhaps theirs was the final and greatest revenge now that they'd created what he had to live. No wonder she had made him come back.

"You should have left me alone, damn it all," he told her, and Avery. It struck him that that was Callie's only desire now. The trouble is, he reflected, no one is ever left alone. In a way he couldn't blame Avery. He'd won the bar; thinking how lucky he'd got, it was natural for him to go on to win the woman and the warm spot in the bed. To the victor go the spoils. Only it wasn't that simple. Avery had come around, a great bear of a man, taking off a soft suede hat and calling Jason's mother "ma'am," speaking gentle. He sat on the edge of the couch in the living room, looking ill at ease, yet uplifted in some painful but gratifying way. He couldn't find a place to fix his eyes, though he managed to keep his hands from getting away from him. The eyes, Jason had noticed, flew everywhere, landed for a moment on his mother's bosom, then leapt away, followed the back of her out of the room when she went after the coffee, met her eyes when she returned, slipped away to her neck, took a moment's rest on her bosom, shot down to the floor, followed an ankle up, landed briefly on her bosom, and flew off to rest on the picture on the opposite wall, of three horses feeding at a trough. Horses of three different colors — white, yellow, and brown — feeding devotedly at the trough — painted by a cousin under the delusion of having talent. Horses whose three eyes watched you go from one side of the room to the other. Avery's eyes met the horses'; the horses' eyes met Avery's. No doubt the horses had only a little less trouble than Jason had at the time trying to figure out why Avery was there and what he wanted.

The next time Avery came, Jason remembered, his mother had fed him supper, and Avery had reminisced about his boyhood. The meal reminded him that food was something you could relish on the way down instead of merely being fodder you threw down to your hunger to get it to leave off and lie down quiet. He'd been in the army and worked in the oil fields and had done some hauling on contract with his own truck, and in all that knocking around, he'd never cared what he put into his stomach, never really tasted it, it went down so fast. When he came around the third time, he said he didn't aim for a fine woman like her to go a-begging; it went against his principles. And didn't the Bible say somewhere to give justice to widows and orphans? He wasn't much of a Bible man, but he did remember something of the sort, and the Lord's Prayer.

It may have been, Jason thought, as he looked back, that his mother's biscuits and fried rabbit had awakened some long-buried instincts. In any case, Avery said that winning that bar had made a changed man out of him. He'd never held onto a dime before, had thrown it away as fast as he made it. But now he was ready to settle down and become civilized. The next time he came he brought his traps.

"Well, boy," he'd said to Jason, and there was that great hand clapping him on the shoulder, "don't stand there gawking. I've come to be your pa. And I brought you a present. Look at that, will you?"

And there before his eyes were a pair of handmade cowboy boots and a B-B gun he'd been half a year trying to wangle his mother into buying for him.

They were waiting for him. Avery was waiting for him to go wild over the gun; his mother was waiting for him to go wild over Avery; and his sister was standing there looking pleased over the new dress Avery had brought for her. Even the horses were waiting. He'd wanted a B-B gun as badly as he'd ever wanted anything. They were all waiting.

Before he knew what he was doing, he'd kicked Avery in the shin and had run out of the room. Behind him, the horses stampeded.

His mother flew down on him like a fury. What did he mean doing that? Somebody trying to be nice and look what you do. "I ought to whale the tar out of you."

She shook him instead.

"Now listen, you're going to be nice to Avery, you hear? If your pa was half a man, he'd be here right this instant, wouldn't he?"

Shake. Shake.

"And why isn't he here — answer me that." Shake. Shake. "Because he did us harm, that's why."

His father? Harm?

"It was him that ran away. Don't you forget that. You think he gives two hoots what happens to us? Avery's going to take care of us. Him a perfect stranger, too. That's who's going to do good for us. And you'd better treat him right, you understand? Now go in there and tell him you're sorry."

He told him. He said the words. But with his eyes he said, "Go away." His father had gone away because Avery had been his bad luck. As Jason thought about it now, it seemed that by a fantastic logic he had been part of Avery's bad luck, though Avery hadn't gone away. Sometimes he had lain in the dark, seeing before his mind's eye how it would be if his father came back and threw Avery out of the house and beat him up and broke his neck. Then things could start all over again from the beginning, fresh and new. And all his daydreams grew from the soil of that stupidity. "Go away," he said to Avery in his mind. "Go away," he said with his eyes.

It was the only thing he could say. What else was there to say to a man you'd kicked in the shins after he'd given you a B-B gun? At first Avery had looked at him with puzzlement, then with a certain disgust, as though at a dog that ought to know better but that has peed on the carpet. And finally that disgust deepened and sharpened to the point where it was a dog he wanted to kick.

"Get out of my sight. If I see you around the next minute, you'll wish you weren't. Get." Whack. Slam. "That's right. You run. Get used to running. You're your daddy's little boy."

And whereas, before, his feelings for Avery had been only as Avery represented his father's bad luck, now he hated Avery purely for himself.

He wondered now whether Avery had been sober those times or liquored up. For having the bar made a changed man of him in more ways than one. It meant that when he poured himself a shot from the bottle, he could pour himself another, as many as he wanted, without his money wearing out ahead of his thirst. It may have been that he'd always had the susceptibility, but that having to work steady, hold onto a job, he'd never given full satisfaction to his thirst. Or maybe it had taken the bar for him to discover it at all, that fatal capacity. At the time it had made no difference to Jason, except that, sober, Avery was steadier on his feet. Avery sober would just as soon have whacked him one as Avery drunk.

But that just proved to Jason that he was right. Aha, he'd known it all along — the secret — and within his heart of hearts he rejoiced. Avery was a VILLAIN, a sure-fire, honest-to-God villain. And there would come a day of reckoning. That's the way it happened in the books anyway: books he read in the library all about the West and books his grandfather had collected and preserved with such loving care, all about Wild Bill Hickok. For wasn't his grandfather the natural son of Wild Bill? Or so the old man claimed in his crazy way. Hoarded away in Jason's room was the collection his grandfather had put into his keeping with tremulous hands — so much rubbish his mother called it: biographies and dime novels and yellowing, brittle newspapers and old magazines: J.W. Buell's *Heroes of the Plains* and *Wild Bill, The Pistol Deadshot* and the February, 1867 issue of *Harper's Monthly Magazine*. Their pages spoke to him, created an image in his head:

> " . . . eyes that have pointed the way to death of hundreds of men . . . "
> "Singular grace and dignity."
> "He shoots to kill."
> " . . . eyes as gentle as a woman's . . . "
> "Quiet manly face . . . "
> "He shoots to kill."
> "Six feet one inch tall . . . quiet manly face . . . "
> "With his own hands has killed hundreds of men . . . "
> " . . . . . hundreds of men . . . . . shoots to kill . . . "

If Wild Bill could handle M'Kandlas and his "gang of despera-does, horse thieves, murderers, regular cut-throats who were the terror of everybody," standing up to them one lone man against ten and killing them all, then surely he, Jason, could take on one drunken bully. Next time Avery laid into him or rough-handled his mother, he'd get something he wasn't counting on. He'd show him. Prove himself. Someday they could write a book about him:

Wildcat Jason
From Boyhood to Manhood
Deeds of Daring, Scenes of Thrilling Peril and Romantic
Incidents in the Early Life of Jason Hummer

She clung to him and he could feel her heart
palpitating as she held his head against her bosom.
"Oh, son, hide yourself," she cried as the tears trickled
down into his face. "Save yourself against him. He is too
strong for a poor child like you. And he is wild as the savages
when the strong drink is on him."

"Oh, Mother, do not fear," said the boy. "When I was a babe in arms,
you were my guardian angel. Now I am a man. And I would be the
most shameless coward that ever lived if I did not stand up to that
brute and deliver my angel."

"Oh, son, now I see what has become of my sweet boy. He has grown
up before my very eyes. He will make me proud of him."

At that moment there came a violent thundering at the door, and the
poor woman nearly fainted from fright. "Oh, hide yourself," she
pleaded, clutching his arm. "He'll kill you."

"Begone, wretch," yelled the boy. "Venture one step over yonder thresh-
old and you're a dead man."

"Haw," came a voice. "You dare to stand up to me, do you, you little
varmint? I'll snap you like a twig. I'll crush you like a jelly." From
within, they could hear him lunging against the door.

Seizing a rifle from the wall, Jason stood, prepared to face the
murderous Avery.

"Is that thing loaded?" his mother cried, growing white as a sheet.

"Quick, behind the curtain," the boy commanded, as the door burst
open and Avery stood before him, a Goliath.

Young Jason fired one shot.

. . .

Fired one shot. Delivered his mother and sister and himself from a drunken bully. Dazed, he stood looking down at the dead man, finally hearing his mother's screams. "You've killed him. Oh, you've killed him. What have you done? Now what'll become of us?" He just stood there, numb all over. There was blood. They turned him over and his body flopped as though it hadn't a single bone in it. The dead man began to moan. Drunk. Falling down drunk. Jason had shot him in the leg.

So it turned out that Avery was right after all: he ran off just as his father had run. And he couldn't have said then whether it was his having shot Avery that sent him off or whether it was his mother's carrying on. All he knew was that he couldn't stay there any longer. For when you've shot a man in the leg for the sake of deliverance and justice and not even your own mother approves, you are a man accurst, despised by the gods and man, and your fate is to wander, with no place to rest your head. But thinking about it now, Jason would have said that it was not they who'd sent him running but only as they revealed to him the gigantic failure he had embraced — a failure that had been beyond his imagination.

His dream had turned to dust. The West had crumbled before his eyes: the roaring towns of the frontier, with the hardy spirits who acted for the sake of justice, against the backdrop of those simplicities of good and evil . . . gone, all of it. And what was left — only the graves in the old part of the cemetery?

All that dream and hope and enterprise and energy and daring that had led that flood of settlers and prospectors and soldiers and ruffians across the plains and over the mountains, enduring what they endured. Then you turned over the other side of the rock and there was all that greed and land hunger and vanity and bloodthirst. All the effort and all the slaughter. The slaughter of the buffalo and the slaughter of the Indian. The Texas War for Independence and the Mexican War and the cattle and sheep wars. The Alamo and Sand Creek and Little Big Horn — all of it. When the dream died and you had to look down at the blood in the dust, what did you do then? Confess — let out all your vileness, wallow in it, maybe even smother in it? Was that the legacy from the past — the vileness and the ugliness and the guilt? A falling down old house with the paint chipped away.

Maybe, he thought, there is nothing so false or stupid as the idea of the second chance, the fresh start. It had sent a whole people chasing across a continent — no doubt that was something. It might even be, he thought, that all those mighty movements of history had come of having an idea stupid enough for a human to believe in. And there was Callie thinking that going to California would make some sort of difference to her. She might as well stay where she was, for all the good it would do her, he thought, as he left the cemetery. He could spare her one more disillusionment. Not that it mattered. He could leave town or he could insist on half the money or he could let her do as she pleased, and whatever it was she'd be bitter about it, see it with the same eyes.

And so, if you had no dream . . . then all you have is the ugliness, the mud at the bottom of the ditch. Either way you were damned, he decided. Either way there was something unreal, as though the human animal were doomed to carry about a certain amount of unreality with him. As for failure, life didn't seem to mind failure. It tucked all kinds of it away in the grave and went on.

He hesitated at the side of the road for a moment and turned and headed back to the house. He was going to be a rich man for a change — rich for him. What would he do with five thousand dollars? Maybe just put it in a bank somewhere and let it lie like an unplowed field. No, he'd bury it, along with the dead. Callie could do what she liked. Finally there were things a man didn't have to prove to anyone, not even to himself.

SENTIMENTAL JOURNEY
Robert Love Taylor

S uch a time. Where to begin. With his mother's displeasure or his father's crazed joy, his sisters' bitterness or his own young emptiness. It was long ago, that is for certain. He remembers the road signs, how you wait for them and then for the towns they prophesy. Always the anticipation of the mountains. The car, a 1952 two-toned blue DeSoto hardtop, was air-conditioned, chilly as a movie theater inside.

He was twelve years old, and so his father would have been forty. His mother, six months younger than his father, was pretty. He had taken a picture of her standing by the blue DeSoto. In that photograph she wore the very short shorts so popular those days, her legs long and slender, the ankles nicely set off, he saw later, by the high, wedge-heeled sandals. She looked like a much younger woman, not anything like his friends' mothers, shapeless and gray figures whose sole purpose in life was surely only to be a mother. His mother had an air about her that suggested she was cut out for something else — just what exactly, he couldn't have said, not in those days, but the special quality certainly did not escape him.

She did exercises every night on the carpeted floor of the living room, rolled, stretched, twisted, jiggled, crouching, kneeling, sitting, standing, or sometimes lying flat on her back or belly, while he sat in the loveseat with his homework in his lap. His father would be in the office, a room several years ago added on to the other side of the garage, a small and separate place, its many shelves cluttered with yearbook samples, order forms, catalogs of rings, company bulletins, copies of *Popular Mechanics* and *Reader's Digest,* musty-smelling books on how to sell, how to succeed, how to win, how to manage, their dust jackets illustrated with photographs of smiling men-in-bow-ties whose hair, only slightly thinning, faintly graying, was always parted in the middle.

There was a big desk with a crook-necked fluorescent lamp that hummed like a radio between stations and made the desk glow with the whitest light you've ever seen, the rest of the room bathed in a darkness so soft that the teeming shelves might have been shadowy altars, the narrow bed beneath the window a pew. Hunched over the desk, his father took a tiny brush and dipped it into one of a multitude of small jars ranged before him just at the edge of the light and touched that brush to paper, just so, touching, it seemed, with the least motion possible, then laying that brush aside, gently, without breaking his concentration on the fine, graceful lines appearing before him on the paper, and taking another brush as delicate as the other and dipping it into the mouth of another jar and touching it too on the bright and smooth surface of the paper.

His father was a salesman, yes, but an artist too. He could have been much better, but there was never the opportunity to attend an art school. In high school, he said, mechanical drawing had ruined him. The boy never knew, not then, what his father meant by that statement about mechanical drawing. It seemed to him that his father's talent was far from ruined; it was immense. The rings he drew, golden and bejeweled, were fit for the hands of movie stars, too marvelous surely for the awkward fingers of those high school students they were designed for, their subtleties beyond the appreciation of even a graduating senior.

Pretending to do homework, sitting on the narrow couch behind the desk until told to go in and get ready for bed, he watched his father draw. Then he went to the loveseat in the living room and watched his mother do her exercises. On the divan opposite, Margaret and Jodie kept their eyes on the big round-screened Zenith console, arguing only during commercials.

That was all long ago.

• • •

One warm spring night his father came in and, instead of scolding them all for still being up, said, We're going to take a real vacation this year. We're going to Colorado.

His mother, her back erect and her arms jiggling, did not comment.

Where's Colorado, said Jodie.

Stupid, said Margaret. It's a long ways.

We're going to spend two weeks in the mountains, his father continued. No sales conference. A real vacation in the mountains. Colorado.

There was a peculiar smile on his father's face, as though the word Colorado gave pain as well as pleasure. His eyes glistened and he held his cigar before him as if it were a special pencil for marking on the air.

Colorado. The word hummed, glowed. Made you feel good to say it. It was where the Rocky Mountains rose from the Great Plains. The Rockies were not like those mountains of Tennessee he had seen two summers ago at the sales conference. Those mountains had lacked snow-capped peaks. They were not majestic mountains. He wanted his mountains majestic.

When can we leave, he asked his father.

We'll see. We'll see.

I want to go tomorrow, Jodie said.

Stupid, said Margaret. What about school.

I'd rather go to Colorado. I don't like school.

A second-grader and she didn't like school. Whatever would become of her, so many years to go. Not enough recess, she said. Dumb games. Mrs. Martin doesn't like me. He believed in doing what you were told to do. It was a lot less trouble. The point was to get through. Next year he'd be in the eighth grade, the first seven years over and done with, only five more to go, and then — then he could do whatever he wanted. Nothing was going to ruin him.

I want to go right away, Jodie said.

. . .

Want, want, want. Was there ever a family with so many wants. His father wanted to go to Colorado. His mother wanted to stay home. A vacation, she said, was only extra work for her. Margaret wanted to bring a friend along. Couldn't Jodie sit in the front seat. Jodie wanted to sit where Margaret sat, by the window. Why should she always have to sit in the middle. Who wants to sit in the middle.

I want you, his mother said to him, to take your accordion.

He wanted to leave it. He was tired of it. At the recital in the Bethany Nazarene Church he had played "The Washington Post March" by memory, hating every note of it. Wasn't that enough.

The accordion would go, but not Margaret's friend, who because of Jodie wasn't invited. Little brat, said Margaret. She always gets what she wants.

Off they went, wanting, wanting, wanting. It was June, it was 1954. Oklahoma City was big, but not so big as it is now. Out on the

Northwest Highway there were no tall buildings yet, neither insurance tower nor condominium nor Baptist Hospital. There were houses, though, new ranch-style ones made of brick, with spacious, as yet treeless, lawns, and thick-shingled roofs and two-car garages. After a while there was Lake Hefner over on the right, a motorboat or two whining across its brownish red surface with a water skier behind. Then you could look back and see the way the city was spread all across the flat but slightly tilted land, in the distance the twin skyscrapers downtown like monuments and all around them lesser roofs and densely clustered treetops, grayish in the early morning haze.

First came Okarche, hardly a town at all, a street past a few brick storefronts with a school at the outer end, then Kingfisher, a bigger version, then Watonga, where you had to make a sharp turn before the highway again opened out across the broad land and, miles later, revealed another town, Woodward. This one had a longer Main Street.

We'll have lunch here, his father said, and pulled up into a gravel lot alongside a bright Dairy Queen. Where were the trees, though. And the grass. The grass beyond the gravel was sparse, growing in weedy-looking clumps with lots of sandy-red dirt all around. The wind kept whipping up this dirt into little pinkish puffs. And what was that blowing across the highway. Tumbleweeds, his father said. They spun around in bursts of speed, round as wheels, and there seemed to be nothing to stop them.

Standing at the window of the Dairy Queen was a tall man in a black cowboy hat. He wore a black vest, string tie, and a thick and elaborately tooled belt, its big silver buckle shaped like the head of a longhorn steer. Clutching his cone of soft ice cream, the man grinned, and his teeth were small blackened stubs, rounded at the edges. Hello, boys and girls, he said, and headed for his pickup, a shiny pink Ford with big dice dangling from the rearview mirror, a rifle rack in the rear window. In the back of the pickup sat a big gray metal box.

That, said Jodie, was a cowboy, Daddy, wasn't it.

No. A welder.

A hayseed, said Margaret, who liked to watch old musicals on television.

It was a quiet drive. Margaret and Jodie rode as though in a spell. After they had gone beyond the suburban developments of Oklahoma City, their wants seemed to have disappeared. It was perhaps magic, he thought, this journey a charmed one, the way to Colorado toward peace, harmony. Jodie slept a lot, her head inching towards his shoulder and finally resting there. He didn't mind. He felt very brotherly towards her. He would certainly protect her if she were challenged by bullies, though he knew he would be beaten up badly. He wasn't little, but he was skinny. Slender, his mother said. Whichever, he had no muscles to speak of. The chest expander he'd secretly sent away for, a thick slice of black rubber with metal handles at either end, never affected, as far as he could tell, a single muscle, and after three and a half weeks of nightly pullings he rolled it up and put it in the back of the drawer beneath his underwear, hoping his mother might, if she happened to see it, take it for a sock.

Still, he would protect little Jodie. Stand up for her. Perhaps the fierceness of his efforts, the fury with which he swung and leaped and darted, would stun his opponent even if the blows themselves caused no harm.

As for Margaret, well, only a year younger than him, she was old enough to take care of herself. She was skinny like him, but it was all right for girls not to be muscular. Besides, nobody picked on her. Even with her teeth braced, she looked tough, seldom smiling, her dark eyes clear and unblinking. She could outrun many a boy, and her girlfriends called her Meg. When they came over, she made them laugh a lot. He could hear their giggles from his room while he tried to practice his accordion. It was distracting. Not that he wanted them to listen, no, but still they might try to make a little less noise. It would be, as his mother would say, only common courtesy. Oh, Meg, they were always saying. Meg, really.

He used to sing duets with her. For the grandparents they sang "The Tennessee Waltz" and "Your Cheatin' Heart." Aunt Esther, a choir director up from Dallas for a holiday, said, My, don't they sound like the Andrews Sisters. Then his voice began to change and he lost interest in singing. It was understood that he would have to begin music lessons of some sort. His mother hoped he might consider the piano because he had such long fingers. She was certain that his fingers were those of a piano player, a pianist. He resisted her encouragement, assuring her that someday he would know what he wanted to play. Maybe it would be the piano, but he wasn't yet ready to decide. Then several of his friends began to take accordion lessons. The accordions rested in dark cases lined with red velvet. There were rows of black buttons on one side and, on the other, keys like on the piano, only much whiter. In between was what made the sound possible, the bellows. The bellows of his best friend's accordion had an *X*-shaped design on them, white on black, that changed into an intricate pattern of Zs continuously expanding and contracting when the music was played. Another set of keys, smaller and fewer, gleamed above the white piano keys — these, his friend told him, were for changing the tone of the note you played. You could make a sound like a clarinet, an oboe, an organ, a piccolo. It was wonderful. Mother, he said, I know now.

And it was done. His friends, after the first year, had quit their lessons, but he kept on. Strapped to his shoulders, his black Polina accordion was heavy and cumbersome, but he was fond enough of the music that came from it, the spirited marches and mazurkas that his teacher, a pleasant young woman affiliated with many churches, taught him how to play. Sometimes he played for hours, in his room among hanging Spitfires and Flying Tigers, vigorously but smoothly pulling and pushing the bellows, pressing the tiny buttons that he had come to know by touch alone while the fingers of his right hand slid across the piano keys in a motion gentle enough to be taken, he liked to fancy, for stroking. For "Lady of Spain" he learned to shake the bellows. His ambition was to master "Malagueña."

Sometimes his mother opened the door and said, That was beautiful. He loved hearing that. Her favorite was a hymn, "Whispering Hope." But it was changing. He found it easy to play less. It was spring and there were other things to do. He wanted to get a job so that he could save his money for a motor scooter, preferably a Cushman Eagle, which had gears and resembled a motorcycle, though with tiny wheels. He wanted to climb up high in the tree in the backyard and watch the horizon. He wanted to ride his bicycle to the shopping centers, Lakewood and Lakeside and Village, and sit at the fountains of the air-conditioned drugstores sipping cherry limeades. He wanted to read novels that were going to be made into movies, then see the movies. He wanted a girlfriend to take to those movies. The book was better, he would tell her as he calmly took her hand in his.

Have you practiced today, his mother asked.

Well, when are you going to practice.

Do you want to quit taking lessons.

The accordion grew heavier, the straps, he now noticed, biting deep into his shoulder blades, clear to the bone. But he wouldn't stop the lessons. He had to go on with the lessons. It would have disappointed his teacher if he quit now, and his mother, and it would have meant that he was not so different from his friends after all.

Of course the accordion would have to go with them to Colorado. He brought it to the trunk while his father was packing. It's all right, he told his father, if it won't fit in. I can leave it here. The trunk seemed bulging with suitcases and garment bags and fishing poles. It'll fit, his father said. Leave it there. I'll find a place to put it. Don't you worry. It'll go.

. . .

Here we are!

His father stood in the middle of a small room filled with chests-of-drawers and straight wood chairs dark as dirt and a huge high bed with a sharply arched and ornately carved headboard. There was a musty smell, though the room was very light, its three windows extending from high up on the walls nearly to the floor, the curtains white and lacy. The linoleum-covered floor creaked and the ceiling above the bed had on it a large brownish stain, whale-shaped if you looked at it close enough, the wallpaper alongside shining with what might have been its own light, pale but steady, the pattern of pink hearts dangling in the stalks of yellowish lilies like faintly glowing bulbs in a tightly coiled cord, the background gray as shadow.

This is where we're going to stay? asked Margaret.

It's dirty, Jodie said.

There were three rooms, the one room, dark and small, between this one and the kitchen, where he and his sisters would sleep, they in a double bed that filled a good third of the space, he in a cot alongside. Every wall bore a calendar, each for a different year, none more recent than 1949. This one, the 1949 calendar, hung in the small room above the cot. It had a picture of a pink lady wearing the meagerest of underwear and a large purple plume in her tightly curled yellow hair. She smiled and looked, he thought, pleasant enough, as though she would be glad to talk to you if, seeing her, say in a restaurant, you spoke to her. The other calendars had ladies on them too. The one in the 1948 calendar looked a little like his accordion teacher in the eyes.

It's cozy, his father said.

It's small, all right, his mother said.

He slept well that night, though awakened once by a strange sound that he realized must have been his father calling from a nightmare. It had been a long day. Mountains galore! Hadn't he seen the mountains, the snowcapped peaks he'd always wanted to see. They had been all around, the road winding through them, twisting along their timber-thick bases, following their swift-flowing streams, crest after crest. Look, his father would say, what a vista. That's what I call a spectacular vista.

You watch, his mother said, the road.

The road was often narrow, twenty of the last forty miles unpaved. Slumgullion Pass. Smell that mountain air. But it was really very dusty and his mother was right to insist on keeping the windows up, even though the air conditioner had been turned off to keep the car engine from overheating on the steep grades. Up the grades they went, the engine whining, his father saying, Come on, Bessie, you can make it, Bess. And then down, to the popping of ears and the whispering of his mother, I've had enough of vistas. You keep your eyes on the road, Bill. She sat stiff, both arms extended to the dashboard, her palms pressed against the glove compartment as if to keep something valuable from falling out. On these downgrades Jodie shouted, Faster, Daddy, faster! Margaret was pale, quiet, a paper bag in her lap in case she should be sick to her stomach. There was no stopping on this road, this Slumgullion Pass.

Not long before coming into the town they came to a historical marker commemorating a man named Packer, who, trapped and starving in a nearby cave during a fierce snowstorm, ate his companions and survived. Very educational, his mother said. I'm sure the children got a lot out of that.

It was late in the afternoon of the second day of the trip when they came down from the Pass and followed a stream into the town, hardly a town, only a couple of streets and a handful of houses. There was a grocery, a bar, a sporting goods store, and, set away from the main street, a group of tiny resort cabins made of brightly varnished yellow logs. The mountains rose high on either side of the town and made such abiding shadows that it seemed hours later than it really was, almost night. As for the mountains themselves, well, they were surely majestic, their gray peaks now round, now pointed, stretching forth from the dark trees as if to boast of what they might do if they chose to, become sharp or smooth, jagged or straight, rising in fact like spectacular muscles, as firm and as proud. They would be sky, but preferred remaining rock.

Jodie wanted to stay in the resort cabins, but their father had already made arrangements. He drove them straight to a little house, the middle one in a row of three at the end of the town's main street. Beyond the street a mountain began, this one somewhat shorter than the others, a weathered-looking church at the base of it, abandoned, they soon discovered, with neither pews nor altar inside.

The owner of their house, their father told them, was a retired sheriff. They found him sitting in a dark room in the last house, a magazine spread open on his lap. He said: Key's on the nail, top of the jamb. He wore furry house slippers and woolen trousers. The chair he sat in was draped in many blankets and the room was very warm, the walls covered with pictures clipped from magazines, desert scenes with palm trees, jungle scenes, photographs of female movie stars, of horses and luxurious automobiles. All around him stacks of magazines stood like pedestals awaiting busts, each stack the same height as all the others, about three feet, some with tin ashtrays on top, the butts in them still long, bent as if to make them look like fingers. The place smelled of tobacco and dust and something else, familiar but not so easily placed, what was it, burnt toast, butter, gasoline. His mother waited in the car.

Well? she asked.

We're all set, his father said.

Did you get the key?

I said we're all set.

I don't see any key.

Taking the key from the nail, his father smiled. It broke off in the keyhole, but the door swung open.

Here we are!

• • •

Evenings he played his accordion at the Last Chance Saloon. An old man played the piano. The duet was arranged by his father, who had met the piano player in the sporting goods store. The barroom was only faintly lit by a pair of what seemed to be old lanterns attached to the wall at either side of the broad mirror that the bartender stood in front of, a steady stream of cigar smoke coming from his mouth. It was a long, narrow room. The piano, a massive dark upright with yellowed keys, began where the bar left off. Along the wall opposite ranged cozy booths above which had been taped travel posters of Colorado, pictures of skiers in midflight, the white mountainside behind them like a great smooth cloud they had just sprung from, and of fishermen knee-deep in white-capped water, casting or tugging their lines, of the fish themselves, silvery and plump and streaked or speckled with yellow, green, and blue, of Pikes Peak and the pink Garden of the Gods.

He didn't like to fish. This was a disappointment for his father, he knew. Dutifully he had gone with his father to the streams, was shown how to cast, how to reel, how to bait a hook, and, when sooner than he had hoped he pulled one in, a small one with tiny black eyes, how to remove the hook. It seemed somehow silly, a little like playing baseball. He tried to like it, wanted to like it, if only for his father's sake, but it was no use.

He wanted to climb the mountains, stand at the top of a peak, see what he would see, and take a picture of it.

You can climb that one, his mother said, pointing to the small one with the abandoned church on its slope. Leave the others alone.

He remembers watching his mother in the kitchen of the little house, the fish floating in the sink before her. He catches them, she said, I clean them. And she grabbed each one and slit its slick belly and gutted it while his father on the back porch cleaned the mud from his hip boots. His father was up early every morning, well before the rest of the family, in fact when it was still dark. He came back at noon, removing the trout from his creel and dropping them into a bucket of water, eating a quick lunch and then driving off again. He drove back deep, he told the family, up the gravel road toward Silverton, then parked the DeSoto and walked the streambed until coming to a good spot, a still eddy where the fish rested, drowsy and hungry.

He's crazy, his mother said, slapping a big fish in the cornmeal batter. It's an obsession. He can't relax. I might as well stay at home. This is my fun. Vacation! No vacation for me.

The fish sizzled and popped in the big black skillet, and when they were served his father pronounced them delicacies, the likes of which would not be found in stores or restaurants. He caught twice the limit every day. A lot of bones, Margaret said, but she said it softly.

His father, disbelief so strong in his voice that it might have had a smell, said it was fine if he would rather climb the small mountain than fish the swift streams for rainbow trout. He'd like to have someone along, but if no one else was interested, why, he guessed he'd just go it alone.

The days were long and warm. His mother walked with them down to the store, no more than a room really, that store, with high shelves and, his mother informed them, high prices. The road to the store was dusty and the peaks of the mountains glistened purplish back of the trees. You could hear the water running over the rocks in the streambeds.

I don't like Colorado, Jodie said. I want to go home.

His mother said little. She wore dark glasses and her mouth seemed fixed forever on the verge of a frown. Once his father said to him: You must understand this about your mother, and it is true of all women. They have times when there's no talking to them. Whatever you say is wrong. You mustn't take it personal. You just have to realize that they have these times and it's always been that way and always will and we just have to live with it and hope we live through it.

This must have been one of those times, all right. There was a crispness to her walking, her steps swift and sure. We must make the best of what's given to us, she told Jodie. When you're home again, you'll wish you were here. Think of it that way.

No, Jodie said.

He and Margaret and Jodie climbed the small mountain. The girls didn't slow him down much. The way wasn't so steep, after all. It would be different on other mountains. The top of this mountain was broad and flat and grassy, the grass not so thick, though, growing in clumps, yellow and knee-high, bending in the stiff cool wind. The three of them sat on a rock — a boulder, he would call it — and looked down on the little town, the house where his mother sat inside alone, and on the stream where, farther up than they could hope to see, his father stalked rainbow trout.

Here we are, he said.

It's like we're on top of the world, Jodie said.

I'm the Queen of the World, Margaret said, and this is my throne. You should thank me for letting you sit on it.

I'm the queen, Jodie said. You're just a princess.

They both tried to look very queenly when he took their picture with his Hawkeye camera, holding their heads high and folding their arms in front of them and crossing their legs daintily.

Lately he was thinking a lot about women. Not girls, but women. He was noticing that there was a difference. Running down the mountainside, Margaret and Jodie screaming behind him, he found it pleasing to think that at the bottom of the mountain a woman, somewhat like the waitress at the Last Chance, watched him. You're quite a mountain climber, she might say, and they would embrace. Kissing her would be like — like nothing else in the world, that's for sure! I'm glad, she would say, you don't like fishing.

You better not drop the camera! Margaret shouted.

The waitress at the Last Chance looked at him while he, with as much feeling as he could muster, played on his accordion "The Stars and Stripes Forever." She was even nicer, he thought, than the lady on the 1949 calendar that hung on the wall above his cot. She stood in the wide doorway between the bar and the dining room, her arms folded across her chest, leaning against the doorjamb in her white uniform, smiling faintly, as though just for him, her lips red — red, he would say, like strawberries, like new plums, some tart red fruit, how could he have said which, lacking the taste of such red lips.

Soon he would be thirteen years old, a teenager. When she asked him how old he was, he said fifteen, then felt his cheeks warm. She smiled a very understanding smile. She was nineteen, a grown woman. He saw the futility of it, but loved her all the same. Maybe she would have mercy. He could play the accordion, and he did, there in the dim light, "Lady of Spain" and one of his teacher's favorites, "Blue Moon." There's a lot more to it, the old piano player said, than just the notes. You have to put feeling into the music. This was hard. He was learning just how hard that was. He believed he had the feeling, but how did you get it in the music?

The piano player, a tall man, a lanky man, sat hunched over the keys, his great gray head hanging low, as though the better to put his feeling into the music, his long tobacco-yellowed fingers dancing atop the keys, now at one end of the keyboard, now the other. Sometimes he sang as well as played. When there were no words, as in the fast polkas, he hummed or whistled. I like the old tunes best, he said, like this one. And he played "Sentimental Journey," the bass notes languorous and steady. His name was John. Some, he said, called him Johnny.

Margaret and Jodie were allowed to stay until nine thirty. Then his mother took them back to the little house, sometimes returning later by herself. The owner of their house, the retired sheriff, sat at the bar, a shotglass and bottle before him. He looked small, though holding his shoulders erect and his head high, and he squinted into the mirror, never looking toward the musicians. There weren't many others in the bar. It's still early in the season, John explained. Later in the summer we'll have the crowds all right. You won't be able to turn around in here.

John drank his wine from a coffee mug, sipping it between tunes.

Watch your step, he said, with women. You got to be real careful.

He had a wife once, he said, and a family, but now he was free. A single man could do most anything he wanted to. You had to watch out for the women, though.

The waitress touched John on the shoulder when she poured more wine into his cup, and John winked at her and the piano music seemed suddenly to hop or leap with something new. Feeling, you bet. The waitress's name was Dolores. He found he was thinking of her constantly. Oh, to be twenty — no, twenty-five would be even better, an older man — and muscular and musical with feeling.

During the long days he climbed the small mountain, sometimes alone. He sat on the rock that Margaret had called her throne and looked down on the little town. Some afternoons he walked back and forth in front of the Last Chance, hoping accidentally to meet Dolores. Almost every evening his mother cooked trout, but still she could not keep up with his father. What they didn't eat, his father took to the freezer at the sporting goods store. We'll pack them in dry ice, he said. They'll keep all the way home. We'll be eating rainbow trout next winter.

Until we're blue in the face, his mother said.

Walking back to the house from the Last Chance, his father and mother held hands. They walked ahead of him, dark and romantic in the stillness, the mountains like strange shadows. His accordion in its velvet-lined case was heavy, but he imagined that he carried it as a demonstration of his love for Dolores and that muscles quietly were taking shape under his shirt. He watched his parents. Someday, he thought, I will have a wife and family. I will not let anything ruin me.

Later he was awakened.

In the next room his mother was saying no. Please, no. Please let me sleep, Bill. Please can't you understand I want to sleep.

An old story, his father said.

Then the stillness came round again.

DINOSAUR

Steve Rasnic Tem

W*here did the dinosaurs go?* The children looked down at their desks. A change of climate, ice age, caterpillars eating their food, disease, mammals eating their eggs. Freddy Barnhill was thinking these answers but was too self-conscious to raise his hand. The teacher waited. But nobody's really sure, Freddy thought. Nobody knows.

Sometimes he thought they might be lost somewhere. They couldn't find their way. They couldn't keep up with the others, the way the world was changing so. So they got left behind. They got abandoned.

Twenty years later, Freddy drove the fifty-nine miles between Meeker and Rangely twice each day thinking about his father and thinking about dinosaurs. Only occasionally were there changes in subject matter, although he would have expected both topics to be exhausted by now. People might call him obsessed; hell, people would call him crazy.

Along Colorado Highway 64, endless streams of yellow-blooming rabbit grass whipped by, each scrub-dotted washout and arroyo threatening to draw his eye up its channel and send him into the ditch. Almost as soon as he turned the pickup onto the road, he would start to see his father's enormous hands pressing down at him from above the bar. He'd feel himself suddenly afraid of his father's instability and scurry under the table to hide. Then he'd hear the sudden crash of his father's huge head on the table as he passed out. An endless crash; his father's head slammed the hard wood again and again the fifty-nine miles between Meeker and Rangely.

There seemed to be little life in the gulleys and low hills. Harsh land which had to be struggled with, which swallowed any failed attempts. Early settlers had named this land with their complaints: Devil's Grave, Bitter Creek, Camp Misery, Bugtown, Poverty Gulch. Rotted houses around clumps of tumbleweed leaned from the hillsides like aged throats, their swollen walls collapsing. The broken fingers of ancient windmills reached toward an empty sky.

Once he reached Rangely, the sense of lifelessness was even more pronounced — gray, lunar sandstone in ridges and flatlands as far as the eye could see. A wind-blasted landscape alive with sagebrush, little else. The oil companies' reservation: new and old riggings, abandoned shacks. His father had spent most of his adult life here, working for one outfit or another.

Mel Barnhill had originally been a cowboy. A drifter. Then when things had begun to change with the oil wells coming in, he'd changed, too. He'd been a mechanic, construction worker, jack-of-all-trades. Freddy remembered seeing him work on some of the early crude equipment, even some of the steam-operated earthmovers. Enormous brown hands working with rough-made wrenches. Smiling, singing — he always had been happy working with machinery. Freddy had helped him, sort of, as much as any very small boy might help his father in his work. But that time had passed. As had the life of the cowboy.

His father had liked to think of himself as an outlaw. "Don't need no laws, no woman to tie me down. Like to do as I please."

Freddy remembered following his father up the street after one of the man's long drinking bouts. The swagger in the walk, he thought now, had been reminiscent of Butch Cassidy or professional killer Tom Horn, who used to hide out not far from there. Cattle were still being rustled at the time, and Freddy could recall more than once his father hinting that he had had a part in some of it. He'd wink at Freddy sometimes when he said this, but Freddy never could tell if that meant he was just joking, or that he really had done those things, and Freddy was supposed to be extra proud. The first time Freddy'd seen a John Wayne movie, he'd thought that was his father up on the screen. The walk was the same. After a time he began to wonder if his father practiced it.

Dramatic gestures seemed to be a lot of what the old-timers in the area were about. Gestures for a fading way of life.

When he thought about it now, Freddy believed his father had known the life was rapidly becoming obsolete, the cowboy and rancher becoming extinct. It was the end of an era. Not long after his father's time, they built that new power plant at Craig, and the old-timers suddenly didn't know every face when they came into town. People had to lock their doors.

"Dumb cowboys! Stupid sodbusters!" Freddy's father had been drunk, screaming hoarsely in a corral outside a Rangely bar. Freddy remembered the incident vaguely; he'd seen only part of it through the bar window. But every time he ran into one of his father's old friends, it was recalled.

His father had been drinking with some of his cowboy friends; there'd been an argument. They'd accused Mel of turning his back on them, becoming a city boy, because he worked for the oil companies.

Little Freddy had shuddered behind the window. His father was dragging a cow out of the barn. Before anyone could do anything, he shot it. The big brown animal collapsed as if in slow motion, its head making a sick thud on the hard ground. One of the waitresses had held Freddy so tightly it scared him, but it had calmed him down.

This was the landscape Mel Barnhill had willed to his son. It provided the backdrop for most of Freddy's dreams. And yet it was at the *outskirts* of Rangely that, every day, Freddy started thinking about dinosaurs.

Fourteen miles north of Rangely was the little town of Dinosaur. And twenty-seven miles west of there, just across the Utah border and above Jensen, was the big Dinosaur Quarry of the Dinosaur National Monument. One of the largest sources of dinosaur fossils in the world. Primitive land, or the way the earth might look after some catastrophe. Freddy didn't go any more. Standing up there looking out over the canyons, where the Colorado Plateau had crashed up against the Uinta range, it was as if his whole life might disappear out there someday, pulled into the emptiness.

Over each street sign in the town of Dinosaur was a little red cutout of a stegosaurus. The streets had names like Brontosaurus, Pterodactyl, Tyrannosaurus Rex. The town looked old, almost as old as the surrounding land, with tar-paper shacks here and there and rough board houses. It used to be called Artesia before the Interior Department set up the park.

But most of the tourists went over to Utah, to Jensen and Vernal. Dinosaur was just a place people passed through on their way to somewhere else; there was no restaurant, not even a half-decent service station. Only a few hundred in population — there hadn't been many people in the first place, and most of them had gone a long time ago. The red on the dinosaur cutouts looked a lot like rust.

Freddy worked in Rangely, just as his dad had, but he lived in Meeker. He liked Meeker, although most of the other men his age complained that there was nothing to do. It was a quiet town; there weren't too many cowboys, and it lacked Rangely's construction and oil workers. Freddy was relieved.

The pickup slid in gravel, and Freddy fought to right it.

You had to be careful driving the roads out here; they lulled you, made you careless. The truck seemed so easy to drive, it had so much power, that you sometimes forgot how dangerous one slip might be. One of the drawbacks to advanced technology, and to evolution. It made you reckless; it became too easy to lose control over the power. And that power could leave you upside down off an embankment.

Again, his father's enormous head crashed into the table. The glasses fell in a rain of glistening shards. His father's shapeless mouth opened to expose rough, broken teeth.

Dinosaurs used to walk the hills here, but it had been different then. Freddy thought about that a lot, how things used to be so different. And how they might be different again, with new monsters walking the barren land: giant rats and scavenging rabbits, but maybe rabbits like no one's ever seen before — long claws and hind legs strong enough to tear another animal apart. Just before the dinosaurs came, low-lying desert then, the early Jurassic Period. No animals. Great restless sand dunes towering seven hundred feet, snaking and drifting like primeval dreams. Fading, dying away in the distance.

The earliest home Freddy could remember was an old boarding-house a few hundred yards from one of the early oil rigs. A white-washed shack, really, several crate-like rooms strung together. He and his father had shared one. He couldn't remember his mother, except as a gauzy presence, more like a ghost, something dead and not dead. He didn't think she had ever lived with them in the rooming house, but he couldn't be sure. It bothered him that he could remember so little about her — a hint of light, a smell, that was all. She had vanished. *She left us. She left me,* he corrected himself. His father had always told him that, but it was still hard to believe.

The land sank. An arctic sea reached in. Millions of years passed, and in the late Jurassic it all rose again. The dinosaurs were coming; the land was readying itself.

He sometimes wondered if he had ever known his mother at all. Maybe his memories were false. Maybe she had died when he was born. Maybe she'd gone away to die, her time done once she'd given him life.

The land just come from the sea was much more humid. Flat plains. Marshy. Great slow streams loaded with silt flowed out of the highlands to the west to feed the marshes and lakes. Dust floated down from the volcanoes beyond the highlands. Araucaria pines towered 150 feet above the forest floor, the tops of ginkgos, tree ferns, and cycads below them. Giant bat-like pterosaurs flapped scaly wings against the sky, maintaining balance with their long, flat-tipped tails. Crocodiles sunned themselves by the marsh.

And yet he did remember his father complaining about her. How she never cleaned, never helped them at all. He held a mental image of his father throwing her out. Her screaming, crying, reaching. "I want my baby, my baby!" Freddy couldn't be sure.

Apatosaurus raises its great head above the plants. Forty tons, plant-eater. Cold eyes. Its head comes crashing.

Freddy loved a woman in Rangely. Because of her he allowed himself to stay overnight there on Fridays. But it scared him, loving someone like that. She might leave. She might vanish. And he didn't like waking up in Rangely; the first thing you saw were those barren white sandstone hills.

He loved her. He was sure of that. His love filled him, and formed one of the three anchors of his life, along with the memories of his father and the thoughts of dinosaurs. But lately something felt lacking. Some crisis, some drama. Loving her didn't feel like quite enough.

He wasn't sure why they'd never gotten married. The time had never seemed right for either of them, but after a time he realized that the time would never seem right. One time she was going to have his baby, but she miscarried. No one else had known about it. Wasn't time for it, he supposed; its time had passed. He didn't believe in God or heaven, but sometimes he wondered if the baby might *be* somewhere. Hiding from him. Or waiting for him.

It was the same all over. They had friends — lovers and married couples — and all of them seemed to be breaking up. Still loving each other, but unable to stay together.

Sometimes his drives from Meeker to Rangely were specifically to see Melinda, but he almost never thought about her during the trip. He thought about his father, and dinosaurs.

Freddy looked out the side window of the pickup. Sagebrush flats, rising sandstone buttes, creek beds turned to sand. Old wrecks out in the fields. Before the oil men there had been cowboys, a few farmers. Before them, the outlaws hiding out.

Before the outlaws, fur traders maneuvering through the canyons.

Before that, Indians trading along the Green and Yampa rivers.

Before that, dinosaurs roaming the hot, wet lowlands.

Freddy had watched his father slowly become obsolete, running out of things he could do, running out of places to live. The drinking had grown steadily worse, his father had gone from job to job, they had moved from shack to shack . . .

His father's great head, his enormous body falling, crashing into wood, Freddy scrambling to get out of the way of the rapidly descending bulk . . .

And then his father had left, vanished. Freddy had been seventeen. He had a vague memory of his father walking away, across the flat into dust-filled air. It had been early morning — Freddy had been trying to wake up, but couldn't quite manage it, and had fallen back into the covers. He'd been abandoned.

Freddy did minor legal work for one of the oil companies. Easy assignments, dealing with the local landowners on rights-of-way, leasing, sometimes the complaints of an especially disgruntled employee. Most of the time he sat behind his desk in Rangely reading a book, or daydreaming. In the office he had a full library on dinosaurs and other mysteriously vanished races and species. Many days he saw no one, and he ate his lunch at his desk.

Today was Friday, and he would be staying over at Melinda's place. Melinda taught school some distance from Rangely — rancher's kids, mostly — and Freddy often wondered why she didn't live closer to her work. But she said she liked Rangely.

Over the weekend they would be visiting her father's grave on Douglas Mountain. Her father had faded after a long, consuming illness. She'd been at his bed most of that time, waiting for him to leave her, but still not quite believing it when he finally abandoned her, his eyes going away into gray.

Freddy felt a bit guilty, but he had to admit he looked forward to it. The wild horses they called "broomies" roamed Douglas Mountain, one of the last such herds in the west. A dry and rocky highland there, over 450 square miles. The herd had been there for more than a hundred years, beginning with horses which had wandered off from the farms and ranches and gone wild. They were beautiful to see, wild and alive. Melinda's father used to catch a few, work with them. Then he'd died.

Melinda's old Dodge was already at her house. Something was wrong; she usually came in an hour after him. He walked inside; she was standing at the old-fashioned sink, her back to him.

"They're closing the school," she said quietly, not bothering to turn around.

"Why?"

Now she turned, looking slightly surprised. "What do you mean *why?* It could have happened anytime; you know that. Enough of the ranchers have moved away . . . there aren't enough to support it now. One of the ranchers bought it; I hear he's going to turn it into a barn."

He felt stupid. "When is all this supposed to happen?"

"End of the term. Three weeks." She looked up at him. "I'll be moving away, Fred. I've spent too much time here; I've exhausted all the possibilities. I . . . " She looked at him sadly. "I can't get what I need here any more."

He couldn't meet her gaze. He walked around the kitchen slowly, looking at things. He knew it was a habit which infuriated her, but he couldn't seem to help it.

"I . . . don't want you to go," he said finally. Then he tried to look at her directly, to show that he really meant what he was saying. He couldn't quite manage it, but he thought he was at least close. Maybe she wouldn't perceive any difference. "Don't leave me," he said in her general direction. "I love you."

"I love you, too, Fred. I really do. But that isn't enough these days, is it?"

"It should be, but it isn't. I'm not sure why."

"I don't know either; things are changing. Everywhere."

He held her for a time, but he knew it was simply a gesture. A last, not-so-dramatic gesture for some kind of end.

They went to see her father's gravesite anyway. It was a rough haul over broken land, and try as he might Freddy found it impossible to think about Melinda, the loss of her. As much as he cared, he found himself again thinking of dinosaurs, imagining serpentine necks rising up over the hills. Again he recounted the ways they all might have died.

Some thought the mountain-forming upheavals at the close of Cretaceous time must have killed them off. But why weren't the other animals destroyed? A favorite theory used to be that disease, a series of plagues, wiped them out. Or racial old-age. Some people claimed it was the wrath of God.

The most popular theory held that they were exterminated because the world became a colder place, maybe when a giant meteorite struck the earth, the resultant dust cloud obscuring the sun.

But no theory seemed quite adequate to explain such a complete, worldwide extinction.

Perhaps they had known it was their time. Perhaps something within their bodies or within their reptilian, primeval dream had told them that their era had come to an end. They had had no choice but to accept. The others had left them behind. He imagined them going off somewhere to die, their great bodies piling up. And the world had gone on without them.

His father's massive head striking the floor, his great weight shaking little Freddy where he hid beneath the table. The large eyes rolling, the mouth loose and shapeless, groaning . . .

They went to her father's gravesite holding hands, not saying anything. Douglas Mountain was beautiful, the broken land made to seem purposeful, aesthetically pleasing in its shape by means of the fields of gray-green sage. There was no one to disturb them; this was real back country. Tooley-wads, the old-timers called it.

The grave was well-kept; they had spent a good deal of time during their courtship on the mountain, and frequently they puttered around the grave and its monument. An old tree crooked its branches above the plain stone, and hanging from it were her dad's stirrups, lariat, a few of his leather-working tools, and a branding iron from his first job as a hand. Like a small museum. Artifacts already ancient-seeming and near-forgotten.

The wind picked up and lifted Melinda's sandy hair off her shoulders. "Sow coon," she whispered, and laughed softly. "Sow coon" was cowboy talk for a bad storm. Freddy thought he'd heard a horse, several, whinnying and pawing at the dirt behind them. He looked nervously around and saw nothing but a gray dust cloud spinning up with the breeze. His father used to say that the "signs" were always there if you just knew how to read them. Nature's secret messages. You could tell what was coming if you just knew what to look for. Freddy imagined his father out there in the dusk with the long lost horses, dinosaurs all, hiding, watching him.

"Where's the broomies?" he asked her.

"Here somewhere. They're a bit shy these days."

Freddy shivered and pulled closer to her. He looked back over his shoulder. A small column of the dust was settling, but for a moment had looked like a horse's leg, bending, then slamming into the dirt. He could hear fiery air being forced through large nostrils. Ghost sounds, he thought. Then all was silent again, the air cleared, and Freddy could see for miles around. No dust, no disturbance of the slopes or barren, windswept flats to be seen. No life.

"I think they're gone," he said to her, staring out over the bare slopes. "My God, I think they're all finally gone."

She looked up at him, but did not reply.

"Love won't save us," he said.

Again the enormous head crashed into unconsciousness.

Hours later, Freddy was ordering another beer, staring at the sleeping cowboy at the table next to him. He hadn't been inside a Rangely bar since his father had disappeared. He hadn't been drunk in years.

The bar was lit by a few yellow lights. Cowboys and oil workers shifted in the dimness, each becoming the other, losing resolution. The darkness of the bar absorbed most of their vague individual shadows, but those Freddy could see seemed much too bulky. They shouted, almost howling, their mouths wide, cavernous, and it hurt his ears.

He found himself examining the tabletop. Ever more closely the more he drank. What he saw there, finally, scratched into the surface, seemed to be some sort of pictograph. Picture-writing. Kokopelli, the flute player. The Fremont Indians, what was it . . . A.D. 1000? Freddy glanced up into the shadows, trying to find someone who might have carved it. He thought he saw a face darker than the others, a painted face, but then the area seemed to soot over again, two cowboys moving into the space. He fingered the carving gently . . . old, worn. Down around the Cub Creek area Freddy had seen a number of them. As teenagers, he and some of the guys used to camp out there, shooting at the pictures. He felt hot shame now, just thinking about it, and even at the time he had felt as if he'd done something dirty. The Fremonts had gone away around A.D. 1150. Vanished into the hills. No one knew why.

"It was their time," he whispered to no one. "Their hearts weren't in it any more."

The shadows in the bar were moving, dancing up the walls. Horses thundering in the dark. Fremont Indians. The cowboys and oil workers seeming to dance with them. And behind them all, the awesome bulk of an ancient, thundering reptile, tilting, falling . . .

"Hey, boy, you look rode hard an' put away wet!" A tall cowboy was slapping Freddy on the back. He blinked, and looked at him. The cowboy grinned back. "Buy you a drink?"

"Sure, sure," Freddy said blearily. It was hard to keep the old fellow in focus.

The cowboy sat down. "Been huntin' coyote up on the White River, thought I'd come into town an' stay out with the dry cattle." Freddy stared at him blankly. "Have a night on the town, don't you know." The cowboy looked around. "Been up too long, I reckon. Last night I was sufferin' the mill tails o'hell, boy, drunk too much I 'aspect, and all the she stuff was just them old sisters . . . made me so swole had to pick a fight with one o'those riggers, just a youngun, put 'em down till he hauled out callin' me to the street. Beat 'em fine, rimfired the kid, but Lord! Stove up today!" He looked at Freddy and winked.

"You . . . trap coyotes? You can make a living doing that?"

"Middlin', for what she's worth," he said. "Hell, it's a life."

"A life . . . " Freddy said sadly, guzzling the beer. "Not much left . . . "

"Now that's a fact! Cobbled up way to live, but it was a livin'. After I'm gone won't nobody know what happened, won't nobody know how I lived!"

Freddy stared into the tobacco-stained teeth. The smile growing wider, expanding, growing lopsided, the rugged, enormous face falling, falling . . .

But it was Freddy's face falling, crashing into the wooden tabletop.

Freddy woke up on Monday with the sun burning his face. He rubbed his dry skin, afraid to open his eyes, certain someone had just dragged him out of the Rangely bar and left him lying in the desert. Then the ground seemed to soften a bit beneath him, he opened one eye, and found himself in his own bed in Meeker, with all his clothes on. "How . . . " he mumbled, then realized the old cowboy must have driven him home.

Freddy stumbled out of the bed and looked around the house, but the man was nowhere to be seen. Freddy's pickup was parked in the front yard. The cowboy must have hitched back into Rangely. Or gone out into the mountains or the prairie, back into hiding. Vanishing. Dying.

He sat down on the edge of the bed and rubbed his neck. The bedtable clock said two. Hardly worth going into work now, but he supposed he should. He didn't have any appointments today, so he doubted they had missed him.

The house seemed unusually quiet. A light breeze ruffled the curtains over the open window, and there were no sounds from outside. No car engines, no children playing. He felt vaguely agitated. A sudden ripple of anxiety washed over his upper body. The hair on the back of his neck prickled. Strange feeling.

His coal-black cat walked into the room. She stopped suddenly, turned her head, and stared at him. He saw her tensing, her back rising. She pinned him with her eyes, unmoving. He started to approach her, but she raced away with a sharp cry. Freddy couldn't understand it. It was almost as if she hadn't expected to see him.

The wind coming through the window seemed to rise, the temperature to drop, so that suddenly he was feeling sharp and cold gusts penetrating the room in an almost rhythmical pattern. He walked to the window to shut it, but stopped and stuck his head outside. The position was too awkward to see very much, but no matter how much he strained his head this way or that, he could see no one, hear no one. A few dogs moved quietly through the streets. Cars were parked, empty.

It took him only a few minutes to slap some water onto his face and get ready for work. He didn't bother with a shower. He slid into the pickup, started the engine, and pulled out onto Meeker's main street, waiting for the images of his father to come once again.

He stopped after two blocks. He got out of his truck.

Cars and trucks were parked awkwardly on both sides of the street, straddling alleys, parked in the wrong direction, pulled up on the curb, stopped too far out in the street. The engines had been turned off, the doors shut firmly, but it seemed as if the drivers hadn't really cared where they left them. Maybe it hadn't mattered where they had left them.

There was no one in sight. He walked around the main part of town; two dogs raced away when they saw him. The doors to the stores and cafes were wide open. Food still on the tables, but the grills and coffee pots had been turned off. Someone had left the radio on, but there was only static. On all channels. "Where are you hiding now?" he whispered softly.

Freddy ran out to the pickup and spun the wheels. He stopped, took a deep breath, then headed out toward Rangely.

Off in the distance, a tall figure in battered hat and faded jeans was walking toward the mountains.

"Hey! Hey!" Freddy shouted, but the figure did not turn.

The wheels took the curves on edge, the arroyos drew him, the washouts beckoned him. He flashed on his broken body, twisted under the wreck down in one of the deeper gulleys, but still he pressed down on the accelerator, spinning the steering wheel.

But the receding figure was always too far away, and the road did not lead there.

"Hey! Cowboy!" Freddy shouted.

The cowboy did not turn, but continued to go away, to vanish.

He passed other vehicles abandoned at the side of the road. He saw no one on the hillsides but an occasional rabbit.

For the first time he could remember, the image of his father did not come to him.

Miles later — he had not kept track of the time — he stopped just within the city limits of Rangely, unable to drive on. A cold wind filled the streets with dust. There were no lights in the buildings, even with the overcast skies. A door banged repeatedly. At the periphery of his vision he was aware of the oil wells pumping on, unattended, unwatched.

He would not go to her house only to find her gone. He would not look at her things, the relics left behind.

It was well past dark by the time Freddy reached the top of Douglas Mountain. He had seen no human beings along the way. He hadn't expected to.

Where did the dinosaurs go? the teacher asked again. Most of the standard answers were covered. The cute little girl in front of Freddy, the one he had such a desperate crush on, said that God had done it, and several in the class agreed. Freddy gave the answer about the plague of caterpillars. He liked caterpillars.

He stood above the old horsebreaker's grave. Her father's grave. She wouldn't have a grave. None of them would. There wouldn't be anyone left to bury them. But maybe there'd be a quarry full of bones, and whatever might be there in the times ahead would dig them up and arrange them in display cases and dioramas.

The metal relics in the tree clanged together in the high wind. It was dark below, but Freddy thought he could see shadows moving there. Reflections of himself, maybe, inverse shadows. He was sure he could hear the wild horses thundering, the Fremont Indians calling to them, the trappers, the outlaws — or maybe that was his father's face in the darkness? Maybe that's where he went . . . all those years . . .

"I'm really the most ignorant of dinosaurs," he whispered to the shadows. "We're already extinct, and here I am talking to the dark. Here I am, again the one they've left."

He crouched down and leaned forward, straining his eyes. Nothing.

"Don't leave me behind!" he shouted. "Don't *abandon* me!" He touched his head softly, then scratched at his cheeks. He had not heard an echo. "I love you . . . " he whispered, but he had lost the names.

The wind seemed to rise, colder, but then he knew it was a wind inside him, and he imagined it starting somewhere near the base of his spine, sweeping up over the intestines, the liver, the heart, picking up odd cells of flesh and bone as it went, taking old memories to the brain . . .

"Take me along," he whispered.

And he felt his head beginning to fall, as if from a great height. Pulling him somewhere.

LEAVE-TAKING

Thomas Zigal

The way I remember it, his wife came here to ski with some wealthy ranch owners from down valley and fell in love with the place. It was virtually abandoned, of course, no more than two hundred inhabitants still surviving, mostly miners' offspring without the ambition or the resources to move on. I knew them all. There were those who kept hoping silver would make a comeback and the mines would be worth something again. Families still owned the claims, you see.

When Mrs. Rumpf spent that weekend here, she stayed in the old hotel my father left me. She and her friends were my only guests in perhaps half a year, since the time a fertilizer salesman from Pueblo wandered over the Pass looking for a shortcut to orchard country. I gave the party my finest rooms, but Mrs. Rumpf was annoyed by dust on the spreads and the lack of adequate heating. She complained of mice in the walls at night. I did my best to spruce up the old place, but so much of it had been shut off for decades, and maintenance was a losing battle. As stipulated by the brochure, I cooked their meals (no audible grievances there) and arranged for a fellow named Tabor, the junk man, to take them by truck to the top of the mountain.

I had learned about skiing from the soldiers in the Mountain Division who trained nearby and who came into town occasionally for liquor. The idea was new to this country and there were no lifts yet, so for two icy mornings Tabor whined his truck up the slope, the poor motor grinding and moaning, and then drove back down to wait for them, offered coffee and the basket lunches I'd prepared for their arrival, and towed them up again for an afternoon run. I remember it as the crispest time of the new year, sunlight glistening on the snow and crystals glassing the evergreens, the sky as clear and blue as the waters of a coral grotto. More than anything else, the glorious weather convinced Mrs. Rumpf that this was a winter paradise and vastly preferable to the gray blizzardy days of Buffalo, where she and her husband made their home, and the headquarters of Jacob Rumpf's awesome corporate empire.

I was married once, a local girl, and my wife had a knack for looking at a broken-down shack and seeing in it the greatest potential. A few coats of paint, some wood varnish, a handful of nails in the right places, and a cozy bungalow would take shape before your very eyes. Mrs. Rumpf was the same kind of woman. She somehow saw in this old ghost town the skeleton for a strange new creature, and one beyond my wildest dreams. If I had had even the faintest glint of vision I might be a millionaire today, instead of what I'm doing now. But in those days, when the Rumpfs and their people were first nosing about in these parts, this ramshackle village was to me simply the accidental repository of my birth and a noose around my neck. All that surrounded my father's hotel were mudhole streets and collapsed fences, the boarded-up shops and saloons that had once pleasured thousands of randy miners, a scattering of baby Victorians with caved-in porches, loose shutters, overgrown lots. An obscure name on the map, wedged in the corner of a remote valley whose beautiful green mountains were scarred by the ugly coring of mines. There was no doubt that I was eager to sell out and escape beyond these confining walls of rock, the only landscape I had ever known. I felt suffocated by the dust of time, the strewn tailings of lost fortune.

It has been written in numerous accounts that a short while after his wife's weekend here, which she praised as the grandest outing of her life, Jacob Rumpf himself stole into town dressed in disguise: some say as a mail carrier, others that he wore a woman's clothing and passed himself off as a traveling seamstress. Those of us who lived here then have always found the story highly improbable. In any event, I am sure he did not stay in my hotel, his only option in those days. So where, then?

Years later Old Man Stuber, the town dry goods merchandiser and my father's longtime card partner, swore that one morning of that fateful season, while shoveling snow along the boardwalk in front of his store, he spied a man fifty yards down the street, peering through the scope of a survey transit, and thought it odd that someone would be measuring property lines in the dead of winter. Stuber has passed on now, like so many of the old-timers hereabouts, so it is impossible to examine his story with a careful eye to the facts. And in the long run, what does it matter? What happened happened, and it is too late now to grieve over our improvidence.

The first man Rumpf sent to deal with us was an agent named Maurice Flavin, a soft little Eastern dandy with chalky coloring and dark worried eyes. When he walked into the lobby of the hotel I was forced to contain my amusement. He seemed to have a dude ranch notion of how to dress out here, and his denim jeans were so new and pressed, his bolo tie so comical, I started to take his photograph for the hotel postcard. He moved about in stiff new cowboy boots the way a little girl tries out her mother's high heels.

I was sitting in an old armchair, reading the morning paper from Denver. "Excuse me," he said. "Are you the proprietor of this establishment?"

He was wearing a Western-cut hat only a picture-show sawbones would wear, and he left it on indoors.

"I'm the owner," I said. "Are you interested in a room?"

He smiled and looked about the bare lobby. "I'm interested in all your rooms, sir," he said. "I represent a man who wants to buy your town."

I snickered at his ludicrous proposition, but he did not change expression. From that moment forward he was all business.

Maurice Flavin produced a map of the town which showed the division of property owners, and another map indicating mine claims in the surrounding mountains. He had purchased the maps, he said, in the county courthouse in Edom.

"Do you know these people?" he asked, pointing out the dozen or so family names responsible for ownership.

"Yes, of course," I said. I had grown up with them. We were the children of the children of the first fortune hunters in this territory, the weak, unworthy seed those great men cast upon this barren ground.

My grandfather was one of the town founders. In 1879, as rumors spread of the silver boom, he sold his stock in a lucrative department store back East and settled here, building Victorian homes, a stunning opera house, the most elegant hotel in the Rockies. But fifteen years later, when Grover Cleveland demonetized silver in favor of a gold standard, the mines were abandoned overnight, workers fled to the gold fields of Alaska, shops and banks closed their doors, the town lost 10,000 inhabitants in less than a year. One winter night, as a vicious north wind howled through the deserted streets, my grandfather locked himself in the garish bridal suite of his hotel and put a pistol to his head. My father was only twenty years old, the inheritor of empty buildings and a few parcels of forsaken land.

"I would like to arrange a purchase of all holdings," Maurice Flavin informed me that day. "But it is a question of discretion, my friend. There are reasons for absolute secrecy in this matter. If land speculators from around the country were to get wind that my client is buying property out here, there would be a rush of the magnitude never before witnessed, and your quiet little town would soon be overrun by great swelling hordes of barbarian fortune-hunters searching for buried treasure."

I was intrigued by the prospect of great swelling hordes. After all, I was a hotelier.

"Why are you telling me these things, Mr. Flavin?"

"Because, my boy," the agent narrowed those deep dark eyes, "my client and I want you to be our negotiator with the locals."

I sat up straight in the armchair.

"We want you to purchase the deeds for us," he smiled thinly. "A price will be set for each lot, based on market estimations, and you may keep anything above the set price. A little entrepreneurial incentive, eh, son?" he winked. "We will also offer you a ten percent commission on all sales. Ten percent off the top. You stand to make a good profit here, my friend. Our only requirement is discretion."

I don't know what gave the man the gall to take me for a Judas. That night I told the boys in the poker group when we met in our usual place, the chamber that had once been the hotel tearoom. I showed them the list of prices the Rumpf organization would offer.

"Where do I sign?" laughed Tabor. The sums were three times what the useless property was worth.

"Are you going to sell the hotel and the opera house?" asked Doc Bradford.

I nodded. Good riddance. Four years earlier, a hobo fire had gutted the inside of the vacant opera house and in all that time I hadn't bothered to clean out the theater or make repairs. On a windy day the odor of charred velvet could still be noted from the street.

"What's the man want with this hole in the wall?" asked Qualey, the garage mechanic.

"Who cares?" said Tabor. "Let's sign before he changes his mind."

I cut the cards. "I think he just wants to own something nobody else knows about," I said.

"You mean he needs a hideout," said Doc Bradford.

"Something like that," I said.

"What's he hiding from?" asked Qualey.

Tabor began to deal. "Progress," he mumbled through his cigarette.

Over the next few months there occurred a series of inexplicable events in our town. On several evenings the old upright piano in the dark opera house could be heard playing a merry rag. Lamplight moved from window to window in the closed-down bordello. A strange man was seen on horseback near the river. Torch flares appeared like twinkling stars high up the mountain in the dead of night. These mysterious phenomena grew in significance with each new telling. They became for us the signs and wonders that precede a great cataclysm of history.

By the end of the summer I had negotiated all the property that could be negotiated. In my name, but with Rumpf money, I bought every building in the commercial zone, most of the liveable houses around town, the dilapidated smelter, all but two of the mine leases. I collected my commissions, a healthy nest egg, and prepared to leave town for good.

"I'm sorry I couldn't convince everyone to sell," I said to Flavin the day we met to transfer deeds into the Rumpf name. In truth I hadn't tried very hard. I wasn't willing to push anyone. "What will you do about the stragglers?" I asked.

Maurice Flavin shrugged. "There are many options at our disposal," he said. "They won't want to stay."

I left everything behind except two suitcases full of clothes, a couple of family albums, and a dozen of my favorite volumes from grandfather's library. I took the tarp off the old Ford my father had bought one year in Denver, Qualey recharged the battery and filled the tank, and I crept out of town, avoiding the awkward emotion of bidding farewell to those I'd known as kin. Saying goodbye would have been a new and frightening experience for us all.

Forty miles away and 3,000 feet lower in elevation, the town of Edom lay at the mouth of the valley, a junction for rail cargo and a rest stop along the audacious highway that traverses the Rockies east and west. The town was known for its natural hot springs, a sacred place to the Ute Indians, and later, the site of a sanitorium where Doc Holliday lost his battle with tuberculosis and where the doddering Buffalo Bill Cody took the waters and fell into a coma from which he did not recover.

When I arrived at the spa it was late in the day, so I checked into the old sanitorium, now a fine tourist hotel, and asked for the room where Teddy Roosevelt stayed during his famous bear hunts in this territory. (My father had joined the President's final expedition, the last great hunt for the last great grizzly roaming these woods.) I had money, you see, and a brooding desire to spend it. It had been a year since I'd last visited Edom, and before that, who can remember?

I ordered champagne and caviar, and for dinner a roasted pheasant with the finest French wine from the cellar. The bellboy brought Cuban cigars, compliments of the house. Afterwards I bathed in perfumed salts in the deep, ornate tub provided with the suite, and then rang again for the bellboy who had been so accommodating. I placed a generous gratuity in his hand, folded his fist around the bills, and asked if he could find me a woman for the evening. He hesitated, lowering his eyes, sputtering with embarrassment. I gave him more money.

"Someone soft and friendly," I said, giving him a little shove toward the door. I hadn't had a woman since my wife, who'd left me three years earlier and taken a train for California.

For several weeks I spoiled the young waitress the boy procured for me. We ate the costliest meals, spent our afternoons lounging in the hot springs, danced away autumn evenings in the hotel ballroom. I bought her the best dresses in town (admittedly a limited selection) and expensive jewelry imported from the East. I told her magnificent lies about where I was going, to the shimmering white cities along the Pacific, to the picturesque lighthouse villages of New England, and she believed me, sweet girl. She wanted only a postcard now and then, an occasional souvenir from an ocean resort. She could not detect my profoundest fears, my lack of heart, and she had no way of knowing that I was afraid of the world, a helpless child who had been swaddled too long in the snug cradle of a beautiful green valley far removed from the commerce of ordinary men. Why did I think I could survive out here, in someone else's hotel? I had been a fool to sell my birthright, damned though it was by lost splendor and seedy dissipation, for a mess of commission money.

From my hotel window I watched as bulldozers, cranes, graders, and heavy earth-moving machinery were unloaded from freight cars onto flatbed trucks, a daily parade of vehicles heading up valley. Noon and night every manner of cement mixer, lumber truck, and storage van roared through town in search of the old country road southward. I counted spools and bales and crates of building materials I was unable to identify. My mind grew confused by what could possibly be transpiring up there in the mountains.

Now and then, as I walked the sleepy sidewalks of Edom, I would run across someone I had known from the old days, a familiar neighbor dazed as I, idling along in a trance of sadness and regret. I would ask when they had left, what they had seen take place. The stories began to assume an outlandish cast, like the mythic tales of a frightened and superstitious tribe. The mountain had been shaved, they said. Boulders removed, groves of aspen and cottonwood felled, wide swaths cut through the spruce. Mine shafts had been sealed, the holes carpeted with sod. Tall steel towers, strung with cable, now formed a gleaming spine up the slope.

For a full year, as the anemic winter snow in these flatland hills melted into the muddy slush of spring, and summer heat prickled with a desert vengeance, I stopped passersby from home, now exiles like myself, and listened to their accounts of strange metamorphosis.

"What about the buildings?" I asked Tabor one day. I had spied his junk truck parked in front of a tavern. "What about the hotel?"

Tabor shook his head. He looked gray around the mouth, gaunt. "Hard to make heads or tails of anything anymore," he muttered into his drink.

I finally decided I had had my fill of hearsay and should investigate the matter myself. I packed a few things in the old Ford and motored off into the valley, the air growing thin and chill as the car struggled up those steep inclines, the roadway hugging marvelous redstone cliffs. In grassy meadows the aspen trees quivered with leaves burnished gold and red, the most splendid vision of beauty imaginable, stirring in me a memory of childhood walks with mother and father along the footpaths of our town. I quickly forgot the modest pleasures of Edom, its heated waters and dear young women, and longed for a night in my old bed, Room 101, the hotel of my forebears.

Near the end of the valley I passed a convoy of diesels bearing goods to Jacob Rumpf's new resort. Within a few miles I came upon a glass guard station where the old vegetable and fruit stands once stood, and a man wearing a security uniform stepped out and raised his hand for me to stop.

"May I see your pass, please," he said. Strapped to his hip was a leather holster from which a pearl-handled grip protruded. Inside the station another man watched with suspicion.

"Pass?" I wondered aloud.

"You have to have a pass to be permitted through, mister," the guard said, straightening his shoulders. "No exceptions."

I tried to act friendly. "How do I get a pass?" I smiled.

He tipped back his hat and sighed a weary breath. "If you don't know," he smirked, "you probably got no business here."

I parked at some distance, in the shade of an aspen stand, and watched surly workers construct an electric fence, long glimmering rolls of mesh extending from the guard station, across the rocky terrain, and disappearing up into the mountains. Another crew was erecting the gigantic support legs for what appeared to be a lookout tower near the base of the slope.

Soon I witnessed an amazing sight, a small silvery airplane buzzing overhead and dipping low to land somewhere just over the ridge. I sat there for hours, till daylight softened into dusk, observing a steady flow of such aircraft, the first I had seen in this valley. They were the private carriages of a new breed, Rumpf's people, the special class of leisured folk invited here to share his seclusion.

As the sun vanished over the mountains and shadows grew longer, an old-time Wells Fargo stagecoach clattered toward the grove where I had stationed my car. The horses reined to a halt, their hooves stirring up dust clouds, and soon the doors opened and a host of passengers emerged, tinhorn dandies costumed like Maurice Flavin the first time he walked into my hotel. A young blonde woman wearing a cowgirl skirt and leather-fringed blouse led them beneath the aspen trees, where the guests began to gather golden leaves.

"Look at this one!" someone exclaimed. "Splendid!"

I walked over to the stagecoach. "Well, well," I said to the driver, who remained up in his seat. It was Qualey, dusty bandana tied around his neck, dark Stetson tipped low over the eyes. He had grown a mustache.

"Hello, Rusty," he said. "Long time, no see." He seemed a little embarrassed to encounter somebody he knew.

"I didn't think anyone was left," I said. "Still running the garage?"

He shook his head, his eyes drifting elsewhere. "Mostly this," he said, nodding toward the horses.

"What's happening with my hotel?" I asked, watching the passengers collect leaves.

"It's a damn sight better looking than when you ran that old fleabag joint," he grinned. "They got a swimming pool now, and chandeliers everywhere. You oughta see what they done with the ballroom."

I stood there in silence for quite some time, unsure of what to say, until the blonde guide hustled her guests back to the coach.

"Take my advice and wise up, Rusty," my old friend said, whipping the reins. "It's too late to fret over this thing. What's done is done. The way I look at it, a man's gotta take what he's given and make the best of it."

I sat on the hood of my car till the stars appeared, icy clear constellations mapping the black sky, the long vague cloud of the Milky Way visible in the darkness of these mountains as it is nowhere else on earth. An autumn wind rustled the leaves around me, blowing them toward the web of fence. In the distance, where my town had been, checkers of light spired high into the night. I thought I could hear music. A merry ragtime piano.

For the briefest moment I wished I had kept my grandfather's pistol. But then, with no clear purpose in mind, I slid from the hood and began to gather the whirling leaves.

• • •

That was years ago, of course, and the best I can remember it. I settled down in Edom and tried to make peace with what I've come to regard as a lost inheritance. The leaves I collected that evening in the mountains still remain pressed between the pages of my family album.

It didn't take long for the commission money to disappear.

These days I work for a man who runs a little storefront tourist shop near the hot springs. He electroplates things, coats them with shiny metals. A silver-plated aspen leaf, with appropriate chain, makes a wonderful birthday or anniversary gift for the little lady.

It's my job to drive up valley every couple of months and collect materials for the business. I spend my days wandering through the aspen groves near the outer boundary of the resort. Sentries stare down through binoculars from the lookout towers. Jeeps sweep along the electric fence; uniformed guards watch my every move. I enjoy putting them on edge. I stroll lazily beneath the shade trees, golden leaves clinging to my ankles. I pretend I'm taking something precious and irreplaceable from them. It's the only thing that gives me satisfaction anymore.

ears popping over la veta pass

Tony Moffeit

you were snoring
in the backseat
marguerita when i
raced the nighthawk
for those high
stakes the radio
blaring the blues
ears popping over
la veta pass and i
drove deeper into
the dark nerves
worn on neanderthal
cliffs body torn
on dead man curves
and you drifted
awake asked if i
was ok and i pulled
out a stick of gum
said yeah i think i
got my second wind

Afterword

J. D. MARSTON — *Capulin Cabin*

I was born and raised in Stamford, Connecticut, where I started photographing microscope samples with a box camera at age ten. A few years later my aunt gave me my first 35-mm camera, which I used when studying photography in high school. I studied journalism and photojournalism as well as education at Boston University, and graduated from Emerson College with a bachelor's degree in speech communications.

After graduation I left immediately left for the Canadian Rocky Mountain wilderness, where I lived alone for eight months in search of the "meaning of life." I then worked in the stress management field for 15 years, and once again the urge to know the meaning of life took me to India, where I lived as a monk for seven years. I returned to live in the San Luis Valley in Colorado, where I own my own home, photographic gallery, and studio.

I continue the search for the meaning of life in the photography I do and try to instill a compelling intimacy in the outdoor photography that is my specialty. My work is well known in Colorado and may be found in galleries and private collections around the country. In May 1992 my work was honored by the Sierra Club, which bestowed on me the Ansel Adams Award for Conservation Photography, an international award.

Regarding *Capulin Cabin,* the cover photograph for this anthology, I had been retained by the Arvada Center for the Arts and Humanities to document folk artists in Colorado. I was in Capulin, recording the work of weaver Senon Martinez. When our session was finished, I stepped outside and noticed the incredible clouds forming. I thought of the adobe cabin that I had seen earlier on my way into town and drove there quickly, hoping that the clouds would provide the perfect backdrop necessary to record the ancient cabin. The clouds kept shifting and growing higher in the sky until they created a form that pointed right into the roof of the cabin and at the same time seemed to emanate the history within the cabin. I had a feeling of spiritual upliftment watching the scene, which I photographed using a polarizer to bring out the intensity in the sky.

TMX   4x5 film   210-mm lens   f 45   1/4 sec

SIMON J. ORTIZ — *Sand Creek*

"I've been writing for a long, long time, probably more than 30,000 years, maybe forever," I said once in a talk. I said that because the source of my creativity, certainly my poetry, short fiction, and other writing, is my heritage as an American Indian from Acoma Pueblo, New Mexico. I give absolute credit to my heritage because of the oral tradition, which is the knowledge, culture, language, really everything that identifies me as Aaqcumeh. Unless I am Aaqcumeh nothing exists — not my perception, not my expression, not my identity, unless I am an Acoma person. I write because of what and who I am. That sounds trite and simplistic but it's true. I wrote *From Sand Creek,* a long poem from which there are excerpts for the present book, by looking at myself as victim, an Indian who's a descendant of a people in the devastating path of Western civilization. I looked at myself also as victimizer, a citizen and a military vet of a nation that has overrun just about everyone in the world. *From Sand Creek* is set in a U.S. veteran's hospital not far from Sand Creek in southeastern Colorado. At Sand Creek one of the most horrendous massacres of Indian people was committed November 29, 1864, by federal troops and Colorado militia. In 1974–75 I was an inpatient in the alcohol–drug addiction rehab ward at the hospital, and Fort Lyon VAH seemed to be a place of last resort for victimizers and victims. It was filled with old men and women from World War I, vets from World War II and the Korean War, and younger ones from the more recent Vietnam War. I learned that in the nineteenth century, Fort Lyon was one place from which U.S. aggression against Indians was launched.

I have a son, Raho Nez; a daughter, Rainy Dawn; and another daughter, Sara Marie. I also have a granddaughter, Krista Rae. They are all beautiful. My latest book is *Woven Stone* (University of Arizona, 1992). I have published *Fightin', The People Shall Continue, From Sand Creek,* and others. I continue to write because of what and who I am.

RICHARD BRODERICK — *The Chinook*

I lived in Colorado for a half-dozen years, beginning with undergraduate work at the University of Denver. A transplanted Easterner, I was immediately taken with the Rockies and only after some time came to appreciate the special beauty and mystical silence of the short-grass prairie. Something of my feelings about both places — the high mountains and the grasslands — runs like an undercurrent through the story.

Like a lot of my fiction and poetry, "The Chinook" was woven together out of dream fragments and personal experience. The house the couple rents is based on a gloomy old place I wintered in one year outside of Allenspark. The dream in which the young woman sees people, houses, and trees tumbling down the mountains was a dream I actually had. The trailer park flattened by high winds was something I witnessed on my way through Boulder. And so on.

"Chinook" is as much about place as people: specifically, the way a place can become part of a relationship between two people. In this case, a troubled and attenuated relationship comes to seem even more tenuous when set against a background of wide-open spaces. The Chinook? Maybe that represents the anger and fears we repress at our own risk.

JOANNE GREENBERG — *The Lucero* Requiem

"The Lucero *Requiem*" is a favorite of mine. Like many of my stories, it combines personal experience and fantasy. For example, the personal experience is that I have sung in a great many choral groups; the fantasy is that I got a chance to be a brilliant soloist.

Years ago I witnessed the cutting off at the knees of a gifted alto by a shrill soprano, but I never thought I would use it in a story. When I began writing "The Lucero *Requiem*" I thought it would be a good incident to use to demonstrate the other side of the music that I so loved — the part where the egos clash. There was then the problem of what work they were going to sing. For a while I considered one of the standard choral masterpieces — Mozart's *Requiem,* Verdi's *Requiem* — but then I thought that it might be fun to write my own, which of course I could make thrillingly beautiful because I was not actually required to do it. What would my choral piece be like? I wanted it to be a Colorado piece, something with a Chicano and Indian flavor from southern Colorado, and so Naçencio Lucero was born. Then, of course, I had to give him a biography; then I had to kill him.

All of my published work has been written in Colorado, and although any work mirrors something that is true or real in a larger experience, everyone, I believe, is a local writer — breathing the air, experiencing the climate and weather of a specific location, engaging in the specific pursuits, and relating to the people of that area.

My love for the state and for being a local in it has developed because I was not born or raised here and didn't come here for the first time until I was twenty-one. Coming back to stay when I was twenty-four, I found a social and intellectual freedom that I had not found anywhere else. I think the pilgrimages that one makes oneself and the treasures that one finds for oneself are the best kinds of pilgrimages and the best kinds of treasures.

ROBERT O. GREER, JR. — *The Can Men*

My stories often begin by setting time and place. "The Can Men" opens with a descriptive, scene-setting passage to draw the reader into the story. The smells, sights, sounds, and weather of the Mile High City trigger the story. I was on my way to Denver's Stapleton Airport to catch a flight to Boston as a snowstorm began pushing in from the West. I was halfway through a sabbatical year of flying back and forth between Denver and Boston, doing recombinant DNA research at Boston University Medical Center and completing the second edition of one of my medical textbooks, which, by the way, was late. About a mile from the airport I saw two heavily bundled street people wheeling a shopping cart full of cans into a Safeway can bank. The story developed from that image and the vision of the approaching weather front. I used my knowledge of medicine and dentistry to give the story its specificity, and my ranching background to give the story its Western frame.

Although I have lived in Denver for twenty years, I grew up in the steel town of Gary, Indiana. The toughness and bonding of the characters in "The Can Men" probably comes from the strength and grit I saw in the working-class people I grew up around. In addition to obtaining my medical training at Boston University, I also have a master's degree in creative writing from Boston University. I found that I needed formal classroom and workshop instruction to become a decent fiction writer. Perhaps my background as a physician/scientist demanded such traditional training.

In addition to writing, medicine, and research, I serve as editor-in-chief of the *High Plains Literary Review* and also raise Black Baldy cattle on my Coyote Creek Ranch just outside of Steamboat Springs, Colorado. It is not unusual for me to use the ranching tradition in my stories.

My most recent stories have appeared in *South Dakota Review, Black American Literature Forum, New Mexico Humanities Review, Writers' Forum,* and *Agni.* "The Can Men" is from a recently completed collection of short stories, *Choosing Sides.* I just completed a novel, *The Devil's Hatband,* set in the West.

KENT HARUF — *Private Debts / Public Holdings*

Though I have lived most of the years since I was eighteen in other places, I consider Colorado my home. I grew up in the northeast corner of the state, in Phillips and Yuma counties. I have also lived in the mountains and twice, briefly, in Denver; but it is the High Plains — that dry flat open treeless sandy country — that I mean by home. It is only there that I feel the religious response to place that makes me want to tell stories.

You will tell me: Okay. But it sure isn't very pretty out there.

And I will tell you: No, it isn't pretty at all. It's beautiful. You just have to know how to look at it.

But I suppose it helps if, when you were a kid, you lived at the absolute west edge of town so that across the street there was nothing hindering your view but grass and gophers and sky and you and your brother had the whole town as a paper route in all kinds of weather and there was a family who lived just north across the tracks who had twenty horses to ride and downtown there were free books at the library and twenty-five-cent movies at the local theater and you had a fifth grade teacher named Miss Keene, who was ugly but wonderful, a spinster who told stories about living in London during the Blitz and who distributed your mimeographed poems to the rest of the school and all the time you had good parents who didn't bother you any more than was necessary, even if one of them was the Methodist preacher.

About the writing of "Private Debts / Public Holdings" I can only repeat what I've said elsewhere. I don't remember what prompted me to write it. But I believe it came out of my fascination for people who are caught in one way or another. I suppose it is a kind of test of character. Sometimes people act in astonishing (and even beautiful and courageous) ways when they are caught.

About its public history I might say a little more, since it seems to have an itinerant and surprising life of its own. "Private Debts / Public Holdings" was first published in *Grand Street* by Ben Sonnenberg, who not only took the story but very generously decided he could pay an additional amount for it two weeks after the original fee was agreed upon. Then the story was chosen by Ann Beattie for *Best American Short Stories*. Then Nancy Cooperstein made a short film of it for Chanticleer Films, which later won a gold medal at the Houston International Film Festival. Then it turned up as a chapter in my novel *Where You Once Belonged*. Then the little film Ms. Cooperstein made was shown on Irish, Italian, and American television. And then Jim Hemesath kindly chose to include it in a Colorado anthology. So perhaps it has come back home now and maybe it can rest.

JAMES B. HEMESATH — *Clare*

For those of us not born in Colorado, I suspect living here has been something of a surprise. We've had to make adjustments. Growing up in Iowa, I thought of Colorado as the West. Just what that meant I wasn't quite sure. During the past fifteen or so years I've lived in small-town South Dakota, Montana, and Colorado.

I've been library director at Adams State College in Alamosa since 1985. My stories have appeared in *New Mexico Humanities Review, South Dakota Review, WIND Magazine,* and various genre anthologies. I am also a book reviewer for the scholarly journal *Western American Literature.* My degrees include a master of fine arts in English from the University of Iowa Writers' Workshop. Recently I received a Creative Fellowship in Literature for my short stories from the Colorado Council on the Arts. I've been writing for twenty-five years now.

"Clare" is my attempt to reimagine the nineteenth-century pioneer journal or diary in terms of the late twentieth-century. The American West has always been a harsh country, be it 100 years ago or last week. "Clare," in turn, is a tale of vast spaces, loneliness, a failed marriage, and a father's love for his son. The story is set in the San Luis Valley because that is where I live. With time "the Valley" grows on a person, and most people who stay find it, as I have, an agreeable enough place.

BAINE KERR — *Jumping-Off Place*

I feel compelled here to admit that, although a twenty-year "native" of Colorado, I was born and bred in a hot, flat state south of the Red River. Little vestigial language disability remains. I've long adopted points of view more appropriate to mountain ethers than the conditioned air of Houston. But surely I settled here as a consequence of the flatlander's yearning for the Rockies. So it has some bearing.

Like other of my notorious countrymen, I first ventured to Colorado as a tourist to Estes Park. At the age of eleven, in 1957, annual summer trips began to the Y-camp outside of Estes, where I also worked on the staff the summer after my freshman year at Stanford. From the overheated Texan adolescent's perspective, Colorado meant liberation. Adventure. Renewal. Life. As it was meant to be lived. As Colorado still means.

Great things are done, according to Blake, when men and mountains meet. This is a verity ex-Texans instinctively acknowledge.

"Jumping-Off Place" was conceived on a flight from San Antonio back to Stapleton. I was returning from my grandfather's funeral. My grandfather was a man of principle. After shaking hands once with LBJ, a man of whom he did not approve (for reasons specific to the hill-country hunting culture), he decorously, yet ostentatiously, washed them in the finger bowl at his table and dried them with a flourish of his napkin. My grandfather did approve of Colorado. His funeral was a kind of closure; I was released to the mountains.

Flight from Texas, liberation, and the flatlander's yearning for the shining peaks are what produced the short story in this book and in a way what keep me here. I practice law in Boulder — this offsets the romance of Colorado — and write when I can. In the early seventies I was editor of *Place,* a periodic book inspired in part by Colorado as a place of the heart. I've published a book of stories, also called *Jumping-Off Place,* and had a story in *Best American Short Stories.* I received a National Endowment for the Arts fellowship in fiction and the 1992 Editors' Prize in Fiction from the *Missouri Review.* I recently published there a story, "Light Sweet Crude," set in the cloud-forest highlands of Costa Rica, where I lived with my family in 1990–91 before returning, as ever, to the place of which my grandfather approved.

RUSSELL MARTIN — *Matter and Energy*

I'm a lifelong resident of far southwestern Colorado, where members of my family have lived for four generations, making me something of a certifiable local. Although I've been fortunate enough to travel fairly widely, somehow I've never succeeded in moving away.

I graduated from The Colorado College in Colorado Springs in 1974, then spent a postgraduate year on a Thomas Watson Foundation fellowship, writing a novel that, quite justifiably, has never seen the light of day. I worked as a newspaper reporter in Telluride for several years, learning how to sit through interminable meetings and how to write rather more concisely than I'm otherwise inclined to do. Then I moved on to magazine work and to books.

I am the author of *Cowboy: The Enduring Myth of the Wild West* (1983); *Entering Space* (co-authored with Joseph P. Allen, 1984); *Matters Gray and White: A Neurologist, His Patients and the Mysteries of the Brain* (1986); *The Color Orange: A Super Bowl Season With the Denver Broncos* (1987); *A Story That Stands Like a Dam: Glen Canyon and the Struggle for the Soul of the West* (1989); and the novel *Beautiful Islands* (1988), from which the story "Matter and Energy" is adapted. The story, as well as the novel, stems from my curiosity about the relationship between scientific and spiritual ways of looking at the world, my conviction that family is a fundamentally inescapable force, and the goading role that guilt plays in all our lives. I do not have a brother, nor is my father an Episcopal priest, and it goes without saying, I suppose, that I'm not an astronaut, so the story is far from that thinly veiled autobiography that so often passes for fiction. Nonetheless, it does seem rather personal in ways that are . . . personal.

A new novel, *The Shapes of Creeks and Rivers,* perhaps will be published someday, and a new nonfiction book, *Out of Silence: A Journey Into Language,* was published recently.

I have edited two anthologies of contemporary western writing, *Writers of the Purple Sage* (1984) and *New Writers of the Purple Sage* (1992), and have otherwise tried to stay entertained and out of trouble.

ANTONYA NELSON — *Mud Season*

I grew up spending winters in Kansas and summers in Colorado, in Telluride, to be exact. Telluride — the box canyon in which the town sits, the incomparable surrounding San Juan Mountains — is the only place in the world to which I have an abiding connection. "Mud Season" came from what I suspect is a common writerly impulse: to write out a worst-case scenario. Simply: I imagined one of my siblings' dying and then affixed that most horrifying fear to a fictional family, one that bears only vague resemblance to my own. While the San Juan range is a gorgeous group of mountains, to a flatlander it has the ability to perpetually stun. Every summer my family would drive through those mountains on our way to Telluride, and I would find myself clutching at the door handle, begging my parents to slow down, imagining time and again a fall down the cliff. The characters in "Mud Season" also come from the midwest; and they suffer the results of a treacherous and bewitching landscape.

This story appeared in my first collection, *The Expendables*. A second collection, *In the Land of Men,* was published by William Morrow in 1992. I live in Las Cruces, New Mexico — within easy driving distance of Telluride — and teach creative writing and literature at New Mexico State University.

KENT NELSON — *Winter Ascent*

Some years ago I was backpacking in Switzerland with a friend from Colorado and was enthralled by the Eiger. My friend's brother had made the first winter ascent of Capitol Peak near Aspen, and I put together some reading about the Eiger with Colorado mountaineering and came up with "Winter Ascent."

Of course, the mountains were already in me before that. I grew up in Colorado Springs, have lived for a time in Boulder and Ouray (where I was city judge for three years), and have spent a lot of time imagining myself in the mountains when I'm not there. My novel *All Around Me Peaceful* was set in the snow in the San Juans and in a fictionalized Ouray (though I wrote the book in summer in South Carolina). Many of my short stories have Colorado settings, including "Ditch Rider," which was reprinted in *Best of the West 5.*

I suppose every writer feels a home landscape in his work, and mine has been the mountains and the plains.

My novel *Language in the Blood,* which was set in Arizona, received the 1992 Edward Abbey Award for Ecofiction.

MANUEL RAMOS — *His Mother's Image*

Every Chicano writer must write at least one *la llorona* story. The fable is so well known and endemic to our culture that it creeps around the backs of our minds long after we have become adults and adopted more mature images of fear and insecurity — bankruptcy, divorce, cholesterol. She may be a cliché, but I enjoy hearing and reading about the crying woman in all of her mutations and progressions.

"His Mother's Image" was my attempt to preserve a story I grew up with in Florence, Colorado, where I was born and raised. From the dim recesses of my childhood, I remember the creepiness of the river, the strange late-night noises, and adults engulfed in a near-hysterical obsession with tracking down whatever it was that haunted the woods. I tried to include those elements with bits and pieces of Chicano drama that have been around me for a long time — the informal adoption of abandoned children; respect and admiration for the older brother; the storytelling old man; hot, almost blinding summers in a rural small town; and, of course, the long-range effects of the Vietnam War. That may be too much for one story.

There are different versions of the *llorona* myth, and some readers have accused me of not telling the "correct" version. What can I say about that? There are as many different versions as there are people who tell them.

I think "His Mother's Image" was my second published short story. My first novel, *The Ballad of Rocky Ruiz*, was published in spring 1993. It, too, takes place in Colorado. *La llorona* is mentioned only in passing. A second novel, *The Ballad of Gato Guerrero*, was just published.

DAN SCHOENHOLZ — *The Black Canyon*

In September 1991, after a week of mountain biking in the San Juan Mountains outside Telluride, I packed up my gear and waited for the taxi to come shuttle me to the airport. When the Jeep 4x4 arrived, a young, redheaded guy with a beard hopped out and helped me load my gear into the truck. He took special note of my fishing pole, and when I was safely belted into the passenger seat, he launched into a diatribe against the mentally deficient brown trout in the nearby San Miguel River. *He* didn't waste his time on the San Miguel, he informed me. He only fished the Gunnison; that's where all the smart old brownies hung out. In the Black Canyon.

Somehow the conversation took a turn from fishing to women. The cabbie had just been unceremoniously dumped by a woman in town, and he was contemplating leaving. In a place like Telluride you can't help but stub your toe on your old mistakes, he told me. It might be time to move on; then again, maybe she'd come around.

As I thought about our conversation on the flight home, the part I focused on was his comparison of the fish in the two rivers. When I started writing the story a few days later, though, I realized that what my character Andy really needed to figure out was his failed relationship. What started as a story about a fisherman's quest for a trophy trout evolved into "The Black Canyon."

"The Black Canyon" is my second published story (the first appeared in the short-story collection *Side Show*). My poetry and nonfiction have also appeared in a number of publications. To supplement the hundred-or-so dollars I earn each year from writing, I work as an environmental scientist for the Port of Oakland in California.

GLADYS SWAN — *Backtracking*

Although most of my fiction is set in New Mexico, where I grew up, I have ties with Colorado as well. My father-in-law came from Cripple Creek, where his father had been a freighter for the D & RG. The family, with its fourteen children, lived at one time in almost every major town in the state. I can remember one wonderful trip back to Cripple Creek, Florence, and Salida, the setting for "Backtracking," when my father-in-law called to mind various scenes and episodes from his youth, and a whole era came to life again. I loved his stories. Perhaps because of my living in the West, and having been raised in Silver City, where Billy the Kid killed his first man, I've always been interested in the legends that have grown up around certain figures and the myths they have engendered, the myths people have lived by. The West itself has a large mythic dimension: the territory that invited people — and no doubt still does — to go for the second chance, to put aside old habits or losses or failures to create a new life and discover a new identity. In a sense, my family, by moving from East to West, tried to do that as well. And because my grandparents came from Eastern Europe, I am accustomed to the notion of crossing continents, and of making extraordinary shifts to something new.

My imagination was formed by the mountains and desert; by a sense of space and distance; by contact with Hispanic culture and food;

by Western humor and tall tales; and by a sense of the Westerner as a person both friendly and independent. Perhaps these influences have made me feel that anything of value has to start with an appreciation of the land one inhabits and a respect for the patterns of life in it, and that ultimately no human good can come of trying to force it under control, exploiting it for purely selfish ends, or violating its spirit.

Thus far my work consists of three collections of short stories and two novels. The novels have moved in the direction of fantasy. The first, *Carnival for the Gods,* is set in a mythical territory between Mexico and the United States, where the Seven Cities of Cibola are located. The Spanish explorers failed to find them, but I have managed to do so. They are the setting for the adventures of a small traveling carnival. Though the second novel, *Ghost Dance: A Play of Voices,* is set in a recognizable town with realistic characters, these ultimately play their roles in fantastic ways. I expect my work to continue to move in the direction of the mythic and the fantastic, with the West as its setting. In this manner I have been able to explore aspects of reality that seem to me valid, though difficult to express in familiar ways, possibilities that can be shaped by the imagination.

ROBERT LOVE TAYLOR — *Sentimental Journey*

Like Billy Haynes in "Sentimental Journey," I grew up in Oklahoma City, a plains city, flat country. The story was written out of an impulse to get down what it was like to travel for the first time from that flat country of Oklahoma to the jagged landscape of Colorado. I wanted to couple the thrill of that travel with my young protagonist's dawning sense of his feeling for women, and I wanted to be true to my own memory of that time in the history of my family, see how little I could get away with inventing. Could the facts be enough? Hardly. Although much of the story's authority may well derive from remembered details — the calendars in the rented house, for example, or the trout in my mother's skillet — those details taught me the necessity of inventing others, taught me how to use my imagination, in fact, and in the end I could scarcely tell which details I remembered, which I invented. At the same time, I felt, and still do, that the story remained true to the feelings that Colorado inspired in me back then.

The story became one of a series of "memory" pieces that later populated my book *Lady of Spain* (Algonquin 1992). Memory was always the starting point in these stories, where the improvisations began. The idea of Colorado is central to the book: the distant white-topped mountains, the high clear streams, the nearness of the sky. To this day I find sustenance in high country, whether in my recollection of the Rockies or, more recently, my hikes in the Alleghenies of Pennsylvania, the Blue Ridge of Virginia, and the Smokies of Tennessee. I write this note from a cabin in Grayson County in southwest Virginia. I'm up high in a hollow near the headwaters of Peach Bottom Creek. It's a good place to write.

STEVE RASNIC TEM — *Dinosaur*

I came to Colorado to study fiction and poetry under Warren Fine and Bill Tremblay at Colorado State University, receiving my master's in creative writing there in 1976. I met my wife, the writer Melanie Tem, and have lived here ever since. We now reside in old northwest Denver, in a turn-of-the-century Victorian. "Dinosaur" was written after a trip through the northern part of the state, which included the small town of Dinosaur and the Dinosaur National Monument. I'd spent part of that summer reading my way through a large stack of small press booklets concerning the colorful local history of that region, so by the time we reached Dinosaur I'd collected enough specific detail to write the story. I've always been fascinated by the way legends and lifestyles are supplanted, how they seem to have their own natural cycle of evolution. The northern Colorado setting provided me with the material to flesh out that idea.

To date I've published approximately 200 short stories and one novel, *Excavation* (Avon Books 1987). I've been nominated for the Philip K. Dick Award, Bram Stoker Award, World Fantasy Award, and British Fantasy Award, winning the British Fantasy Award for best short story in 1988. My short fiction has appeared in *Asimov's, Shadows, Twilight Zone Magazine, Year's Best Fantasy & Horror,* and many other publications here and abroad. I'm the editor of a forthcoming volume of Colorado writings in the fantastic.

THOMAS ZIGAL — *Leave-Taking*

I was born in Galveston, Texas, in 1948 and grew up on the Texas Gulf Coast and in central Texas. I graduated from the University of Texas at Austin, and in the early seventies I received a master's degree in creative writing from the Stanford Writing Program. My short fiction has appeared in the *Missouri Review, New Letters, Minnesota Review,*

Texas Quarterly, South Dakota Review, and other literary magazines and anthologies. My story "Curios" in the *New Mexico Humanities Review* won Best Story of the Year in 1983 from the Texas Institute of Letters. Delacorte Press is publishing my novel *Into Thin Air,* a murder mystery set in Aspen. At present I live in Atlanta with my wife and son.

From 1986 to 1989 my wife and I lived in Aspen, where she was the executive director of the Aspen Art Museum. Our son, Danny, was born in Aspen. It was during that period that I wrote "Leave-Taking," my rumination on the origins of leisure-class resort towns in the American West. The history and development of Aspen has continued to pique my curiosity, primarily because it is the age-old story of despoiled innocence played out in a uniquely American context. My feelings about the consequences of greed and improvidence are made very clear in the story.

TONY MOFFEIT — *ears popping over la veta pass*

"Ears popping over la veta pass" is a poem about a journey I regularly take: a drive through southern Colorado to Taos, New Mexico. The highest point of the journey is La Veta Pass in southern Colorado. When you're driving along, the radio blaring the blues, the drive can be a long one, particularly at night, but the country is spectacular and the ghosts come alive, inspiring poetry, which I create in my head as I drive. It is always a journey of renewal.

I am director of the Pueblo Poetry Project and poet-in-residence at the University of Southern Colorado in Pueblo, Colorado. I received a National Endowment for the Arts fellowship in 1992 and the Jack Kerouac Award in 1986. My most recent book of poems is *Neon Peppers* from Cherry Valley Editions, Cherry Valley, New York. I perform my poems and songs regularly, accompanying myself on conga drum, to the guitar of Rick Terlep. I am an essayist as well as a poet, and a book of my essays and poems, *Poetry Is Dangerous, the Poet Is an Outlaw,* will be published by Floating Island Publications, Point Reyes Station, California. A work-in-progress contains essays about different models of the poet and the therapeutic value of poetry.